Bridg

A FELLHOUNDS OF THESK STORY

MOON CROSSING

by
Cathy Farr

BITE
Publishing

About
Bridge Readers™

Designed by BITE Publishing, Bridge Readers© help
improving readers to develop their reading skills as they
move towards Young Adult and Adult fiction.

Ideal for weaker and improving readers,
reluctant readers and those learning English
as a second language.
No bad language or sexual content
– *they're just really great reads.*

Bridge Readers™
bridging the gap between learning to read
and reading to learn

Author Notes

Cathy Farr first saw and fell in love with Irish Wolfhounds as a teenager but she had to wait over twenty years to own one. Her first novel, *Moon Chase* was inspired by Cathy's first wolfhound, Finn: like a lot of Irish wolfhounds, Finn stood at eye level with most children, and it was their reaction to her giant hound that inspired Cathy to invent the Fellhounds of her stories. Cathy also works as a part-time teacher at a local primary school, concentrating on creative writing as a key tool to improving literacy. She firmly believes that no child should leave school unable to read.

Cathy adapted *Moon Crossing* as a **Bridge Reader**™ after working with ESL and SLCN children in local schools and with the charity Afasic Cymru*. The first in this series, *Moon Chase* Bridge Reader version, was published in 2014.

*Afasic is a parent led organisation representing children and young people with specific language impairment (SLI) and speech, language and communication needs (SLCN); their work has helped open the world of words to many who would otherwise still find that door firmly closed. To find out more about SLCN and Afasic's work, visit www.afasiccymru.org.uk or www.afasic.org.uk

For Abbey & Sam

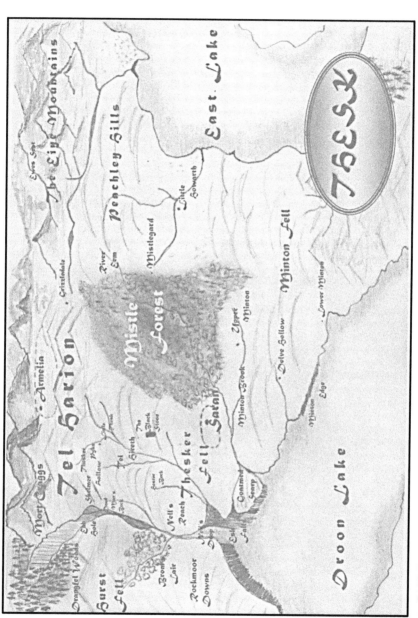

CHAPTER ONE

The One Left Behind

Godwyn Savidge was standing in front of the fireplace in Lovage Hall. A portrait was hanging on the wall behind him with three people in it: the Hall's owners, Lady Élanor and her younger sister, Tally, with their father, Lord Lakeston. It had been painted before he died, when Tally was still a baby.

'I just can't believe you've brought Wil Calloway back after what he did to my son!' Godwyn was saying.

Lady Élanor's housekeeper Martha put another log on the fire and offered slices of honey cake to the people gathered in Lady Élanor's sitting room. No one was smiling.

'He was going to marry Olivia!' said Godwyn.

Morten Mortens, the Grand Wizen of the Order of the Magewizen, took a huge piece of cake and gave Martha a polite smile. Oswald Beck declined Martha's offer of cake with a wave of his hand. Agatha Peasgood took a very thin slice of cake but didn't eat it. Godwyn was still talking.

'If Calloway hadn't been so busy trying to be a hero... We should have hung him when we had the chance... We were too soft, Mortens.' Godwyn pointed his finger at the group of people. 'I warned you but you wouldn't listen!'

Lady Élanor was sitting next to the fire. She interrupted before Godwyn could speak again.

'We are all so sorry that you have lost your son, Godwyn.' Her voice was soft and quiet. Oswald, Agatha and Morten Mortens nodded. Godwyn stared into the fire. 'But Giles was an experienced Fellman. Wil is not to blame for what happened.' She nodded towards a teenage boy sitting quietly, eating a piece of honey cake. 'I asked Wil to come, Godwyn, to help rescue my sister.'

'Well, I don't see how–,' Godwyn hissed. Lady Élanor did not let him finish.

'Godwyn,' she said with a kind smile. 'You know it wasn't Wil's fault – Giles made a huge mistake.'

No one spoke. Godwyn's only son had been attacked during a moon chase and no one knew what had happened to him.

Wil's own father had been taken away by Lord Rexmoore's men six years ago because Wil's parents couldn't pay their taxes and he, too, had no idea where his father was now. Suddenly Wil felt very sorry for Godwyn Savidge.

**

A knock on the door made everyone jump. Martha rushed to answer it.

'Master Merridown!'

She stepped aside and a tall young man strode[1]* into the room.

'Hello, Martha, my lady,' said Mortimer, nodding as he looked around the room. Then he spotted his old friend. 'Wil! I *knew* we'd see you again! How's that Fellhound of yours – Apophinis? Is he behaving himself?'

'Oh, Phinn's fine –my mother *might* one day forgive him for chewing her favourite bedspread – well actually, it was her only bedspread!' Wil answered. Mortimer laughed.

'Well, where is he? I bet he's grown! Mia – Phinn's sister – remember? She's brilliant – big, too, like her dad – Tarek would have been so proud!'

Mortimer suddenly looked sad. Wil spoke quickly.

'Phinn's as big as Farrow!' He held his hand up to his waist to show Mortimer. 'He's up in the stables with Pickles and Alana–'

Lady Élanor interrupted.

'Gentlemen, we are here to talk about rescuing Tally and Tanith.'

'Sorry, yes, Lady Élanor,' said Mortimer, suddenly serious. 'Actually, that's why I'm here. I want to help.'

(* When you see a tiny number like this [1] take a look in the back of this book)

Wil sat and listened while they talked about how to get to Armelia and who might go. Lady Élanor was holding a scrap of paper in her fist. Wil knew the words on the paper said: *'Give up the legacy or I will make your precious sister tell me where it is!'*

He also knew that only three people knew where, and what, Saran's legacy was, and that Tally was not one of them. He watched Lady Élanor push her long silver hair back over her shoulders and look at the map. Earlier Godwyn Savidge had stepped on it, leaving a big muddy print of his boot on the corner, although nobody mentioned it.

The map showed the kingdom of Thesk. Wil could see his village, Mistlegard, and Mistle Forest with the River Eem going through it. He could also see Tel Harion, where the Wraithe Wolves lived. Wil couldn't forget their smell... or the Moon Chase he had been forced to join the previous autumn... or the terrifying howls of those wolves. He could also see that it was the quickest route to Armelia, and so could Mortimer.

Morten Mortens leant forward to look at the map, still clutching his plate which was empty apart from a few crumbs.

'What concerns me,' he said, giving Martha his empty plate as she tiptoed past, 'is more that Rexmoore's wife will soon realise that Tally doesn't know where the legacy is. Eli, this is very serious.

'When your mother died, Imelda was convinced your father had hidden a huge pile of gold from her. She was wrong, but Rexmoore had been in love with her for years and suddenly she realised he might be useful so she married him. If Rexmoore thinks he is getting close to finding that gold for his wife, he is not going to give up easily.'

A tear trickle down Lady Élanor's cheek and dripped onto the paper she was still holding. Godwyn Savidge, who had been silent for some time, sniffed loudly.

'Well, I just don't understand why you are so worried about an old horse and a fourteen-year-old girl – who is not even from Saran!' He spoke with gritted teeth. 'And as for this legacy of yours, *your worship* – even as a member of your own Order, I don't know what it is!'

For the first time that evening Morten Mortens looked angry. 'Now, really, Godwyn, that's– '

But Godwyn Savidge was not to be stopped.

'No, Mortens! I've only ever done my best for Saran – bought things with my own gold, too! And how do you repay me? You keep secrets and you have my son destroyed. Well, I'm telling you,' he turned to Mortimer, 'Rexmoore's men will destroy you before you even reach Tel Harion!'

And with that he marched to the front door, grabbed his cloak and stormed out – leaving the door wide open behind him. As Godwyn left, Martha came out of the kitchen with a tray of glasses filled with ruby red elderberry wine.

It was finally agreed that Tel Harion was the best route because it was the quickest; Mortimer, Wil and Phinn would leave at dawn the next morning with Fellmen Leon Beck, Curtis Waller and Becky Lum. Oswald had insisted he was going too, although it was obvious that Mortimer was not happy about this.

Wil was very surprised that no one had mentioned Gisella, not even when they had discussed the other bit of news – the mysterious disappearance of her mother, Fermina Fairfax. Seth Tanner had, however, been considered, but the general view was that Seth's mother wouldn't let him go – particularly after the last Moon Chase! Wil couldn't help but agree.

CHAPTER TWO

Dawn Flight

Freezing air hit Wil's face like a wave of icy water. Struggling to breathe, he was sure he was travelling *very* fast – *downwards* – and kept his eyes tight shut. Suddenly he changed direction – upwards. The wind roared in his ears; his nose burned in the cold. Another dive. He instantly regretted eating three pieces of honey cake, retched, fell sideways...

...and landed with a loud thud on the floor-boards of the bedroom in Lovage Hall.

Confused and bruised, Wil could hear heavy rain beating on the window. It was dark. Someone was running.

'Wil, are you alright?' It was Lady Élanor. 'Can I come in?'

Wil climbed back into bed shaking. 'Er... yer... er...'

The bedroom door opened. Lady Élanor was holding a lamp – its candle flickered and made her shadow dance on the wall.

'What was that noise? Wil – are you alright?'

'I... I'm fine... I... think...' Wil stammered. He could feel his cheeks going red. 'I fell out of bed. I... I thought I was flying.'

A sudden, sharp tap on the window made them both jump. The rain sounded heavier. The tapping got louder... and more impatient. Something peered through the tiny glass panes, something dark... and...wet... Then Wil saw the shape of a raven.

'Pricilla!'

He crawled to the end of the bed and opened the window.

'Crronk! Crronk! Prruk!'

The soggy raven hopped onto the bed, spread her wings and flapped, and Wil hid behind the bed covers until she had finished. The visions from his dream began to make sense.

'Well, if letting me fly with you was your idea of a welcome, Pricilla, I'm very glad it was dark! You know I hate heights!'

The huge bird gave Wil's big toe a light peck and flew over to the washstand where she took a long drink from the water jug.

Lady Élanor didn't seem to notice. She stood at the open window and stared out into the drenched black night. Rain trickled over her hand. Pricilla splooshed[2] water over the floor.

'I was dreaming I was flying – must have been reading Pricilla's mind while she was coming here,' said Wil, although he didn't think Lady Élanor was listening. 'Gosh, it's cold up there!'

Lady Élanor didn't answer. The rain splashed off the windowsill onto the brightly coloured quilt at the end of Wil's bed. Wil tried to guess what she was thinking. He could just about read the minds of animals if he concentrated really hard; it was only Lady Élanor and Tally who could read the minds of humans.

'Don't worry about Tally, my lady,' said Wil. 'I'm sure she's OK.' He knew this sounded weak but he didn't know what else to say. The candle in the lamp flickered again in a sudden gust. Lady Élanor closed the window.

'I hope so, Wil,' she whispered and walked to the door. Without looking back she said softly, 'Pricilla, I have a dead mouse downstairs. Would you like it?'

Much later, Wil was woken by a loud banging on the front door downstairs. He could hear a gruff man and Lady Élanor's housekeeper; Martha did not sound very happy at all.

Wil got out of bed as quietly as he could and dressed quickly, grabbed his hunting knife and cloak, and hurried out of the bedroom carrying his boots to avoid making a noise on the wooden floor.

To his surprise, Mortimer was at the bottom of the stairs. He put his finger to his own lips and pointed towards the living room. Wil nodded and listened.

Lady Élanor was talking now, not Martha.

'Sorry, er, Wil Calloway? No, there is no one here with that name, sire.'

A man's voice replied.

'We know he's here, my lady. There's no point lying. We must take him to Armelia. Lord Rexmoore is waiting.'

As Wil was wondering how Rexmoore even knew his name – or that he was in Saran – a second man spoke. His voice sounded familiar, but Wil couldn't remember from where.

'Look, woman, give 'im[3] up or we'll come in and get 'im!'

The next sound Wil heard was the creak of a door hinge – Lady Élanor must have opened the front door wide, although, to his surprise, she didn't sound cross at all.

'Come in and search, gentlemen! Where would you like to start?'

'Right, where's the stairs? I heard something up there just now. I bet he's under the bed – they're always under the bed... unless you've got an attic!' said another voice.

Lady Élanor's voice sounded very strange when

she answered: 'Before you start, gentlemen, would you like a cup of mint tea... and some breakfast, perhaps? It is still very early. You must be *starving.*'

As she said the word 'starving', Wil thought about a plate piled with slices of warm bread spread with butter and sweet raspberry jam. His stomach rumbled. Just as he took a step forward, Martha's chubby hand grabbed his arm. She was holding Mortimer's elbow with her other hand.

Wil could hear Lady Élanor's voice. She was telling Rexmoore's men about hot buttered toast, homemade marmalade, scones, scrambled eggs...

Without saying a word Martha pulled the boys away and by the time they reached the library Wil had forgotten about breakfast entirely.

'What happened back there?' whispered Mortimer, nodding back towards the stairs.

Martha chuckled. 'Oh, that's one of Lady Élanor's little tricks. They won't even remember why they came here! I've seen her do that with naughty children before now... although it doesn't seem to work so well on Tally, now she's a bit older!' She frowned. 'Not sure how the one with only one hand'll cut his bacon though? Or butter his toast!'

At Martha's words, Wil remembered when and where he had heard that man's voice; Wil had cut the man's hand off when he tried to stop Wil and Gisella escaping from the deer rustlers on the Thesker Fell, after the Moon Chase. He must have told Rexmoore about Sir Jerad Tinniswood's theory that Wil was a seer[4]. Of course! Maybe Rexmoore thought Wil could read Tally's mind? But Wil knew Rexmoore was wrong: whenever Wil and Tally linked minds, Wil was so badly affected that he seriously thought he was going to die.

Bryn was waiting at the stables, just as Martha had said, and standing with him were Seth and Gisella. Wil was about to say a friendly hello when Mortimer spoke.

'Seth, where are the others?' He did not sound in the least bit pleased to see them and didn't even look at

Gisella, who was standing beside a pure white Fellhound.

Wil felt very awkward, although Seth didn't seem to notice.

'Rexmoore's men took them – they're all over the village, Mort!' The young boy's eyes shone with excitement. 'I heard them asking about you, Wil. Martha woke me up. She told me to meet you here to help rescue Tally. D'you think Farrow looks good, Wil? Her ear's better now.' Seth patted the shoulder of another much bigger, grey Fellhound that sat next to him. Even sitting down she was nearly the same height as Seth. 'I've just seen Phinn – he's massive! What've you been feeding him?'

While Seth continued to chat away Farrow got to her feet and wagged her long tail lazily. Wil could see a neat split down her right ear – an old battle wound. She, too, was wearing an iron collar – a collar Wil knew had once saved her life while she fought to protect Seth.

Wil was confused by Mortimer's sudden bad mood. Gisella remained silent, but at least Farrow seemed pleased to see him. Gisella continued to fiddle with the hound's collar. Hoping he sounded friendly and relaxed, Wil asked, 'So, is this Mia?' But Mortimer answered before Gisella could open her mouth.

'Yeah, this is Mia. Why is she with you, Gisella?'

Wil was stunned. Gisella answered without looking up.

'Seth asked me to help. Rexmoore's men were arresting everyone – I thought I might be needed. Seth's brought Rhoani, too.'

Bryn looked at Mortimer, then Gisella, then back at Mortimer. He shook his head sadly and turned towards the stable block. 'Martha, come and help with Pickles, he's still not eating – missing his mistress too much, I think.'

Martha looked relieved to be called away; Wil was very tempted to follow, too – this certainly *wasn't* the reunion[5] he'd been hoping for!

Mortimer glared at Seth. 'Do your parents know where you are *this* time?'

'Er, yeah... well... Martha said she'd tell them. Anyway, they'll understand that I didn't have a choice. Everyone except for Olivia and Gisella were being taken away!'

'So, why didn't you bring Olivia?'

Wil could see that Seth still hadn't realised anything was wrong.

'Well, I didn't think Olivia would come, Mort. You know what she's been like – she's still missing Giles. And anyway, Gisella was closer and, well, you two have been training Mia for most of the winter. I thought you were... um, well... I thought you two were, er... going out?'

'What?' said Wil and Gisella together.

Mortimer went very pale. As he answered he jabbed his finger towards poor Seth, who stepped back.

'I can assure you, Seth, we are NOT going out. And *you* should have just come alone!'

Mortimer turned towards the stables. Mia walked over to Gisella.

'Mia, come!' Mortimer shouted without turning around. Mia did as she was told.

Seth looked like he might cry.

'Oh dear, I'm so sorry, Gisella. I didn't realise. But with your mother gone… well… you and Mortimer have spent so much time together over the last few months that everyone just assumed…'

'Well, they were wrong,' snapped Gisella. 'You were *all* wrong! And it looks like *my* assumption that we were all friends was wrong, too!'

CHAPTER THREE

A Bitter Reunion

Mortimer's mood had got worse during the morning; he didn't even thank Martha for the four saddle-packs, each one stuffed with blankets, food and flasks of water and elder wine.

'Lady Élanor made me pack these last night,' she had muttered, pushing another plump pasty into Wil's bag. 'I think she knew something like this would happen. I've put your first aid kit in, Wil... Mortimer, I packed some extra herbs and spices in yours.'

Mortimer didn't seem to hear so Wil nodded a thank-you – the very special first aid kit had been extremely useful during the Moon Chase.

Bryn had given them all new crossbows together with as many bolts as they could all carry.

'You still got that hunting knife Tally gave you for the Moon Chase?' he had asked, handing more bolts to Wil.

'Don't worry, Bryn – I wouldn't be without it!'

'I put a collar on Phinn, too,' added the

gamekeeper. Phinn was lying on a patch of grass at the end of the stable block, rubbing his neck along the ground. His face and the collar were covered with fresh mud. Bryn laughed. 'I don't think he likes it much though!'

Mortimer had not smiled once.

'Right, come on. Wil, you ride with me,' he had said eventually. 'We've got to get to the Black Rock before it gets dark.'

Now, it felt to Wil like the rain would never stop. Shadow and Rhoani splashed over the soaking ground while Mia and Phinn followed, looking utterly miserable; Farrow did her best to stay under the trees – no matter how low the branches got. Wil pulled his cloak over his head.

Suddenly all three Fellhounds stopped and stared at the same patch of the gloomy forest. Mortimer pulled Shadow to a halt and held up his hand for Seth to do the same just as a branch sprang towards them. Rhoani leapt sideways. Seth and Gisella tumbled off the startled horse and landed on the mud with a soggy *splat*[6].

'Who's there?' demanded Mortimer.

Gisella was already on one knee, her bow loaded and ready to shoot. Seth tripped but managed to grab at the reins of his frightened horse. Farrow gave a warning bark.

'Do not be alarmed,' said a familiar voice and a

slender figure appeared through the trees in front of them.

'Lady Élanor!' exclaimed Seth. Gisella lowered her bow. Farrow gave a sweeping wag of her tail; Mia and Phinn wandered off to shelter under a leafy branch. Lady Élanor pushed her hood back and opened her mouth to speak but Mortimer spoke first.

'Are you alright, my lady? Rexmoore's men – Seth said they've arrested the Fellmen. What about Leon? How–'

Lady Élanor held up her hand for quiet.

'I am fine, thank you. The Fellmen are in Saran jail, but Leon and Olivia are not among them. Morten is trying to find out why the others have been arrested, although Rexmoore's men seem only interested in you.' She nodded towards Wil. 'And as for my visitors... they had a bit too much of Martha's gooseberry gin porridge and are now enjoying a restful nap. They will not wake for a while yet.'

'So what happened to Leon and Olivia?' asked Wil.

'I am told that Olivia has gone to stay with an aunt in Lower Minton – she left yesterday afternoon. Leon got away with Oswald. They will meet you at the Black Stone.'

She glanced over her shoulder and then took another two steps forward.

'There is something else I must tell you... I assume that you have all heard of the Alcama?' She rested her hand on Rhoani's nose.

Mortimer, Gisella and Wil nodded. Seth looked as if he was trying to remember something.

'Isn't that when the twin moons do something weird?' he said looking around the sky as if he was expecting to see Thesk's two moons at that moment. 'My mother told me about it. I missed the last one 'cos I was in bed with mumps. I can't really remember what happened.'

'Yes, Seth – once every seven years the two moons cross and for a brief moment they become one. Long ago the people of Thesk believed that the Alcama was a time of evil. They would sacrifice animals and lock their doors on the night of the Moon Crossing.' Her face became sad. 'Children born on the Alcama were cast out as witches.'

'So, what's the Alcama got to do with us rescuing Tally?' asked Mortimer.

'That is a reasonable question, Mortimer,' said Lady Élanor. 'There are some who wish to keep the fear of witchcraft alive – my aunt, Imelda, is one of these. People can be controlled when they are frightened.' She paused, stroking Rhoani's nose in long sweeps, then added, 'She knows this... she also knows that my sister was born on the night of the Alcama.'

'Oh,' said Mortimer.

'The Alcama is in three nights' time,' continued Lady Élanor. 'Imelda will use Tally any way she can to find out what and where Saran's legacy is, and I cannot imagine what would happen if she was successful.'

Seth looked confused.

'Legacy? I didn't know Saran had a legacy. Does that mean there's loads of gold hidden away somewhere?'

Lady Élanor's vague answer did not surprise Wil.

'The legacy ensures that the people of Saran are kept safe and well, Seth. *What* and *where* it is are nothing to be concerned about. Tally is as ignorant about this as you and, in fact, me. I want her home because only then can I be sure that they are safe – at Lovage Hall – with me.' She turned then turned back. 'You can only help her if you are acting as one.'

CHAPTER FOUR

Friends No More

It had stopped raining at last, and the ride through Mistle Forest was made a lot more enjoyable by Phinn and Mia: son and daughter of Tarek – the Fellhound that Mortimer had tragically lost on that doomed Moon Chase. They galloped through the trees and bounded into the long grass at the edge of the forest.

'Well, they certainly seem to like each other!' said Wil.

'Yep!' was Mortimer's curt reply.

There was a yelp from somewhere behind them. Wil turned. Mia had Phinn pinned to the ground with her huge jaws around her brother's throat.

'Mia, gentle!' roared Mortimer. Mia immediately let go and with a single booming bark jumped backwards, lazily wagging her huge tail. Free from his sister, Phinn ducked behind her and nipped her bottom. It was Mia's turn to yelp. Then both hounds raced around in a huge circle, darting between the trees, their massive strides covering the ground at breakneck speed[7].

Wil tried again to get Mortimer to talk.

'It's great to see Phinn playing with something his own size. At home he's got the choice between the Peachley herding dogs or the tiny Grizzledale Terriers – or the sheep, of course… well, he *thinks* the sheep are one of the choices anyway!'

Mortimer didn't say a thing. Wil gave up. Instead he watched Phinn and Mia in their own mad game. Stretching every muscle, Phinn caught up with Mia, tucked his nose under her ribcage and lifted her clean off her feet. Once she was brought down, his massive jaws closed around her throat; then, almost as if he had counted to three, he jumped away to let her chase him.

As the sun rose higher over the trees the young hounds were finally starting to get tired when Farrow galloped off into the dark forest. She returned only moments later with something limp and dead swinging from her jaws; it was a plump, deer-like creature covered in red feathers.

'There we are, Mortimer, we can have marbussal for lunch!' Seth grinned. 'My aunt cooked one for us last yulefest[8]. I was really surprised; it was yummy!'

But Seth wasn't smiling for long.

'There's no time for cooking. Martha gave us food. Eat that. The hounds can share the marbussal later!'

A long time later Wil noticed that the trees were not as tightly packed. They were right at the edge of the forest. Wil's thighs ached and his bottom was completely numb. All he wanted to do was get his feet back onto solid ground so that he could stretch his legs.

'I really think we need to stop for a break, Mortimer,' he said hopefully.

Mortimer's reply was reasonable but still sullen.

'No. We've got to get to the Black Stone before dark. You heard Lady Élanor, Wil. Leon and Oswald'll be waiting for us – it's too dangerous for them to be that close to Tel Harion without any hounds.' He paused then added, 'And it's not as if our own support is that great!'

Wil had heard enough. He let go of Mortimer's waist, slid backwards over Shadow's rump[9] and hobbled[10] around trying to get some feeling back into his legs and feet – he simply could not understand why people rode horses for pleasure!

Mortimer looked down in complete astonishment.

'What the…! *What* are you doing, Wil?'

But before Wil could say a thing Seth slowed Rhoani and swung his leg over the horse's neck. 'Well, I agree with Wil!'

He jumped to the ground and darted[11] behind a bush. Farrow followed him.

'Go on, girl! Can't a boy have a little privacy?' said Seth from somewhere in the thick greenery.

Beaten for now, Mortimer slid to the ground and untied the saddle-packs. Wil looked around. Rhoani was standing on his own – Gisella and Mia had also disappeared.

Starving, Wil munched on a soft bread roll from his pack. He really wasn't looking forward to the ride across Thesker Fell.

'Oh, no!' Seth's horrified tone dragged Wil from his own worries. Seth was holding a sandwich that was missing a large bite-sized chunk. 'Martha's put tomato chutney on my ham – *I hate tomato chutney* – yech!'

Seth spat bits of chewed sandwich into the grass and threw the rest into the long grass, where Mia took an immediate interest. Gisella was on her feet in a second.

'Seth, you know you're not to give them food just after exercise!'

She grabbed at the hound's collar and bent to pick up the bread. 'No, Mia!'

A bolt thunked[12] into the ground only a few inches from her outstretched fingers.

'What the…!'

Mortimer held his bow steady; his face was as white as a sheet.

'If I want you to interfere with the training, or welfare, of *my* Fellhound, Gisella Fairfax – I will ask you! OK?'

Wil and Seth watched, speechless – Wil was barely able to breathe.

Gisella unwound her fingers from Mia's collar,

picked up the bread and walked towards Mortimer. When she spoke, her voice was so calm Wil was actually scared.

'Oh, I'm sorry, Mortimer. Did *you* want this?' And she hurled[13] the food straight into Mortimer's face.

'Whoa!' whispered Seth. Wil didn't move. One of the bread slices left a trail of tomato relish down Mortimer's nose before it dropped to the ground.

'*That* wasn't funny!' Mortimer growled and raised his hand.

'*NO!*' shouted Wil. Mia leapt between Mortimer and Gisella and growled. The hound was utterly confused – Wil could feel it: the two people she loved most in the world were fighting and she didn't know which one to protect.

At the sound of Mia's growl Mortimer lowered his hand.

'It's alright, Mia. Down.' His gentle tone surprised Wil. The hound looked from Mortimer to Gisella, then back to her master. Gisella continued to glare at Mortimer. He repeated his order as softly as before. '*Down*, Mia.'

Wil could feel the hound's heart rate slowing down as if it was his own, and she lowered her body and lay down in the grass – but Wil knew she was still confused.

Farrow and Phinn were watching their own masters.

Without another word, Mortimer wiped the tomato relish off his cheek, turned and walked away towards the horses. Wil and Mia followed, leaving Gisella with silent tears streaming down her cheeks. Wil heard Seth's frightened voice behind him.

'Gosh, Gisella, what was *that* all about?'

Wil was so angry he wanted to punch Mortimer, and for a moment he really believed he would feel better it he did. But instead, he took a very deep breath and tried his best to sound calm.

'Is Mia OK, Mort? She didn't eat any of the bread, did she?'

'She's fine,' answered Mortimer. Wil could see his friend's hands were shaking.

'Good job Gisella got there in time then, wasn't it? We don't want a hound with bloat just now, do we?'

Mortimer continued to fiddle with one of the buckles on his pack and didn't look up.

'Yeah. It's a good job she's so quick. She's always looked after Mia like that. Though...' he hauled the pack into his saddle, 'I know why, now!'

He said those last words so quietly that Wil thought he'd misheard.

'What do you mean, Mortimer? You know why – *why, what?*'

'Look, Wil, just leave it. It's got nothing to do with

26

you! We need to get a move on. Leon and Oswald need us!'

'Yes, and so does Tally! But if you and Gisella don't sort this out, no one's gonna to get rescued!'

Mortimer turned and looked past Wil to where Seth was comforting Gisella.

'She's trouble, Wil. She's trying to make Mia obey her instead of me so that she can get me killed on the next Moon Chase!'

Wil felt as if someone had just clutched hold of his heart and squeezed it with both hands. He could not believe what Mortimer had just said.

'Mortimer, I don't know who you've been talking to, mate, but they're messing with your head!' Wil was whispering now. He could hardly believe what he had just heard. *'You don't honestly believe that Gisella is planning to get you killed?'*

Mortimer's jaw twitched.

'Olivia told me that–'

Wil could stop himself from laughing.

'Olivia! Olivia Drews? *Giles Savidge's girlfriend? Ha!'*

Gisella and Seth looked over. Wil tried his best to keep his voice to a whisper. 'For goodness sake, Mort – she blamed Gisella for what happened to Giles!'

'Look, Wil, you haven't been here. Gisella's been around so much since I've had Mia that some days it's all I can do to get Mia to listen to me. I tell you – if I'd let it go on any longer... I'd definitely have lost control of that Fellhound and goodness knows what might have happened on the next Moon Chase!'

Mortimer climbed back up onto Shadow's saddle.

'Come on,' said Mortimer, his voice loud enough for the others to hear. It was clear that his conversation with Wil was over. 'Try to keep up – they'll be waiting.'

CHAPTER FIVE

The Black Rock

The ride across the Fell was horrible. The freezing wind made Wil's eyes stream and every time it felt like they were slowing down, Mortimer just made Shadow gallop faster. Wil clung on.

Rabbits and deer ran in all directions as Mia, Farrow and Phinn bounded over fallen trees and swerved around boulders. Rhoani jumped right across a stream instead of galloping though it – Gisella was fine although Seth very nearly landed in the water!

Mortimer finally slowed Shadow to a walk just as Wil was seriously considering falling off and walking the rest of the way – no matter how far it was. The sun was setting and the clouds shone pink and gold. All around them the ground was white with frost; Wil could see snow amongst the barren[14] rocks. Up ahead a huge rock stood like a black tower against the sky.

'The Black Rock,' said Mortimer.

***

It was almost dark when they climbed the gentle slope that led up to the huge rock.

A voice growled, 'You're late!' and a dark figure with a loaded crossbow stepped out of the gloom. Phinn stopped and sniffed but the other two hounds padded towards the voice, their huge tails wagging from side to side. The speaker was Leon Beck, the Bearer from the Moon Chase. Wil knew that Leon had always blamed him and Gisella for what had happened to Giles that night.

Leon acknowledged Mortimer with an abrupt nod; he ignored Wil.

'What took you so long?' Then Leon noticed Seth and Gisella. 'What the hell have you brought these two for?'

Mortimer swung his leg over Shadow's neck and slid down the saddle.

'Rexmoore's men,' he said. 'They got Emmet and Curtis so Lady Élanor made a few changes.' He spat on the ground near Shadow's feet. Wil carefully dragged his aching leg over Shadow's bottom, gripped the saddle with both hands and very slowly lowered himself to the ground. Leon watched Wil's painful dismount.

'Yeah, we saw them take Emmet. They got Becky, too. I reckon *someone* tipped them off after yesterday's meeting – *can't think who!*'

Gisella dropped her bag close to the fire and

stomped off towards the sound of running water – a stream, Wil guessed.

Wil stood on the high bank of the gully. He could see Gisella below, up to her knees, splashing water over her face and arms. The shallow brook tumbled noisily over the rocks making any surrounding sounds impossible to hear; now was the time, Wil decided, to find out what was really going on with her and Mortimer.

The climb down wasn't easy in the dark. Wil grabbed every tree branch to stop himself falling while Phinn kept his body so low that his deep ribcage brushed the ground.

As they reached the water's edge Gisella looked up. There were two splashes; one was Wil falling off a rock; the other was Phinn who obviously thought that Wil was playing.

'Well, that's one way to get my attention!' said Gisella as Wil spat out a mouthful of the river.

'It wasn't quite what I had in mind,' grinned Wil. Gisella didn't laugh… she didn't even smile.

Phinn ducked his nose into the icy water and blew bubbles. When his lungs ran out of air, he jerked his head up and coughed loudly. Then he did it again.

Wil tried very hard to stand up. But his cloak had wrapped around a tree root and he fell for the second time. This time Gisella did laugh.

She waded over and untangled the cloak. 'There, you should be able to get up now. Here!'

Wil took her outstretched hand[15]: cold and slender, it felt weird in his rough palm – nice, but weird.

Back on his feet and very soggy, Wil waded to the bank, plonked down on a twisted tree root, leant backwards and lifted his legs into the air. Water poured out of his boots – together with half a dozen bolts that he had jammed in there earlier. Gisella laughed again.

'Well, as long as someone thinks it was funny,' said Wil, with a good-natured grin.

Gisella's smile vanished. She waded back to the bank and picked up her boots.

'Well, it's certainly the funniest thing I've seen all day!'

Wil squeezed about a bucket of water out of his cloak.

'Just what *is* going on with you and Mortimer?' he said.

'I would have thought that *you* knew the answer to that, Wil!'

Wil continued to squeeze his dripping cloak.

'Well... if I did, I wouldn't... be asking... would I?'

Gisella gave a disbelieving snort.

'You don't honestly expect me to believe that, do you, Wil?' She was standing in the stream waving her boots over her head. 'Maybe *you'd* like to tell *me* what's going on because I *really* haven't got a clue!'

'Look, Gisella, I'm asking you because Mortimer just won't talk about it. Seth's as confused as me and, to be honest, unless it gets sorted out, I really don't think we've got any chance of rescuing Tally. In fact, I'm worried she'll be in more danger if we go!'

Gisella stopped flinging her boots around and stared into the stream.

'Do you think I hadn't thought of that, Wil? Look – all I know is that Bryn asked me to help Mortimer with Mia – after he, you know – lost Tarek so suddenly – then next minute he's best friends with Leon and I'm all on my own!'

'So, you and Mortimer... you aren't... I mean... you weren't... well, of course – you were just helping him with Mia, weren't you?' Wil's words tumbled out in a rush. Gisella frowned.

'That's what I just said, Wil.'

'Yes, but Seth... er... Seth said that he thought that everyone else assumed–'

'Wil, for goodness sake!' Gisella was waving her boots around again. Wil ducked in case she let go – accidentally, or on purpose! 'I am not *now* – and *never was* – going out with Mortimer Merridown, if that's what you are so clumsily trying to ask!'

'No... No! Of course not... I didn't think..., of course – I just thought, you know, I'd better check, er...

to make sure there was no… um… misunderstanding.'

'The only misunderstanding around here is that I thought I was coming to help my friends rescue Tally – but apparently no one wants me here!'

Gisella hurled one of her boots into the water right in front of her.

Wil watched the boot bob a little way downstream before it caught on a fallen branch, filled with water and sank. *I want you here!* he thought.

After a moment's silence he nodded to the spot where the boot had sunk and said out loud, 'Do you want me to go and get that?'

Gisella was still clutching the other boot. 'No, I'll get it!' She took a careful step and put one bare foot on a rock in the middle of the stream. 'Honestly, Wil, you've got to believe me. I told Bryn that I want to train as a Chaser. He was already worried about Mortimer taking Mia on so soon after Tarek so he suggested that I help Mortimer train Mia; that way I could keep Mortimer company, and learn about Fellhounds at the same time. And my mother was…' she frowned and took a deep breath, 'wasn't well… so it was a great excuse to get me out of the house.' She sploshed her foot back into the water. 'Mortimer seemed fine then one day I went to join him out on Nell's Reach and he completely ignored me. It was awful, Wil. I don't know what I've done and now he won't even look at me…' She stopped talking, retrieved her boot and swooshed a handful of water over her face.

Wil sat on the bank.

OK, so she does want to be a Chaser, he thought. *But that doesn't mean she wants to take Mortimer's place... and it certainly doesn't mean she wants him dead... Does it?*

'Did you tell anyone else about Bryn's idea, Gizzy?' he asked.

'Only Olivia – I went to see her. I know she said some horrid things about me on the Moon Chase after Giles... you know... but I'm sure she didn't mean them. We were always OK before.' Gisella clambered back along the rocks and tree roots that cluttered the riverbank. 'She doesn't want to be a Fellman any more, Wil. Now Giles is gone she wants to leave Saran for good when she gets to her eighteenth summer. She told me but she made me promise not to tell anyone, so I haven't... until now. That's next summer, Wil. I could take her place without upsetting anyone – and we already know that Seth would prefer to be a Bearer than a Chaser, so he could take *my* place – as long as we could convince his father, of course!'

The root Wil was sitting on bounced as Gisella plonked down and emptied her boot into the swirling pool below her feet.

'Well, it certainly sounds like a good plan, Giz. Why didn't you tell Mortimer?'

'I promised Olivia I wouldn't tell anyone... and,

anyway, I wanted to make sure I could handle a Fellhound first. If I was hopeless I wouldn't stand a chance, I'd look stupid. So I asked Olivia not to tell anyone until I was ready and she said that she wouldn't.'

Wil stared down into the dark water below him as he listened; he knew she was telling the truth. Olivia must have broken her promise and told Leon and somehow the truth got twisted; so all Wil needed to do was to tell Mortimer what had happened. But how? Especially as Leon was about to go with them up onto Tel Harion!

CHAPTER SIX

A Gift from Above

'Where've you been?' Mortimer demanded when Wil walked back into the camp. Gisella was already back and seemed to be concentrating very hard on something right at the bottom of her pack.

'Went for a wash but I slipped – it took ages to wring out my clothes.'

Wil draped his wet cloak over a bush to make the point and delved[15] into his own bag.

Leon nodded towards Gisella. 'But *she* went down there, too?'

'Did she?' said Wil. He bit into a pasty that Martha had packed for him – it was absolutely delicious. He spoke again with his mouth full. 'Didn't see you, Giz... now you mention it Leon,' he swallowed, 'I did hear splashing further upstream. But it was so dark I couldn't see who it was.'

Wil took another bite; even though the pasty was cold, he could feel the food warming him up.

'Did anyone else have one of these pasties,

they're really good!'

'What was in yours, Wil?' asked Seth. 'I had corned beef – *my favourite!*' He was looking a lot happier now he had a full stomach.

'Pork and apple – I think?'

'Eew! That sounds yech!' Seth stuck his tongue out in disgust.

'I thought you might say that!' Wil grinned and popped the last scrumptious[16] piece into his mouth.

After supper, Mortimer told everyone to get some rest before they headed off. The fire was still glowing but Wil wasn't sure he was going to get any sleep at all on the frozen ground. He glanced over at Seth. The sleeping boy's hair was coated with frost that glistened in the moonlight. Wil pulled his damp cloak around him; within less than a minute he was fast asleep, too.

Wil was being chased by at least a hundred Wraithe Wolves. An eagard had just picked up Phinn and taken him over Mort Craggs; Phinn was yelping. The eagard flew over the ruins of a castle and let go–

Wil opened his eyes and sat up. He was being watched, he knew it. He shook his head and blinked into the dark. Everyone else was still asleep – he could hear their steady breathing. In the moonlight he could see Farrow and Mia sprawled out next to Seth and Mortimer; they were covered in ice crystals. Phinn though, was not asleep – Wil could see the hound's shining eyes watching him – his long eyebrows were sparkling with frost. Wil grinned. The young hound stayed with his chin flat on the floor between his huge, outstretched paws. Wil closed his eyes again but questions kept popping into his head – questions about Gisella and Mortimer, the journey they were about to make, and Tally: *How would they know where she was? Was she even still alive? What was Armelia like?*

Wil pulled his cloak up under his chin and tried not to think of anything. Suddenly something hit his cheek. He brushed his face in case it was an insect and shut his eyes again. Something else his forehead – it hurt.

'What the...?' he hissed and sat up. Phinn raised his head as well. A third stinging tap right on the top of Wil's head made both him and Phinn look up.

'Crronk!'

The familiar noise came from right up on the top of the Black Rock, high above them. Phinn sat bolt upright on his haunches[17].

No, DROP! Wil thought. Phinn lay down immediately and watched Wil intently.

'Well, that's a first!' Wil muttered, remembering all the times he and Phinn has spent in the sheepfold at Mistlegard when training sessions had not gone to plan – well, not *Wil's* plan anyway!

Another impatient *Crronk!* echoed out of the dark. Wil heard something hit the Black Rock just before it bounced off his shoulder. He grabbed it before it hit the ground. At the same moment, Wil caught sight of Oswald; he was lying on his side staring directly at Wil.

Not knowing what else to do, Wil shrugged his shoulders and smiled, holding out the long, straight stick he had just caught as the explanation for why he was dancing about in the freezing moonlight. But Oswald didn't even blink and after a few seconds he snored loudly and turned over.

Wil held his breath. No one else moved. He looked at Oswald again – the man was fast asleep. Wil decided not to check if Oswald's eyes were still open.

In the clear sky the twin moons cast a pale light across the sheer granite of the Black Rock. Wil knew that in a few nights' time the moons would cross and, for only as long as it took his heart to beat a dozen times, they would shine as one huge silver orb[18] – the Alcama. Wil wondered what the Alcama would be like in Saran. He remembered the last one in Mistlegard. It was his ninth spring. His parents had taken him to Garth Fengal's home where everyone in the village had gathered for the event. The house was round and built of stone like all of the houses in the village although it was a much bigger than most. The main house was surrounded by a cluster of little extensions, like a troop of mushrooms[19]. Each wall had a deep, tiny window, and on each windowsill was a sheep's skull lit up with a candle – put there for this special night. Wil's mother had told him that if the candles burned all night they would all have good luck for the next seven years. Later that evening when Wil opened the door to get some more pear juice from the larder one of the candles had blown out – just over a year later Rexmoore's men had come and taken Wil's father away and Wil never saw him again.

Wil shook his head to try to get rid of his sad memory. He looked around for Pricilla but the jet black raven was impossible to see in the dark, even if she was throwing things at him! Wil gave up and looked at the stick in his hand. To make sure he didn't wake the others, he tiptoed around to the other side of the Black Rock. Phinn padded after him.

'So, what've got here, Phinn?' Wil whispered. The stick felt surprisingly light. Phinn sniffed it. Wil gripped the thicker, smooth wood at one end – it was worn… it was also warm, as if the hand that had carried it for many years had only just let it go. The hairs on the back of Wil's neck prickled. He ran his hand down to the other end of the stick – or staff, or whatever it was? The other end was almost pointed; it was cold, too, some sort of metal; it was square with sharp corners and a flat base. With the metal tip on the ground the wooden head came up to Wil's elbow.

The staff, Wil decided, must have come from Lady Élanor – after all, it wouldn't be the first time she'd got

Pricilla to deliver something to him out on the Fells. But why? He had no idea, although he was sure he would find out soon enough.

CHAPTER SEVEN

Eagards!

'Where've you been?' asked Leon when Wil returned. He was trying to carry the staff in a way that he hoped no one would notice he was carrying a staff he hadn't had before.

'Oh, you know... just needed a private moment.' He tightened his belt to hint at what he meant. Leon nodded.

'Oh, yeah, er... right. Well, you'd better get packed up – we're not waiting!'

Wil picked up his flask and pushed it down into his pack. Right at the bottom of the deep bag his fingers touched something soft. It felt like fine rope but there was too much food on top of it to get a proper look at that moment. He was about to slide the staff into the pack when he heard Mortimer right behind him.

'What's that?' Mortimer had been a lot happier since they had met up with Leon.

'Not sure yet,' whispered Wil. 'I reckon it's from Lady Élanor.'

'Hmm, well, if it's *half* as useful as the first aid pack she gave you on the Moon Chase, it'll be worth trying to hang on to it!' Mortimer watched while Wil first tried to jam the staff into his bag only to find it was too long; then he tried to tie it to his bow but the cord snapped and both bow and staff clattered to the ground.

'Oh, well done, Wil! Look! You've broken it!'

Mortimer was pointing down at the staff. It was lying on the ground, snapped in two places and bent almost into a triangle.

'Oh, great!' Wil sighed and snatched up the broken staff. It immediately became a perfectly straight rod again.

'Whoa!' said Mortimer, stepping back. 'How did you do *that*?'

'Don't know,' answered Wil. He bent the staff gently – it did not break. He held it out in front of him and let go: as it hit the stone, the rod flicked back into the shape of a triangle. Wil had an idea. He carefully picked it up and squeezed the triangle into a neat bundle, about a third the length of the original staff and, with a grin, tucked it neatly into his bag.

Mortimer raised his eyebrow. 'Hmm, I have to admit, Wil, I'm not sure I can think of any uses for a collapsible stick just at the moment!'

The journey through the rest of the night was fast and extremely uncomfortable, although they did manage to get across the river on Tel Hireth without Seth falling in!

By dawn, Mortimer seemed happy with progress and agreed almost immediately when Oswald suggested they should stop for a rest.

With sweat pouring down his face, Oswald was the first to dismount. He stood for while with his hands on his knees, breathing very heavily, before he carefully sat down and leant back against a rock. He straightened his leg and winced[20].

Leon bent to speak to his father and although Wil couldn't hear what Leon said, Oswald's bad-tempered answer was loud enough for everyone to hear.

'For the last time, boy – I'm absolutely fine!'

Leon turned away, looking worried. He dragged a package from his saddle pack and stomped off to join Mortimer, who was sitting under a tree devouring[21] one of Martha's pasties; his broadsword and crossbow were leaning against the trunk of the tree behind him.

'The hounds'll need time to rest and eat,' said Mortimer, dropping pastry crumbs down his chest, 'So once we've eaten we might as well all try to get some sleep.'

'Good plan, Mort!' said Leon, waving a chicken leg in mock salute[22].

Wil still wanted to talk to Mortimer about Gisella, but with Leon always there, it was proving impossible.

Wil munched on a piece of honey cake and

thought about Lady Élanor's words: '*Not if you are not acting as one,*' she had warned, then he thought about Leon and Oswald bickering and the row between Mortimer and Gisella. At that moment the prospect of them all working together was seemed impossible.

'When do you think we'll get to Armelia?' Leon asked with a mouthful of bread.

'Well, we're right above Skelmer Hollow now,' replied Mortimer. Suddenly Wil didn't want the rest of his breakfast: just the name of the place brought back very bad memories. Mortimer didn't notice. He pointed to a hill in the distance. 'Once we get to the tip of Thesker Pyke we'll be able to see Mort Craggs. The city's not far then.'

'So where's the castle? Is it actually *in* Armelia?' asked Seth. He and Gisella were sitting on a rocky ledge a little way off. Gisella was staring out over the frost-coated grassland. Mortimer raised his pasty in Oswald's direction.

'No! Mortimer, *LOOK OUT!*' A shout from Gisella drowned out whatever he said. But before Mortimer had time to raise his head a huge grey and black shape swooped down and grabbed at Mortimer's wrist.

'*Eagards!*' yelled Seth.

Mortimer cried out. The great bird wrapped its talons around Mortimer's arm and tried to take off again.

Leon was on his feet in a flash. But, as if something had lifted him up and thrown him away, Leon suddenly flipped backwards and lay flat on the ground with his arms over his head.

'*NO!*' Oswald yelled and ran to his son. The eagard continued to flap its massive wings– each one easily the length of a full-grown man – but Oswald didn't seem to notice.

Wil grabbed his bow… and cursed; his bolts were

still on the river bank! Any spares were packed away in his bag but Rhoani and Shadow had bolted out onto the Fell as soon as the eagards had attacked. Mia was frantically leaping and snapping at the huge bird. Wil yanked his knife from his belt. He could see Mortimer trying to reach for his sword. His desperate fingers touched the hilt just as the monstrous bird hauled him into the air. Wil heard a clang and the sword toppled away, out of reach.

Mia leapt for the eagard's neck but she was knocked backwards by an easy beat of the bird's giant wing. Gisella called out. She was standing on the ledge above Wil jabbing her finger to his left.

'Wil – my bow – *use my bow!*'

Wil whirled around – Gisella's bow was only a few feet from him and there in the stock, ready to fire, lay a silver-tipped bolt.

'Gisella Fairfax,' Wil muttered, 'you are truly wonderful.' He dived for the bow. Two more eagards came out of the sky – Farrow and Phinn were ready for them. One swerved to avoid Farrow's snapping jaws, crashed straight into Gisella and took off into the safety of the sky.

The other eagard wasn't so lucky – Phinn snapped his jaws around its throat; with a gush of dark blood it died before the Fellhound had dragged it to the ground.

There was no sign of Gisella, and Mortimer was now being dragged away. Mia, back on her feet, was joined by Farrow. They charged after her master and, with a lunge, Mia grabbed a mouthful of tail feathers in her teeth and held on.

Adrenalin burned through Wil's veins. He dragged the string of Gisella's bow back until it clicked. An ear-piercing screech made him look around. Hurtling straight towards him on an absolute collision course was the third eagard. It streaked through the sky with its wings in a dive position – Wil took aim and was just about to shoot when Seth stood up in front of him facing the stooping bird. Seth's bow was ready too. He hadn't seen Wil. Wil yelled at the back of Seth's head.

'Seth, get out of the way!'

It was too late. Seth released his bolt. The bird screamed and went into a spin. Seth ducked: Wil, however, didn't.

CHAPTER EIGHT

A Stitch in Time

Wil woke up with a headache, a very bad headache.

'Wha... what happened?' He felt a cool hand on his arm.

'You were run over by an eagard,' answered Gisella. 'I think you might have a few broken ribs.'

Wil tried to sit up, realised it was a bad idea and lay back down.

'So what happened to the eagard?' he asked, looking around – everything looked very blurred.

'Seth shot it,' said Gisella. Wil could hear Seth and Mortimer's voices. Then he heard Oswald; he sounded very upset. Wil had a horrible thought.

'Oh no, Giz! Leon? Did they get Leon?'

'Yes, Wil. It's OK, he's not dead.' Gisella looked over her shoulder again. 'Well, I think it's OK.' Gisella spoke in a whisper. 'He's still unconscious. Oswald won't let me near him. Honestly, Wil, what does he think I'm going to do?'

Seth must have heard Gisella talking.

'Wil! Welcome back! You OK? I really thought you'd duck!'

He nodded in the same direction Gisella had looked. Wil could see three very blurred black and white mounds and realised they were eagards – dead ones. One didn't appear to have a head. Phinn and Farrow were guarding their trophies and Wil was also relieved to see Rhoani and Shadow tied to a tree. He hoped they had recovered from their fright.

Then Wil heard a groan: it came from Mortimer.

'Mort, you OK?' Wil was trying to see by blinking really quickly – it wasn't working. He could just see Mortimer waving – his arm was glistening crimson.

'Is that blood?' he whispered to Gisella. Seth seemed to be turning something tied to Mortimer's arm. Each time Seth moved, Mortimer gasped in pain.

'Is that a tourniquet?' asked Wil.

Gisella kept her voice to a whisper. 'It's really bad, Wil. It won't stop bleeding.'

'Have you looked in my pack?' asked Wil, just as quietly.

'No. Why would I do that?' Gisella sounded slightly offended.

'Because Martha packed another first aid kit – she told us at the stables!'

'Er, oh, I... I must have missed that,' answered Gisella.

'Can't think why!' sighed Wil. But Gisella was already on her way to Wil's pack. She came back clutching a familiar pink silk bag – even with his blurred vision Wil recognised it immediately.

Right, let's see if it works this time, Wil thought to himself. He put his hand into the little bag and immediately felt cool glass. It was a tiny clear phial[23] with a glass stopper in one end; swinging from the stopper was a label. He handed it to Gisella.

'It's no good, I just can't see the words properly.'

Gisella peered at the little label and read the words out loud:

'For Feather Blindness:

Apply once and keep eyes bound for four full days.

Do not allow sun or moon light to shine on eyes during treatment.

Best before: The next gibbous moon[24].'

Wil was confused. He glanced over at Mortimer and then back at Gisella.

'How're his eyes?'

Gisella pressed her lips together as she thought. 'I don't remember him saying anything about his eyes; he certainly looked horrified when I went to help him, so I'd say his sight is pretty good.' She looked directly into Wil's eyes. 'Must be for you then.'

Wil shut his eyes and looked away.

'It can't be. They're a bit blurry but they're getting

better all the time!' It was a lie: his sight wasn't a bit blurry, it was *very* blurry. 'I'll have another go.'

He put his hand right down into the bag again, this time he concentrated on Mortimer's blood-soaked bandage. A sharp pain shot through his finger.

'Ouch!' He dropped the bag.

A pack of needles and a twist[25] of fine golden thread fell out onto the ground. But this time there was no label.

Gisella looked down and then back at Wil. Her eyes were wide with surprise.

'Gosh, Wil... I think you're meant to sew him up.'

Wil gave a quick nod.

'I think you're right. Only problem is – I'm not sure I could find Mortimer's arm at the moment, let alone sew it up!' He blinked up at her. 'You're going to have to do it, Gisella!'

'NO! Absolutely no way!'

Mortimer tucked his injured arm behind his back. Oswald looked over but Leon was still unconscious and Oswald didn't really seem to care about anything else. He used a rag to wipe his son's face then held the rag to his own eyes – Wil guessed the man was crying.

Wil turned back to Mortimer: blood was now dripping off his elbow onto the grass.

'Look, Mortimer, this really is the only way.

You know how Lady Élanor's bag saved me – and remember Gisella's leg? So if the bag's given us this,' he held up the needle and thread, 'well, it probably means that if we were back at Lovage Hall, Lady Élanor would be stitching you up… but we're not!'

'I know that, Wil, but you can do it!'

'I've already told you – I can't see! I'd probably sew your fingers together!'

'Well, it's you or no one!' insisted Mortimer. Sweat was trickling down his white face. Wil sat back against a rock and chucked the pink bag aside. This was Olivia's fault – Olivia and her stupid lie. It was a good job that Leon was already unconscious, Wil thought, because if he hadn't been–

'Wil, can you come here a minute?'

Gisella was standing by the Fellhounds. In one hand she was holding the silk bag, in the other was a small square of clean white cloth with a label dangling from it. Mortimer was now stumbling over to Leon and Oswald. Seth was following, ready to catch him if, or rather when, Mortimer passed out.

Once again the words on the label were too much for Wil's poor eyes.

'Sorry, Gisella.' He handed the cloth back.

Gisella read in a whisper, 'Chloroform: for emergencies only. Ideal for minor operations, *stitches*, extracting teeth or foreign objects. Get patient to take one deep breath and then work quickly! Best before: Eternity.'

Wil glanced towards Mortimer, Leon and Oswald.

'OK..., so we get Mortimer to put this over his nose and breathe in... and everything else will be easy!'

'Look, Wil, maybe you could show him this and tell him that Seth will do the stitches... once he's out I can do them. He'll never need to know!'

'Seth! Do you honestly think Mortimer would trust Seth with a needle?'

Gisella looked defeated.

'Well, we could just wait until he passes out from loss of blood!' As if he had heard, Mortimer fell against a tree. He was ghost-white. Wil knew he had to convince Mortimer that Seth would do the stitches. But first he had to speak to Seth.

'Needles! Oh, no. I faint at the sight of needles – always have! Sorry!'

Seth did look genuinely sorry. He had perked up significantly at the thought of helping Mortimer until Wil and Gisella told him their plan.

'Look, you're not going to actually do the stitches; just let Mortimer believe you are. Once he's had the chloroform Gisella can do them!' Wil begged – his sight was clearing, but not quickly enough.

'What about Oswald?' demanded Seth. 'He's not going to let Gisella anywhere near his son's new best friend with a needle in her hand!'

Wil grinned.

'Gisella's already thought of that,' Wil said, sounding a lot more confident than he felt.

'How is he, sir?' asked Wil quietly.

He knelt next to Oswald. Leon was as still as a stone; he had three dark red lines, like deep scars, across his face and eyes. He looked terrible.

Oswald wiped his son's face and then dabbed his own eyes again with the same grubby cloth. He blew his nose.

'I couldn't do anything,' he whispered. 'I'm so sorry, son. I just couldn't...'

'Why don't you come and help us, sir? Seth is going to stitch Mortimer's arm,' said Wil gently. 'Come on, sir. We could do with some help over here.'

Wil waited, praying that Oswald would refuse. If Oswald agreed, Wil would have to resort to his back-up plan[26]... which he hadn't quite come up with yet.

A tear ran down Oswald's cheek. Wil did his best to sound desperate, which wasn't hard.

'Please, Mr Beck. We really need your help.'

Oswald suddenly glared at Wil. His eyes were bloodshot with tears.

'Did you say that *Seth Tanner* – the clumsiest Chaser that ever rode in a Moon Chase – is going to stitch

56

our best Fellman?'

Wil was taken aback[27].

'Yes, er, yes, sir – Lady Élanor, um... gave us some... er... stuff – over there, sir.' Wil waved vaguely in Mortimer's direction; he wasn't at all sure how much Oswald knew about Lady Élanor's first aid bags.

'*No!*' snapped Oswald. Wil jumped. '*I'll* do it!'

Oswald was on his feet in a second. Wil scrambled to follow. This was not the plan at all. Wil needed Oswald to refuse to leave Leon; he needed to give Oswald the new cloth, hoping that Oswald would blow his nose again and breathe in the chloroform, leaving Gisella to do Mortimer's stitches. *Oswald* doing the stitches was definitely not in Wil's plan at all!

'Er..., j-just a minute, Mr Beck. You... er... you'll need one of these.' Wil held out the chloroform-soaked cloth. 'To... to clean your hands, you know... to do Mortimer's stitches. Lady Élanor showed me, um, back at the Infirmary.' He held out the soft white cloth and smiled politely. 'She... er... sh-she said it was *really* important with open wounds. And, er, well, she did a pretty good job with Giles Savidge, didn't she, sir?'

Oswald hesitated then took the cloth and gave his hands a quick rub before dabbing it over his tear-stained face. His eyes suddenly widened. He held the cloth to his nose took a deep sniff... and collapsed forward into Wil's arms.

Gisella turned the tourniquet tighter. Mortimer didn't flinch. The blood continued to drip but Mortimer barely noticed the pain or the blood now. Seth was white with worry.

'I don't think we can leave it any longer, Wil,' said Gisella, trying not to kneel in the growing pool of blood.

'Right, here's the cloth, Seth. Where are the needles?' Wil asked.

Mortimer's eyes suddenly opened.

'What's that?' He pointed at the cloth in Wil's hand. 'I know what you're doing! All of you! Well, you won't kill me that easily, Gisella Fairfax!'

He smashed his good arm into Gisella's shoulder and punched Seth in the face. Wil dragged him backwards and, before Mortimer could do any more harm, pressed the chloroform cloth over Mortimer's nose. The Fellman went limp.

'Sorry, Mort,' panted Wil. He was trying to undo the bandage but the blood quickly made his fingers sticky and the tight knot was impossible to undo.

'Who tied this?'

Using his hunting knife, he sliced through the knot in one sweep. The bandage loosened. Blood immediately started to pump from the open vein in Mortimer's arm.

'Seth, press on this. Gisella, where's that needle...? Gisella?'

Wil looked up, expecting to see Seth and Gisella

ready to help. They weren't. They were just sitting there. A huge bruise was already coming up on Seth's cheek and Gisella was holding her shoulder.

'Hey, come on!' Wil pressed down on Mortimer's wrist and felt warm blood ooze between his fingers.

'It's only a bit of blood! Surely you've seen plenty of that before?'

'What did he mean, Wil? He said I'm trying to kill him!' Gisella said quietly.

'He thinks we're *all* trying to kill him!' added Seth.

'I know. I think it's the fever,' answered Wil without looking at either of them. 'I'm sure he didn't mean it.'

'No, Wil!' said Gisella. 'He meant it. You've seen how he's been with me since we set off. Now I know why!'

She seemed to have forgotten the needles in her hand. Mortimer moaned.

'Look, it's what you told Olivia, Giz. But we really haven't got time now. Can we just do this and then you and Mortimer can have a good chat later, hey?' begged Wil. He waved the chloroform under Mortimer's nose again. If they didn't do something soon, Gisella might never get the chance to have that chat.

'But he doesn't trust us!' said Seth with a hurt look.

Wil was starting to get angry now.

'Look, no one trusted me on the Moon Chase – but

I still helped!' he snapped. 'And if I hadn't, at least one of you three wouldn't be here now! Just give me the needles, Gisella. I am *not* going to sit here and watch one of my best friends die in front of me – even if you are!'

He thrust out his hand. Gisella looked as though she'd been slapped. She sat for a second and then got to her feet. 'No, Wil. I'll do it.'

Mia walked over and licked Gisella's hand.

'It's OK, girl,' said Gisella softly. 'He'll be OK, I promise.'

It had taken Gisella quite a few attempts to get the golden thread through the needle's tiny eye[28], but once she started sewing Wil was impressed. Seth had passed out just as he said he would.

'Wow, have you done this before, Gisella?' asked Wil.

'No!' she answered. 'The needle seems to know what to do!'

With each stitch the blood stopped dripping and very soon there was only a neat red line down Mortimer's arm where the wound had been. Gisella was almost finished when Seth woke up.

'Is it over yet?' he asked, looking like he was about to be sick. The bruise where Mortimer had punched him was dark purple now and his cheek was swollen. Seth opened his mouth and carefully pressed his teeth with his finger. 'I think he loosened two of my teeth, you know!'

Wil grinned. He was much happier now Mortimer wasn't going to bleed to death.

'I'm sure you'll live, Seth. And yes, it's over. Mortimer's OK – thanks to Gisella!'

Her hand was in the pink bag again.

'I think we're supposed to give him this,' she said, holding up a little bottle of dark green liquid. She looked at the drying pool of blood next to Mortimer. 'The label says it's for heavy blood loss.'

Wil kicked the pile of soggy crimson bandages.

'Well, I'd say he's the ideal patient then!'

CHAPTER NINE

Time for the Truth

'As I've already said, I really am very sorry, Mr Beck. I must have given you the wrong cloth!' said Wil, apologising for the third time.

Oswald had woken up just after they had poured the thick, green liquid down Mortimer's throat. Mortimer was still unconscious and it had been quite difficult to make sure he swallowed the liquid instead of choking on it.

Oswald, though, didn't seem to remember or notice that Mortimer had been injured; he was far too worried about his son.

Suddenly Leon coughed and sat up. He opened his eyes, closed them, and opened them again. Then he started screaming.

'My eyes – they're burning! I can't see, I can't see!' He grabbed Oswald. 'I can't see! I can't see!'

'It's OK, son. You've had a bit of a knock. Just sit back, you'll be OK. You'll be OK,' Oswald repeated as he tried to calm the panic-stricken[29] boy.

But Leon wasn't listening. He kept blinking his eyes.

'I can't see. *Why can't I see?* My eyes – they're burning, arggh! Help me!'

Wil looked at Leon face; Leon's eyes were blood red. Then Wil felt the cool glass of a phial being pressed into his hand.

'Wil, use this!' Gisella offered him the phial of feather blindness potion.

Wil grabbed Leon by the shoulders and spoke as calmly as he could.

'Leon, it's me, Wil. Listen to me. Calm down and listen!'

But Leon wouldn't stop shouting. Wil tried again.

'Leon, please! It's me, Wil. I think you've got feather blindness, Leon… we can help you!'

'No! It's a trick! You did this! You and her! Oh, the pain. I can't see, I can't see! Get off me! Arrgh!'

He pushed Wil backwards. Wil managed not to fall but dropped the phial. Then Oswald joined in, yelling, 'What are you doing to my son? I know what you–'

'Oh, for goodness sake!' said an exceptionally calm voice, and a slender hand held a small white square of cloth over Oswald's nose. Oswald went limp. A second later Leon stopped shouting, too.

***

'I'm sure that much chloroform isn't good for you,' groaned Wil. Seth and Gisella lifted poor Oswald off him.

'Well, I had to do *something!*' Gisella said waspishly[30]. 'Just in case everyone's forgotten, we're supposed to going to rescue Tally!'

With Oswald and Leon both knocked out by the chloroform it was much easier to drip the feather blindness ointment into Leon's eyes. Gisella had then carefully wrapped clean bandages around Leon's head and eyes to keep out the light, as the label on the bottle had instructed, although Wil knew Leon would not be any happier when he woke up – especially when he found out that the dressings had to stay on for the next four days!

Mortimer was still lying with his back against the tree. The chloroform was wearing off and his cheeks were now a much better colour. He turned his hand over and flexed his fingers.

'Who did this?'

Wil and Seth answered at the same time.

'Seth.'

'Me!'

Wil carried on speaking before Seth said the wrong thing.

'Don't you remember, Mort? It was the first aid bag – the needle and thread? You've had something for the blood you lost, too.'

Mortimer inspected the thin scar.

'Hmm, well, it feels OK... so far... I guess I owe you a thank-you, Seth.' And for the first time in a very long time, Mortimer actually smiled at Seth. 'That's one heck of a bruise, by the way! Did one of those birds get you, too?'

For a moment Seth looked surprised then he beamed.

'Yep! Luckily I got out of the way before I got really hurt!'

Surprised by Seth's lie, Wil was also grateful. It was now late morning; they needed to get back to trying to rescue Tally, which meant that Mortimer needed to be told about Leon. Wil began talking.

'The thing is Mortimer, Leon didn't – er, well, he didn't get out of the way, I mean.'

For a moment Wil thought it was going to be OK.

'What! He's not dead, is he?' But then Mortimer was on his feet. 'Where is he? Where's Oswald?' He grabbed the front of Wil's shirt and pointed at Gisella without looking away from Wil's face. 'Did *she* have anything to do with this?'

Wil had had enough. He swiped Mortimer's hands away and pushed him as hard as he could. Mortimer tumbled backwards into Seth.

'What the–' Mortimer started, but Wil didn't let him finish.

'This... stops... now!' He marched over to the rocky ledge where Gisella was pretending to keep a lookout for more eagards. 'Gisella, come down here! You and Mortimer are going to have that chat!'

Without waiting, Wil turned back to Mortimer. Now he had started speaking he couldn't stop.

'Right, to start with, Gisella is NOT trying to kill you! Olivia lied to Leon. Second, Gisella wants to be a Chaser – Bryn told her to help you with Mia! For some very strange reason these people care about you! Third, it wasn't Seth who stitched you up, it was Gisella. And before you say *anything* – she probably saved your life, so I suggest your next two words are – *Sorry* and *Thanks*!'

He stood panting and unclenched[31] his fists. Mortimer opened his mouth. Then he closed it again. Seth stepped between them, looking very nervous. Mortimer eventually spoke.

'Is this true?' he said in barely a whisper.

Seth nodded.

'Well, the bit about the stitches and saving your life is – I was there! But Gisela didn't tell me about the other stuff,' he said and quickly added, 'I believe her though! Mia trusts her and that's good enough for me... and it *should* be good enough for you too, Mort.'

As if she understood what was happening Mia licked Mortimer's hand and then walked over to Gisella and sat down, pressing her long back against Gisella's leg.

Gisella scratched the hound's ear and took a deep breath.

'It's true, Mortimer. Olivia told me that she wants to leave Saran. I told her I wanted to be a Chaser then I spoke to Bryn. He suggested I help you with Mia – he was worried... you know, because you might still be missing Tarek. I was supposed to learn at the same time.' She was struggling not to cry now. 'True, I love Mia. But she's *your* Fellhound, Mortimer. All I wanted to do was ride with you and the others on the Fells and one day maybe... have my *own* hound.'

Tears were now flowing down her cheeks.

Mortimer suddenly looked lost.

'Why would Leon do this?'

No one answered: Wil knew no one knew the answer.

'Why didn't you tell me you wanted to be a Chaser, Gisella?' Mortimer asked eventually, keeping his eyes on Mia.

'Because I had to make sure I could do it first – I... I didn't want anyone to laugh,' Gisella answered. She was trying to stop her tears.

'And you did my stitches – even though I've been so horrible to you. Why?'

Gisella swallowed and tried to speak but tears were streaming down her face again and no words came. Wil answered for her.

'Because, like the rest of us, she cares about you,

you complete idiot! And, because she didn't know what she had done. She believed it would be alright in the end!'

'You didn't tell her, Wil?'

'You must be joking! This all happened because of Olivia's lie – I just didn't know how to get you both talking to sort it out!'

Mortimer looked into the sky. 'Well, I never thought I say this, but – thank the moons for those eagards!'

He gave Gisella a sheepish[32] grin.

'Sorry, Giz... and... thanks.'

Gisella smiled and kept crying – again, words failed her.

'Right,' said Wil with a sigh of relief. 'Now that's sorted that out – can we *please* get on with rescuing Tally?'

With Gisella and Mortimer speaking again, it was much easier to discuss Leon. Both he and his father were still unconscious but Wil didn't think it was a good time to ask Gisella just how much chloroform she had put on that cloth.

'How long did you say those bandages had to stay over Leon's eyes, Gizzy?' he asked instead.

'Well, the label said four *full* days.'

Mortimer glanced towards the horses.

'Well, in that case, the way I see it Oswald should

take Leon home. Leon can't carry on with us. It's better if they go back now – much safer for everyone.'

As it happened, breaking the news to Leon and Oswald had been helped by a bottle of dark purple liquid that Wil had come across in the first aid bag. The label said simply, '*FOR PANIC! TAKE THREE DROPS!*'

Oswald was very confused when he woke, but at least he was calm and agreed without argument to Mortimer's suggestion that Leon should be taken home.

As Leon came around it was clear he still couldn't see, but the pain seemed to have gone, and he listened calmly while Mortimer explained about the bandages and the plan for him and Oswald to head home.

'Just take it steady, sir,' Mortimer had said once Leon and Oswald were packed and ready to head south. 'Once you get to the Black Rock you'll be able to see Mistle Forest. You'll be back in Saran tomorrow.'

CHAPTER TEN

Another Attack

From the snowy top of Craggston Tor, they could see the dark line of Mort Craggs on the horizon. Below, Armelia's city wall completely surrounded buildings so close together they looked to be stacked on top of one another.

As they got nearer Wil could see a half-built castle tower, shining golden in the late afternoon sunlight.

'I think Rexmoore's doing some home improvements!' said Mortimer.

'Well, Mort,' said Seth. 'Any ideas how we're going to get the hounds in there?'

'Please tell me *someone* mentioned that wall?' said Gisella. 'Didn't Lady Élanor tell you how to get in?'

'Ouch!' said Seth, slapping his hand onto his neck. 'What was *that*?'

'What was *what*?' asked Mortimer, looking around.

A second later he, too, was holding his cheek.

'What's wrong with you two?' asked Gisella.

'Not sure,' Mortimer answered, waving his hands around his head. 'I think I've just been stung.'

'Well, I don't think it was a midge!' said Gisella examining a red mark the size of a walnut that had appeared on Mortimer's cheek.

This time it was Gisella's turn to cry out. 'Ow!'

Mortimer grabbed at the missile as it bounced off Gisella's thigh. It really was a walnut!

With that, Wil felt a sharp sting on his own neck – a hazelnut rolled across the ground. At the same moment, in a thick copse[33] of battered, snow-dusted trees to their right, someone giggled.

Mortimer pointed towards the copse. 'Mia, Go!'

Mia took off towards the trees. Phinn was right behind her.

'Got your knife handy, Wil?' whispered Mortimer.

Wil patted his boot. 'Yep, safe and ready for action.'

'Good, hold on!'

Wil hardly felt Mortimer move but Shadow went from a stand to a gallop in a heartbeat[34]; in three more, they were under a huge pine tree in the middle of the thick copse. Mia was on her hind legs. Towering above Mortimer, she stretched up the trunk, gripping its orange-brown bark with her finger-long claws. Phinn sat on his haunches and let out a single bark that echoed over the barren hills.

'Call them off! Call them off!' wailed a boy's voice

from high above them.

Mortimer dismounted.

'Who's there? Come down and show yourself!'

'Not until you call off those dogs!'

'How do I know you won't shoot us?'

The voice didn't reply. Mortimer's eyes flicked to Wil's boot. Wil nodded and silently slid out the hunting knife.

After a few minutes something else clattered down through the branches. Mortimer jumped backwards with his arms over his head. A small tin whistle, several nuts and a slingshot[35] landed at his feet. Mortimer bent to pick up the whistle but Mia got there first.

'Leave!'

Mortimer retrieved the dropped items one by one and tapped the whistle on the back of his hand.

'If you have no more weapons you can come down. But I warn you, my friend here has a knife... and he's very good with it!'

'But how do I know those dogs won't eat me?' said a nervous voice.

'You don't!' Mortimer answered. He winked at Wil.

'Well, in that case I'll stay up here, thanks!'

Seth steered Rhoani through the trees towards them.

'What's going on?' asked Gisella. Farrow padded behind them. Mortimer grinned.

'Seth! You got your bow handy?'

'*NO!*'

The terrified shout was followed by a shower of twigs, needles and pine cones raining down over their heads.

'I'll come down. Don't shoot! I... I was only messing around!'

They waited. After a lot more falling leaves, pine cones and twigs, a body, dressed entirely in black, crashed through the lower branches and landed with a dull thud between Wil and Mortimer: the body was followed almost immediately by a black hat.

'Elegant!' observed Mortimer.

Phinn went to investigate. The body let out a pathetic cry.

'Oowee! Nooo, don't let it eat me!' it squealed. 'Please! I gave you my stuff. Pleeeease... call it off!'

Phinn sniffed the crumpled hat and gave it a nudge with his huge nose. The hat rolled away in a half-circle on its brim. Phinn took a surprised step back and stretched his head as far forward as he could without moving his feet. He sniffed again and opened his mouth to investigate further.

The boy on the ground curled up and whimpered.

'Down!' ordered Mortimer. To Wil's absolute amazement, Phinn obeyed immediately – so did Farrow and Mia. Wil felt a twinge[36] of envy: Mortimer was just

73

so good with those hounds – he could even make Phinn
do things!

The boy started to sob.

CHAPTER ELEVEN

The Jackal

Mortimer stood over the boy with his hands on his hips.

'Right, I'm going to ask you some questions. We're in a hurry so I suggest you answer quickly – if I believe you, I might not let my friends kill you. OK?'

The boy stopped sobbing and nodded.

Seth took aim again and Wil flicked his thumb across the point of his knife; Gisella looked skywards and walked away.

Mortimer walked slowly around the quaking[37] boy.

'Who are you?'

The boy swallowed. His tears had left clean lines down his filthy cheeks.

'I... I'm... The Jackal.'

'Really!' said Mortimer raising one eyebrow. Wil could see that Mortimer was trying hard not to laugh.

'Yer!' said the boy, suddenly brave again; but then his shoulders dropped. He looked younger than Seth. 'Er... but, well, er, my real name's Colin.'

Colin glanced at Seth's bow. 'I prefer The Jackal though!'

'Is that what your friends call you?' asked Mortimer. 'What about your parents? I bet your mother just loves calling, "Come on, *The Jackal*, your supper's ready"!'

Seth chuckled.

'I don't have any parents.'

Seth stopped chuckling.

Mortimer frowned.

'Oh, sorry about that… what, er… what happened to them?'

'Dunno. The cook, y'know[38], at the castle – the old one – the cook that is, not the castle… that's so old it's falling down… she died last year – the cook – she found me on some sacks of flour when I was a baby. She called me Colin.' The Jackal spoke nervously, watching Seth's bow. 'I grew up in the castle, scavenging, y'know, in the kitchens and I help with the pigs, too, y'know, for my keep.'

'Oh!' gasped Gisella. 'That's terrible.'

'Nah, reckon I was lucky – least I never went hungry! There's always stuff to steal, y'know, in the castle kitchen. Folk[39] hardly ever notice!'

Gisella looked shocked. 'What! You mean no one actually looked after you?'

The Jackal sat up. He tucked his skinny knees

under his chin and hugged his long shins. His pointed boots were scratched and grey from lack of polish. Wil could see a hole in one of the soles.

'Well, no – I mean, y'know, they taught me right 'n wrong. They cared about me, too… cook used to hit me with a wooden spoon, y'know, if she caught me stealing stuff… and, er… the baker clipped me round the ear once 'cos I nicked a bowl of raisins that were supposed to go in some cake he was making!'

He smiled at the memory and hugged his knees closer.

'How does being beaten show that someone cares about you?' asked Gisella.

The Jackal looked surprised.

'Cos[40] if they hadn't cared they would have told Rexmoore. And he would have flogged[41] me for stealing and then, y'know, he… he would have thrown me out!'

He nodded to confirm this fact and then reached into his long, grubby jacket. In one quick movement Mortimer drew his sword; Seth, who had lowered his bow, took aim again and Wil got ready to throw his knife. They were all looking at the boy's hidden hand. The Jackal didn't move.

'What!' he said, and very slowly drew a golden pear from his tattered pocket. 'Oh, sorry, I've only got this one. Never take more than you can eat in one go. Less likely to be noticed and if you do get caught, running away's easier!'

With another wise nod The Jackal bit into the pear and munched. Seth lowered his bow and Wil slid his knife back into his boot.

'Yes, Wil, but he's a half-starved urchin from the castle kitchen,' said Gisella. 'You saw how quickly he ate that pie I gave him!'

Mortimer, Wil and Gisella were standing at the edge of the tiny wood trying to decide what to do with the boy. Seth was playing with the slingshot and had already hit Phinn on the bottom with a lump of mud: Phinn was now sitting on the floor some distance away. Wil watched Seth load the slingshot with another lump of dry earth. He pulled it back ready to fire.

'Well, I don't believe him,' said Wil. 'He said he'd stolen a horse to come up here. So where is it now? Surely we would have seen it.'

Wil looked through the trees and out over the hills. Seth looked around, too, and seemed to forget the loaded sling. It slipped out of his fingers: the lump of earth hit a branch above them and soil sprinkled down on their heads.

'Oops!' said Seth, pushing the sling into his boot.

'Well, I think we should give him a chance,' said Gisella, pulling earth out of her hair. 'We can't just leave him here. Anyway, Wil, we've got the hounds, the horses and all the weapons. And at least if he's with us we know where he is!'

'You've got to admit it, Wil,' added Mortimer. 'He might have a stupid name but he could be pretty handy if he knows his way around Armelia! He might even know where they're keeping Tally.'

Wil shook his head. 'What if it's a trap?'

'Nah,' said Mortimer, flicking a tiny bit of earth back at Seth. He looked over his shoulder; The Jackal was snuggled against Farrow's back – both were dozing peacefully. 'He's just a kid with a tin whistle and a slingshot.'

They decided to tell The Jackal that as long as he got them into Armelia, Mortimer would not order the Fellhounds to rip him apart.

'But that's right into the city, mind,' warned Mortimer in a voice that would have chilled ice[42]. 'All the way!'

'Well, I don't think that's going to be too difficult,' called Seth before The Jackal could speak. 'There's a gate. Look, over there!'

Armelia looked less welcoming the closer they got. Wil had been glad to leave the wild, barren fells but the path didn't get any easier. Old snow lurked[43] in the rocks; loose stones on the frozen ground made the horses stumble and odd-shaped boulders on the path cast weird shadows that made the horses shy[44]. Wil had a very strong feeling that they were being watched.

Mortimer had decided that The Jackal should ride with him so Gisella had volunteered to walk with Wil, which cheered Wil very much. But when Shadow tripped and slid down a bank on his rump, Mortimer insisted that they all walk, which did not cheer Seth at all!

They made their way in silence. Taking care where he put his feet at every step, Wil began to worry; if The Jackal didn't know what Fellhounds were... well, did that mean that Armelia didn't have them? After all, Wil hadn't seen them before the Moon Chase – Mistlegard was just too poor and Peachley Hills didn't have Wraithe Wolves to worry about. So, if Armelia didn't have Fellhounds, Wil thought, how were they going to get into the city with three enormous hounds that each stood shoulder high to a grown man, without attracting a lot of attention?

High up on their left Mort Craggs towered over them like rows of crooked teeth – Wil guessed that the only way to get out that way was with wings. Much further to the right, and a long way away, the sharp peaks of the Eiye Mountains stabbed through the clouds in the ice-blue sky. Around him, boots, hooves and paws crunched, slipped and tripped over the frozen ground but even though he was with his friends, Wil felt lonely and helpless.

Gisella broke the silence.

'I don't know if it's the light,' she said squinting into the distance, 'but that tower down there looks like it's actually made of gold!'

'Oh! That's because it is!' said The Jackal with a wide smile. 'Been building it for years. It's for his wife – she just loves the stuff, y'know – Imelda's Golden Tower, that's what he calls it – Lord Rexmoore, y'know. You should see the rest of the castle, it's falling down. All the gold that's collected, y'know, in taxes – they melt it down for bricks – every scrap!'

'What?' Gisella gasped. 'You mean all the gold our parents hand over to Rexmoore's henchmen... it's used for building that!'

Wil suddenly felt sick.

'So what did they do with my father? He couldn't pay them,' he muttered almost to himself.

'Prob'ly made him work up there,' answered The Jackal. 'Yeah, they bring them in all the time, y'know – the ones who can't... or won't pay.' He smirked. 'Make them work, y'know until, well, until they drop dead... or fall off the wall, y'know.'

'Oh!' breathed Gisella.

Wil's world went red[45]. He grabbed The Jackal and threw him to the ground.

'No, actually I don't know.' Wil's jaws were so tightly clenched his teeth went numb.

'Take it easy, Wil,' said Mortimer carefully. He, Seth and Gisella knew about Wil's father being taken away by Rexmoore's men; they also knew that Wil had been told that his father was dead.

Consumed by anger, Wil pressed down on the boy's throat.

The Jackal clawed at Wil's arm.

'Gurnnn!'

Gisella grabbed Wil's shoulder. Beside her, Phinn was barking loudly but Wil was too angry to notice – or care. He put all of his weight on his elbow. Phinn dropped low, ready to spring.

'No, Phinn, leave!' shrieked Gisella.

'No!' yelled Seth, Mortimer and Gisella.

But Phinn's master was in trouble. He opened his huge jaws and leapt.

Whether it was the three alarmed voices yelling in unison or Phinn's misjudged dive that took Wil off his feet, but something got Wil's attention and brought him back to his senses. Once again The Jackal lay whimpering in the dirt.

Phinn waited, his tail wagging to and fro in great sweeps, his eyes fixed on the boy.

Wil crouched on all fours, trying to catch his

breath. His heart was pounding.

The others watched. No one moved.

'Just tell me,' Wil panted, without raising his head. 'Just tell me... What happens at the tower?'

The Jackal looked up at Mortimer as if he was asking for help.

'Tell him,' ordered Mortimer.

With his eyes on Mortimer, The Jackal spoke.

'Well, from what I've seen, y'kn-,' Mortimer raised one eyebrow. 'Er, yer... well, er, they bring them in and set them to work. Some go straight up to the wall and some go to the foundry, y'–, er, that's where they make the bricks.'

He stopped.

'That can't be all,' said Gisella. She looked appalled. 'Where do they sleep? What do they eat?'

'Oh, yer. Er, well, they sleep in the tower and, y'know, Cook makes them porridge and...' He swallowed. 'And... um...'

'Go on,' said Mortimer.

Reluctantly, The Jackal continued.

'They take the bodies to a field on the edge of the city... There's a man, y'know, up there. He, er, carves their name on a stone – with the words 'Taxes paid' underneath. They put the stones, y'know, on the, er... g-graves...'

After a long time Seth spoke.

'How does he know their names?'

'They tattoo each man's name on his arm when he's brought in – just the last name, y'know… to save ink.'

Wil lifted his head. He was sure he saw the boy grin but this time he was too shocked to do anything about it.

Rexmoore's men had taken Wil's father and two other men from their village when Wil was eleven; afterwards Wil's mother kept telling him that if they earned enough to pay the tax then Lord Rexmoore would let Wil's father come home. But every time Rexmoore's men came, no matter how much they paid, Wil's father was never with them.

It was Wil's father who had taught Wil how to handle a knife. His mother hadn't approved. But from the day Wil's father was taken away his mother never tried to stop him from practicing his throwing… and now he was very good.

CHAPTER TWELVE

Plan 'B'

'Blimey, Cecil, you seen these?' called a voice from high above their heads. It was now very late in the afternoon; they were tired and hungry and the gate into Armelia looked depressingly solid close up. Wil's feet were numb from hours walking; and Gisella had a badly grazed elbow and a cut lip after slipping on the snow-covered rocks.

A few seconds later they heard another voice from the other side of the gate.

'Seen wha'?'

'Tell you what, boys,' the first voice called down, 'You should put a saddle on them an' ride 'em!'

A face appeared over the top of the gate.

'By the moons, 'Arry, now that's what I call a dog!'

Mortimer stepped forward with a patient expression on his face.

'Good evening, gentlemen. Would it be possible for you to open the gate and let us in?'

'You 'ere for the Alcama Festival?' called a voice from lower down behind the gate.

'Er, yes,' said Mortimer. The man on top of the gate peered down at them.

'You got gold?'

'Er, no.' Mortimer turned to the others – they all shook their heads. Wil felt suddenly angry again – for him, 'gold' was now a dirty word.

'Well, unless you got gold we can't let you in.'

The Jackal had not spoken since Wil's outburst. Now Gisella gave him a gentle nudge. He stepped forward and took off his hat.

'Hi, Harry. It's me, The Ja-, Colin,' he called. 'Look, these are my friends. They've come for the Festival. Just met them over at Thesker Pyke – I forgot about the gold thing. Can you just let us in anyway?' He flapped his arms at his side and bounced[46] on his toes.

'Colin? Colin from up at the castle? They've been looking for you all day, you little–. Said you nicked[47] Lady Imelda's quail's eggs. Mhaddphat's gonna string you up when she finds you! If I were you I'd stay out there with yer mates!'

'Quail's eggs?' whispered Gisella.

'Long story,' The Jackal whispered back.

'And who's Mhaddphat?' whispered Seth.

'The cook – she's a bit weird,' whispered The Jackal.

A second face appeared on the wall above them.

'I hope all that whispering's about how you're gonna get those eggs back to her ladyship?' the face said.

'Er, well, yes actually,' answered The Jackal, sounding suddenly confident. 'I've got them here in my pocket – all twelve of them.' He tapped his pocket. 'Let us in and I'll go straight up to the castle to return them.'

The two faces ducked back behind the wall.

'Weird, how?' asked Mortimer, still looking up to where the gate-keepers' faces had just been.

'Weird in a, y'know, dangerous kind of way,' answered The Jackal, also looking up.

The face of Harry reappeared.

'I 'eard you're gonna need a lot more than twelve. You sure you got no gold? What about on those dogs? Those collars – are they gold?'

'Oh, no,' Seth answered cheerfully. Wil was nearest but there was no way to shut Seth up without attracting attention. Seth carried on. 'It's wrought iron. Gold's not nearly strong enough to hold a Fellhound!'

He shook his head proudly and patted Farrow hard on the shoulder. Mortimer looked skywards.

'Seth!' hissed Gisella.

'What?'

But it was the man on the gate who spoke next.

'Sorry, no gold, no entry. Shame actually – I reckon those dogs would stand a good chance in the Unexpected Pets contest, eh, Cecil?'

'What?' called Cecil, from somewhere lower down and clearly no longer next to Harry.

'These dogs – Unexpected Pets – would have given that dragon a bit of competition.'

'Dragon?' called the muffled voice.

'You know – that noisy little thing we let in earlier. A Lesser Crested Ridge Creeper, if I'm not very much mistaken – it's the call you know – very distinctive.' Harry let out three loud squawks and nodded in an "I know my dragons" kind of way.

'So can we come in then?' asked Seth brightly. 'You know, for the contest?'

'If it was up to me, boys, I'd open the gate now. But can't go against orders, see.' And, with another shake of his head, he disappeared. From behind the gate Wil heard a disembodied voice 'Blinking big dogs, mind! Bet they take some feedin!'

Mortimer stood looking up at the solid oak gate, it was locked. They were going to have to find a different way to get into Armelia. Mortimer turned to The Jackal.

'Well, you said you would get us into the city – not just outside the gate! So I hope you have a Plan B?'

'Plan B?' The Jackal looked genuinely confused.

'Yer, you know, Plan A didn't work, so now we go to Plan B – and the moons help you if we have to go to Plan C!'

'Oh, you mean like another way in!' For some reason The Jackal's sudden smile did not fill Wil with any confidence. 'Round the back, y'know, er, by the market – that's the way I usually get in and out.'

'So why didn't you take us that way in the first place?' asked Wil. He wanted to get off the Fell: Tel Harion was still far too close.

'You didn't ask,' said The Jackal. 'You headed for the gate so I thought you, y'know, had gold with you. I mean, everyone around here knows you need gold to get into the city!'

'Well, we aren't from around here, in case you hadn't realised,' growled Mortimer.

'Oh, well, n... no... of course. Should have guessed after that thing, y'know, about the tower... and the... er, gold... um,' stammered The Jackal.

Mortimer looked like he was seriously contemplating shooting The Jackal where he stood, and although Wil was very tempted to let him, he also knew they needed the boy's help to find Tally.

'Look, we don't have any gold but we, the horses *and* the hounds really need to be on the other side of this wall as soon as possible. Can you help us?'

The Jackal pressed his lips together, walked a few paces forward and inspected the two huge gates. He turned back to face them.

'You know Plan B?'

'Yeess,' replied Mortimer slowly.

'Well, er, there's good news and bad news.'

Plan 'B'

'I think we'd better have the bad news first,' said Mortimer with a quick glance towards Wil.

The Jackal took one more step away from them and said simply, 'Plan B won't work.' He took another step back and pressed his back against the gate. 'It's the animals. They'd never, y'know, climb the wall.'

'Climb what wall?' asked Seth from behind Mortimer. He was standing with Rhoani and Shadow. All three Fellhounds had already got bored and were lying in the grass waiting for orders.

'Well, you never said anything about the animals before! Get us into Armelia, you said. Get us in and we won't shoot you, you said!' The Jackal waved his arms up at the gate as he spoke. 'Now you say you don't have any gold to get through the gate but you want to get two horses and three of the biggest dogs I've ever seen in my life into the city.'

The Jackal closed his eyes tightly.

'And what's the good news?' asked Gisella. 'You did say there was good news.'

The Jackal didn't open his eyes.

'I was really hoping that you'd just shoot me after the bad news,' he said, bracing himself against the gate, his eyes still shut tight.

'Why?' demanded Gisella.

'Because there is no...' The Jackal opened his eyes and beamed. 'Hang on. Can you swim?'

CHAPTER THIRTEEN

Troubled Waters

Seth peered down into the canal.

'Oh, great!'

A few feet below, the dark water drifted under the city wall through a low culvert[48].

'The *last* time I came out with you lot I nearly drowned!'

Mortimer frowned down into the murky blackness.

'Mmm, but luckily for you Wil was there!' He turned to The Jackal. 'And the plan is?'

'Well,' said The Jackal, looking very pleased with himself. 'The river flows right round the city – well, y'know, under it actually. There are wells along it. It goes to the foundry. There's two, y'know, mill wheels. We can get out just before the first one.'

'And what happens if we don't, *you know*, get out?' asked Wil, knowing he wasn't going to like the answer. The Jackal waved his hand.

'Oh, don't worry, you'll get out. It gets really shallow. I fell in there once – only went up to my bu- ackside.' He glanced at Gisella.

'Yes, but what happens if you *don't* get out?' Gisella insisted.

'Weeell, y'know, the wheel... chguh.' The Jackal coughed but didn't say anything else.

'Great!' Mortimer muttered, shaking his head.

Wil looked at the culvert. Back home Wil couldn't persuade Phinn to go over his knees into East Lake. Mortimer plonked down on the grass and pulled off his boots.

'Right, Wil, you and I'll go with The Jackal,' he said, folding his cloak. 'We'll take Mia and Phinn. Seth, Gisella; throw our books and cloaks over the wall up there,' he nodded to trees The Jackal had pointed out as being in the kitchen garden of the castle, 'then get back to the gate with Farrow and the horses. We'll get you in somehow. At least with dragons around we shouldn't have to worry about the Fellhounds attracting too much attention!'

The Jackal nodded enthusiastically.

'You'll see the top of a big tree just up there – y'know, a plum. There's a bit of a hump on this side. If you stand on that you should, y'know, be able to get the stuff over. Er, you can throw, can't you?'

'What?' said Gisella.

'Er, well, y'know, it's just that you're a..., y'know, girl.' He wrinkled his nose. Gisella didn't move.

'Look, I really think we should be going now,' interrupted Wil – he'd seen the look on Gisella's face before and it never ended well. Mortimer came to The Jackal's rescue.

'Right, that's it then, in you go... er... Jackal,' he said with a grin.

The Jackal lowered himself carefully into the water; his teeth started to chatter before he was up to his knees.

'Right, Wil, you next,' said Mortimer. 'Just get in and call Phinn. He'll come in after you. If not, just swim away – he'll definitely get in then.'

Wil wasn't sure but he slid down the bank anyway. The water was so cold he was surprised it was actually flowing. Within seconds he couldn't feel his hands or feet; his heart beat as if it was about to pump out of his body.

Gisella called from the bank, 'What's it like, Wil?'

He took a deep breath. 'F-Fine,' he shivered. 'B-but I'm not sure I want to s-stay in l-long! Ph-Phinn, come on.'

Phinn stood on the bank and peered down at him – as Wil's body temperature dropped he couldn't focus on the hound's mind.

'Phinn, c-come on!' Wil called again. But Phinn simply jumped over the canal onto the other bank and barked loudly. Mortimer frowned.

'I'll get in with Mia, Wil. Phinn'll see what she's doing and get the idea.'

Mortimer plopped into the freezing water; Mia trotted a little further down the bank, found a gentler slope and splashed in. Within seconds she was happily swimming around Wil and Mortimer.

Phinn stayed on the bank.

'I don't like to c-complain, guys, b-but I'm f-freezing my b-backside off here!' called The Jackal. He was already swimming towards the gap under the wall. With wide powerful strokes, Mortimer set off in the same direction – Mia followed.

'It's OK, Wil,' Mortimer called over his shoulder.

'Just follow us, he'll come.'

Wil kicked his legs hard and followed. The Jackal was now at the wall, with Mortimer and Mia not far behind. Thanks to the many hours swimming with his friends on East Lake, Wil was a strong swimmer; he caught up with Mia in a few powerful strokes.

The silence from behind him was embarrassing.

'Don't worry, Wil, he'll come,' shouted Mortimer. Wil swam on.

Almost at the culvert Wil could feel the current getting stronger. He grabbed at the slimy stone of the wall to let Mortimer and Mia go through first.

Suddenly something on the other bank caught Wil's eye – a movement in the shadows. An image flashed across his brain and his blood ran even colder. Then it was gone. There was the sound of pounding paws... and a huge splash. Ice-cold water surged over Wil's head and into his mouth – his eyeballs felt as though they were going to freeze in the cold.

When he got back to the surface the first thing Wil saw was Phinn's nose only inches away, then a huge tongue as Phinn gave him a warm lick. On the bank, Gisella and Seth looked like they were trying extremely hard not to laugh.

'See, I said he could swim,' Mortimer called, and he ducked down and swam under the city wall.

***

The journey was longer than Wil had expected; although he was sure the water was getting warmer which made breathing a lot easier. It was pitch black. Wil could see light in the distance and swam towards it. Phinn stayed close, moving through the water as if he'd been born to it. Wil hooked his fingers under Phinn's iron collar.

'So, you like swimming after all then, hey?'

Mortimer called out in the dark. 'You OK, Wil?'

Wil could see his friend's bobbing head silhouetted against the little strip of light way off down the tunnel. 'If you grab Phinn's neck–'

'Already worked that one out, Mort. The water's not so cold now.'

The Jackal's voice echoed off the walls from somewhere ahead of them.

'Oh yer, I forgot to say, keep your mouth shut!'

'Why?' called Wil.

'Let's just say, not everyone uses this water for drinking!'

'But you said there were wells,' said Wil, with a sudden desire not to be in the water anymore.

'Mmm. Well, they're also used for y'know, disposal, as well as collection,' said The Jackal's voice somewhere up ahead.

It was a while before they spoke again. Wil kept his lips pressed firmly together as they neared the light patch which was obviously a 'well'. But they passed by without incident and swam on.

With the light from the well now behind them, Wil could hear every drip, sense every trickle and – unfortunately for Wil – feel every heart that beat that fluttered or pounded in the darkness. Suddenly very nervous, Wil felt his fingers tingle. His legs felt as if they were on fire as he tried to control the fear surging[49] through his body.

'Er, how much further, d'you think?' Something slithered across the wall above Wil's head. He heard The Jackal in the distance.

'Not far now, we've ju–'

Silence.

'Sorry, didn't catch that,' Wil called. Phinn and Wil suddenly collided with Mia. 'What the–'

'Is that you, Wil?' said Mortimer. 'Can you see The Jackal? Hey, Jackal... Colin, hey!'

Still silence.

'I think it's time we got out of here, Mortimer.' Something slid between Wil's feet – it was big, cold and very slimy. 'Yep! We *really* need to get out of here!'

At the end of the tunnel Wil felt thick, slimy goo squeeze between his toes. Within seconds Phinn and Mia were powering through shallower, faster flowing water, dragging Wil and Mortimer who clung to the hounds' collars as they fought to stay on their feet.

'Look for somewhere to get out,' Mortimer called, now wading chest deep. 'That's got to be the mill, look, there.'

Mortimer was pointing towards a huge tower – and attached to it was a mill wheel – a *spinning* mill wheel.

The sound of crashing water was almost overwhelming now. The wheel squeaked and groaned; its battered buckets seemed to hurl[50] more water back than they carried. Wil frantically scoured[51] the canal sides, looking for a way out. Phinn slipped. Wil realised that the water was gathering speed because it was falling.

'We've got to get out of this now,' he shouted.

'I know!' Mortimer yelled back. He was pointing towards a narrowing channel. 'There's a gap – over there. I think it's an overflow.'

But they were caught up in the unstoppable water. Wil kicked against the current. He slipped and slid on the slimy rocks of the bank, desperate to avoid another crash that might cost them their lives. Mia headed straight for the slim gap, dragging Mortimer with her as she disappeared. Phinn, too, headed for the tiny opening – just as Wil lost his footing. He let go of Phinn's collar. The Fellhound went one way – to join Mortimer and Mia, Wil went the other – straight towards the spinning mill wheel... *this was not how it was meant to be!*

***

'Now do you see how useful a Fellhound can be, Wil?' panted Mortimer. 'Thank the moons that wall was low enough for Phinn to reach you! We'd have been picking bits of you off that wheel for weeks!'

'Thanks, Mortimer – I'm gonna have nightmares as it is!' said Wil. But he was grinning at Phinn, up to his knees, taking great gulps and blubbing water through his nose; Wil knew there were tooth marks across his back but he really didn't mind.

Away from the bubbling mill water, at the edge in the reeds below bobbed a dark shape; a horrible thought crept into Wil's mind.

'I don't think The Jackal was so lucky,' he said, pointing. 'Look, isn't that his hat... down there?'

Mortimer waved his hand dismissively.

'Nah, he told us we'd get out. We must have just missed a gap earlier that he knew about. I bet we bump into him again. He's probably at the gate already!'

It was soon clear that Mortimer and Wil had no reason to worry about standing out in the crowd; the Alcama Festival might still be one night away but in Armelia the festivities had already started.

Everywhere Wil looked, people were dressed – or nearly dressed – in strange costumes. Bright orange and purple silk seemed to be very popular; there were also some strange people and even stranger animals.

'Wow, isn't that a troll?' Wil whispered, pointing towards one of the many bars that lined the shabby streets. 'Haven't seen one of those for ages!'

Despite the cold evening, people were coming out of dark doorways and gathering around battered tables. Wil knocked over a chair and, as he bent to set it upright, something hissed at him from under the table; a pair of scarlet eyes blinked slowly and a bright green forked tongue wound around the chair leg. Wil jumped back, banging his head on the table.

'I do hope you aren't trying to steal Sebastian?' asked a soft voice.

The abandoned chair rose up into the air and settled slowly back, the right way up, on the ground.

'Er, no. No!' said Wil backing away. 'What is it – he?'

'Oh, it's a surprise,' said a woman wrapped from head to toe in orange silk. She smiled. Whatever Sebastian was, he stayed hidden under the table. 'If you stick around for the competition tomorrow you might just find out. Are you entering that?'

'Sorry?' said Wil. Then he realised that Phinn was standing just behind him. 'Er.. um, probably. I, er, haven't decided yet.'

'Well, I hope he does tricks then,' said the woman, looking very unimpressed. 'I mean – a Fellhound... hardly unexpected, even for Armelia.'

Mortimer reappeared in the crowd.

'Today, Wil!'

Up ahead, Wil could see a crooked sign hanging from a single hook. The sign read *The Olde Mule*. Again there were people everywhere, and as Wil and Mortimer got closer a man charged out of the crowd and ran right up to them, yelling right into Mortimer's face. Mortimer stood still. The man, covered from head to toe in orange and purple tattoos, stuck out his tongue then sprinted back to his friends. They cheered, downed[52] huge jugs of frothy black ale and banged the empty vessels down on the nearest table.

'What're they drinking?' Wil asked. He was fascinated and horrified at the same time. In Mistlegard, Wil swept the floors of the tiny inn. Everyone there drank mead or barley beer – they also drank out of goblets.

'That'll be rat beer,' said Mortimer with a knowing grin. 'Makes you mad and keeps you *bad*!'

'Rat beer! Please tell me it's not made out of real rats!'

'They've got to do something with them, Wil. Flying rodents; the city'd be overrun otherwise!'

'*Erch!* I bet it's disgusting!' said Wil.

'The Fellmen from Little Thesk bring it when they come for the Moon Chases. I tried it once – made me want to fight with everyone,' said Mortimer with a grimace. 'You're right – give me barley beer any day, or Lady Élanor's elder wine!'

Back at the bar, the orange and purple man had another overflowing jug. He stood swaying and spilling rat beer while his companions sang a very rude song; when the song came to a very loud end, the tattooed man drank the beer in one go. As his friends roared and clapped, he ran down the alley at the side of the bar and vomited over his feet. They walked away from *The Olde Mule* just as a fight began behind them.

CHAPTER FOURTEEN

Plan 'C'

The two moons were high in the night sky by the time they reached the castle's kitchen garden. The gate into the garden creaked loudly when Wil tried it but no one came to investigate so he pushed it wide and they simply walked in.

As they searched for their belongings, the massive, part-built tower above them glistened in the light of hundreds of torches now burning across the entire city. The smell of smouldering candle wax drifted through the evening air.

'D'you think Tally's in that tower?' Wil whispered, still searching for his own clothes. It was then he noticed that all of the fruit trees in the garden were covered with blossom; the garden seemed oddly warm, too, and... he listened... he could hear the gentle hum of bees – very odd so soon after such a hard winter. Wil concentrated on the bees for a moment; for them, here, this day was like all others, always warm and there was always blossom.

Mortimer pulled on his boots and looked up at the part-built tower. Next to it, the crumbling walls of the rest of the castle looked like they might fall down at any moment.

'Well, I'll bet she's in there somewhere, Wil,' he said wrapping his cloak around his shoulders. 'But I haven't come up with a Plan C yet. Let's go find the others. I can't think properly until I've had something to eat!'

Their journey through the city was not easy; people kept offering them beer, someone tried to pick a fight with Wil, and a very friendly young lady tried very hard to persuade Mortimer to go to a party with her. By the time they got back to the main gate both Wil and Mortimer were hot and very hungry – although nobody seemed to take much notice of Farrow and Mia.

As they got closer a man said something to Mortimer but his voice was drowned[53] by shouting up ahead.

'Great!' said Mortimer. 'That's all we need – a fight right by the gate. There'll be guards down here in no time!'

Then the people in the crowd nearest to them stepped back and Wil heard a familiar, though slightly odd-sounding voice.

'Get your handsh off me, you… you oaf! I could knock you down with one punsch… and don't try and stop me!'

A tall, blond boy put both his hands up and backed away, muttering something about a tambourine.

'Gisella?' said Wil.

'Wil, Mortimer! At last!' Seth appeared from the orange and purple crowd. Behind him, a young man was playing a flute while people around him smiled and clapped in time to the tune. Two other people were plucking at small harps, and while they showed more enthusiasm than skill, the sound wasn't actually too bad.

Gisella suddenly shrieked.

'Wil!'

Gisella charged forwards, waving with her hands as if fearing he might not spot her.

'Wil, Wil, Wil! I'm sooo glad you've come! Oh, and Phinney too. Phinney, oooh, look. Theshe are my new friendshsh – well, mine and Seth'sss,' she slurred, and held out her hand to Phinn who backed away. Gisella twirled back to face Wil and beckoned him closer with a hooked finger. 'But to be honesht,' she whispered conspiratorially and pointed vaguely, 'he'sh being a big meanie. He took away my tambourine… and my drink! Shaid I couldn't have any more!'

As she breathed over Wil, all became horribly clear – Gisella was drunk!

Seth forced his way between the two people with the harps, neither of whom took any notice of him, Farrow, or the two horses he was pulling along behind him.

'Who are your new friends?' asked Mortimer. He was watching Gisella trying to cuddle Phinn.

'They were at the gate when we got back,' said Seth.

He was holding the horses' reins in one hand and clutching a tambourine in the other. Every time he waved his hand the tambourine jingled – and in his present flustered state it was jingling a lot.

'The guy over there – Jev – he saw Farrow. His father used to breed Fellhounds over in Grizzledale. The guys on the gate weren't around so Jev invited us to join them while they waited to be let in. That's when they brought out the mead.' Seth finally took a breath. The tambourine jingled again.

Gisella stood beside him, swaying slightly and smiling at anyone who passed by.

'So why didn't you just say no, Seth?' asked Mortimer while still watching Gisella, who clearly wanted to re-join her new friends. 'Gisella, no, stay here.' He reached to grab Gisella's arm but missed. Gisella took the tambourine from Seth's hand as she went.

'I did!' Seth said in answer to Mortimer's question. 'But Jev gave Gisella some of his drink – I think it was some sort of beer – very dark, smelt awful! And, well, she didn't seem to like it at first but Jev kept talking to her and being really friendly–'

'How friendly?' demanded Wil. He was trying to keep an eye on Gisella and listen at the same time.

'Oh, *really* friendly. She kept giggling – I've never seen Gisella like that before – then she had more to drink and then…er, then she started dancing.'

'What!' said Mortimer. 'On her own?'

'Oh no, they were playing music – it was really good actually and Gisella and Jev were dancing. And then they fell over–'

'I don't think I want to hear any more,' said Wil.

'Oh, no,' Seth insisted. 'Once she fell over I managed to get her to sit down with me. But then they opened the gates – just now. We've only just got in and … er… as you can see, she's… er… livened up again.'

Seth's voice trailed off. All around them people were laughing, singing, or shouting to one another; some were buying bulging pies or glistening slices of roast boar from nearby stall holders. The air was full of the smell of smouldering charcoal, burning meat fat and stale beer. Gisella's tambourine had disappeared; she now had a harp and every now and then she stopped walking and brushed her fingers across the strings. Wil watched. Jev offered Gisella his flask. Beaming, she lifted it to her lips; at the same time Jev slid his arm around her waist – Wil had seen enough.

'Right, that's it!' he said and marched into the crowd. Mortimer made a grab for Wil's arm, missed, but managed to stop Phinn from following.

'Wil!' said Gisella, as if she was seeing him for the first time that evening. 'When did you get here? Thish is Jed, my oops..'

She swayed slightly and Wil saw Jev tighten his hold.

'Jev, it's Jev,' corrected Jev quietly. He looked directly into Wil's eyes with an almost-smile but Gisella gave him a vague wave and threw her arms around Wil's neck.

'Oh, I'm so happy to see you, Wil! I've really, really, really, really missed you.'

Jev stepped back. Gisella hugged Wil tighter.

'Did I ever tell you Wil, I really, really, reeeeeally like you. Did you know that?'

Much as it *really* was very nice to see the look on Jev's face and to have Gisella snuggled so close, the smell of beer was overpowering. Wil gently unwound Gisella's arms from his neck and turned in search of Mortimer and Seth.

'Oh,' said Gisella, suddenly sad. 'Wil, you don't like me!'

'Look, Giz, of course,' he turned back, 'I do.'

But Gisella didn't seem to be looking at him, or anything else for that matter. She swayed again and flopped forwards. Wil caught her before she hit the floor and lifted her up over his shoulder. The people around them cheered.

'Nice one!' said Jev. 'I was planning to have had a go at that one myself, but after all that rat beer – nah, I'll leave her to you.' And with a grin he patted Gisella's bottom. With the unconscious Gisella over his shoulder, Wil turned… and turned back. He punched Jev in the ribs – just once – and waited just long enough to see his drunken opponent collapse before marching out of the crowd into the nearest alley. Everyone else cheered again.

'Oh dear, this is my fault,' moaned Seth. 'If only we hadn't spoken to those people. If only I'd stopped her from drinking that beer.'

'While I do hold you partly responsible, Seth Tanner, Gisella really should have known better,' said Mortimer angrily.

They had found a quiet corner next to a blacksmith's forge which was closed for the night. Gisella had already been sick once; she was now fast asleep a pile of hay. Wil had hoped that the first aid bag would have come up with something to help but instead it had produced an empty bottle. A tiny label swung from the stopper with the words:

For excess alcohol: Accompanied by sickness, headache and feeling like death – suffer and learn from the experience! Best before: If Nothing lasts Forever, this cure will last a very long time, though few will only use it once.

Wil was busy being cross with Gisella for letting that Jev bloke chat her up, when a voice as rough as a bucket of gravel rattled above the hubbub[54] of the crowd.

'NO! Are you thick or *what?* I said quail eggs – get them now!'

'I... I'm so sorry, Ms Mhaddphat, they told me you would be here last evening. I, er, I thought you had changed your mind, or gone somewhere else...' said another, much quieter and slightly frightened voice.

'What!' yelled Mhaddphat. 'A hundred and forty I ordered– DON'T tell me you sold 'em!'

The sky was now a faint pink colour – it was nearly dawn and the city was still wide awake. A small child started to grizzle.

'An' you can be quiet,' she growled. The child continued to whine. 'SHUT UP!'

Mhaddphat's shout was so loud that Gisella jumped up and peered around through very bleary eyes. Mhaddphat continued to bellow.

'What am I gonna do now? YOU can tell her ladyship. I ordered them an' *YOU* let me down!'

'I... I can see if Cecil has some... over on Bell Street. If... if you'd like?' The voice was very scared now.

There was a moment of peace before Mhaddphat shouted again.

'Get over there then! Go on! NOW!'

The child whinged. The yelling got louder.

'An' *when* you got em, bring 'em up the castle. I'm no' wasting any more of *my* time! I go' things to do!'

The child started to sob. Mhaddphat was some distance away before she called to the child.

'Faerydae, GET 'ERE!'

Gisella slumped back onto the hay and instantly went back to sleep. Mortimer sat up.

'That's it!'

'That's what?' said Seth, who had also dozed off.

'Plan C!' said Mortimer.

'Plan C?' repeated Seth with a yawn, but Wil had already guessed.

'We buy some quail eggs and deliver them to the castle?'

'Not quite, Wil. But not far off. We find that poor guy and offer to *deliver* the quail eggs he's going to buy,' said Mortimer. 'I mean, he won't want to go himself, not after that!'

'And what about the horses?' asked Wil. Rhoani and Shadow were happily munching on a mound of hay that Gisella hadn't been sick on.

'Someone will have to stay with Gisella. Seth, Mia, Farrow and Phinn need to be fed anyway. Wil and I'll deliver the eggs, get into the castle and find Tally.'

Wil wasn't convinced but, unable to think of anything better, he kept his mouth shut and nodded.

'And, Seth,' Mortimer added, looking at Gisella,

'If Gisella wakes up and can stop being sick for long enough, you need to find Tanith. You might want to start with the castle stables if you can find them.'

CHAPTER FIFTEEN

Special Delivery

Bell Street was even busier than the market around the city gate. There were rickety[55] stalls piled high with honey, cheese and delicious smelling hams; others were overflowing with jewellery made of anything from brightly coloured gem stones to carved bone. There were also a lots of sheep skulls.

'You want to buy a lantern, boy?' whispered a scruffy little man, as Wil walked past. 'Put one in your window tonight, boy. It'll keep the Alcama evils at bay when the moons cross.'

'Er, no thanks,' said Wil. 'I, er, I haven't got a window.'

'Well, evil be upon you, boy!' the man hissed. Beside Wil, a woman picked up one of the skulls. The man smiled at her. 'You want to buy a lantern, lady?'

Wil moved on. The next stall was much more interesting. It had the biggest selection of knives Wil had ever seen, including a very ornate display of cream-coloured daggers. Something sparkled red. Wil leant forward. He could see a very odd shaped dagger – like a stretched 'S' that finished in a deadly point. Close to the tip Wil could see what looked like a drop of blood. It sparkled again; Wil guessed it was a ruby.

'It's a dragon's tooth,' said a cheerful voice from behind the table. 'Giant Redback – left that in my dad's favourite bull – absolutely no fear, your Redback. If you ever get chased by one, best thing to do – throw yourself off something high and hope you hit the ground before it catches you in mid-air. Once a Redback can smell you, believe me, you're dead!'

The girl pulled a woollen shawl around her shoulders and nodded. Another ruby sparkled in her nose and a similar but much shorter tooth dangled from her left ear.

Wil picked up the tooth dagger and turned it over in his hand.

'So what happened to the bull?'

'Managed to stitch it up. It's fathered fifteen calves since!' she beamed proudly.

'Gosh, I bet your father's pleased!' The tooth was twice as long as Wil's hand. It felt surprisingly rough – like it was covered in tiny scales.

'Dunno,' said the girl. She looked up at the sky. 'Redback swallowed him in one gulp. He's up there somewhere – the dragon, not my dad.'

Wil hastily put the tooth back in the fan-like

display. 'Oh, I... I'm sorry,' he stammered and, not knowing what else to say, moved away from the table. Up ahead, Mortimer was standing outside a shop; unlike a lot of the others which were still closed at this time in the morning, this one was brightly lit and open for business. Wil could hear something clucking.

'She needs them urgently, you see,' Mortimer was saying to a tiny man as Wil joined them.

'W-well, yes, I could see that,' answered the man. As he spoke he jerked his head back and forth, eying[56] the boys suspiciously. 'She really was very cross, wasn't she?'

'Yes.' Mortimer nodded. He looked so confident that even Wil started to believe him – and Wil knew his friend was lying! 'She's making quail egg soufflé. It's a new dish for the festival – a surprise for Lord and Lady Rexmoore. It's absolutely delicious. Cook really must have them as soon as possible.'

The man twitched his head upwards – he reminded Wil of a tiny, frightened mouse.

'Oh, dear, this really is awful. I can only get eighty – they're just not laying at the moment. It's the moons.' He seemed to be talking more to himself than to Mortimer. 'Everyone knows quail don't lay when the moons cross – just like the cows won't give any milk. And anyone eating moonpig meat during Alcama is asking for trouble. Oh dear!'

He pushed his shaking hand through his thin hair.

'Mmm, sounds like you've got a problem – and you know what Mhaddphat's like,' said Mortimer, crossing his arms over his chest.

'Oh, don't,' said the little man, covering his face with his hands. 'I just can't face her. She'll roast me alive!'

'Look, tell you what,' said Mortimer. 'We could deliver them for you? We'll say that Wil here dropped some on the way, which is why there are only eighty.' He leant towards the man and whispered, 'My friend here is one of her favourites, treats him like the son she never had.' He winked again.

'Oh!' gasped the man. 'But what about Galorian? I know he's a little brat, but surely she hasn't given up on him already? He's only three!'

Wil was impressed by how quickly Mortimer corrected his mistake. 'Older son, of course! I mean, a three-year-old's not going to be much help around the kitchen now, is it?' Mortimer put his arm around Wil's shoulder. 'No, Wil here is her little helper – fetching, carrying, peeling, plucking – she hates plucking, did you know–'

'Mort!' interrupted Wil.

Mortimer dropped his arm. 'Well, anyway,' he said, standing so upright that he looked even taller than usual. 'We are offering to take those eggs up to the castle... but if you want to do it yourself we'll be off.' He turned, grabbed the edge of Wil's cloak and pulled Wil around with him.

'No, wait! Yes, I mean – *please*,' begged the man.

'Keep walking,' whispered Mortimer.

The tiny man burst into tears. 'Please, s… stop. I beg you.'

Both Mortimer and Wil turned back towards the sound of clucking, quacking and squawking. The little man grabbed the handle of a large wicker basket and, still sobbing, handed it to Wil before throwing his arms around Mortimer's waist. Mortimer looked slightly embarrassed and patted the man's shoulder. Then without saying another word, the man dashed into the crowd weeping loudly as he disappeared.

Mortimer gave Wil a triumphant grin.

'Right, let's go deliver some eggs!'

The gate that led into the castle's kitchen garden was wide open. In the pink light of the rising sun Wil could see old bee skeps piled up against the wall. They smelt of rotting straw mixed with cow dung; although Wil was sure he could hear the soft hum of bees coming from somewhere close by. Mortimer could hear them too.

'Watch you don't get stung, Wil,' he said, ducking under low-hanging branches of apple, plum, damson and cherry trees.

But Wil knew that the bees meant no harm; he could feel their contentment[57] so strongly that his mouth suddenly filled with the taste of Martha's delicious honey cake.

'Just be careful where you put your feet,' he replied in a whisper. 'Bees are a very close family and they don't like having their relatives squashed!'

'Oh, right-oh!' laughed Mortimer. 'And what do you think they'd do then?'

'You really don't want to know, Mort. Just watch where you're putting your feet!'

Wil could see a door in the old stone part of the castle. This, like the gate, was wide open and the dark, damp entrance looked very unwelcoming against the glowing golden tower behind it: the gravelly voice that bellowed from somewhere beyond the doorway was even less welcoming.

'I told you already, Galorian, I'm busy. I go' things to do, I 'aven't got time now!'

'But Faerydae took my barey[58] sugar. She won't give it back,' replied a young boy's voice.

'No I didn't!' objected another voice – a girl – still young but older than the boy – Galorian, Wil guessed. 'He said I could have it!'

'I didn't gi' you my barey sugar! I never said nothin'!'

'Did too, you liar! Mmm, it's reeeeally yummy! Baaaarley sugar, my favourite,' said the girl, exaggerating her own correct pronunciation of the word *barley* as if to taunt her brother all the more – it worked.

'Yaaarghhuhuh,' sobbed the boy. 'I want it. I want my barey sugar. Yhaaarghhuhh!'

'Right, that's it. Ger out, both of you! Ger out and don't bother me 'til breakfast time! I said I'm BUSY!' Mhaddphat's voice echoed out over the garden. Wil could feel the bees becoming agitated.

'Do you want to do this?' he said, offering the hamper of eggs to Mortimer. But Mortimer held up both hands and grinned.

'She'll be fine, Wil. You'll see... and don't forget, we're here to help her with a problem – she's bound to be pleased!'

'Yes,' said Wil, unconvinced. 'But if you remember we've only got *part* of the solution!'

Another bee skep lay upturned on the doorstep, together with an old sheep's skull. The black wick of a cold candle was just visible through one of the eye sockets. Next to the skep was a water trough, overflowing with thick, green water, above which hung a bell that Mortimer was about to ring when two tiny figures ran out through the open door. Mortimer jumped out of the way but the skep and the skull were knocked over. One of the figures was waving a twist of barley sugar high in the air and the other was sobbing – very loudly. As they disappeared among the fruit trees, another, now familiar voice came after them.

'Oh my gaawwd! If I get my hands on you two – just SHUT UP, WILL YOU!'

Mhaddphat appeared in the doorway clutching a rolling pin in her fist; Wil nearly dropped the hamper.

'Whoa, a hobgoblin!' he said before he could stop himself.

Mortimer looked as surprised as Wil but managed not to say anything.

The tiny woman glared at Wil. 'Yeah, and what of it!' she demanded. Her top lip was barely visible under her bulbous nose and her beady black eyes were almost hidden, too, under bushy, black eyebrows.

She raised the rolling pin higher above her head, making it waist-high to Wil and Mortimer. Wil lowered the basket for protection and Mortimer closed his hands across his breeches. The hobgoblin glanced at the basket. 'What d'you want?'

'Eighty! Oh my gaawwd! What I am supposed to do with eighty?'

Mhaddphat, now clutching a carving knife, stomped around a huge pine table in the middle of the even huger kitchen – her huge bottom swinging from side to side with each heavy step. She was still shouting. The kitchen, that moments ago had been full of busy staff, was suddenly empty.

'I said a hundred and twenty. You bring me eighty

– I can't believe it!' She stopped and pointed the knife at Wil and Mortimer. 'You sure there's eighty? You counted 'em?' She glared at them suspiciously and began counting the eggs in the hamper.

'I thought you were going to tell her I dropped some,' whispered Wil.

'I was,' Mortimer whispered back, his lips hardly moving. 'But she's got that knife and there are a lot of parts of us both I'd rather stayed attached!'

'Seventy-six, seventy-seven, seventy-eight, sev-' Mhaddphat stopped counting. Her head popped up from behind the wicker lid of the hamper. 'Eighty! There's only eighty! Oh my gaawwd! What do you expect me to do with eighty?'

'I think it's going to be a long night!' said Mortimer, but as he spoke there was a crash and a high-pitched squeal from the garden.

'Was that one of you?' demanded Mhaddphat with an accusing glare. She moved away from the quail eggs and cocked her head to one side. Her pointed ears turned, trying to locate the source of the disturbance.

'Wow,' breathed Wil. Of course, he had heard of hobgoblins before – every wealthy household in Thesk had at least one – but he had never actually seen one. They certainly didn't have any in Mistlegard because everyone was much too poor; but his mother had told him about a very rich man who lived on the other side of

121

Grizzledale who had three. She had told Wil that hobgoblins were exceptional cooks, owing to their own huge appetites; this also made them quite expensive to keep – and looking at Mhaddphat, who was once more bending to count the quail eggs again, Wil could certainly believe that! They also had very long arms, which made them very useful at harvest time.

Outside there was another crash.

'Ger them off, Faerydae. They's 'urtin me. Argh, i' 'urts! Mama, argh! Mama!'

The cries of the little hobgoblet were so high-pitched that Wil and Mortimer had to put their hands over their ears. On a shelf next to the fire a bottle of oily, yellow liquid exploded, splattering its sticky contents up the wall.

'Mamaaaa!'

Mhaddphat slammed the hamper lid down and waddled towards the kitchen door, her knuckles swinging just above the floor. At the same moment, two terrified hobgoblets charged into the room – followed by a dark buzzing cloud.

'Run!' yelled Mortimer. But Mhaddphat was in the way.

With her mouth wide open – easily the size of Wil's head – she was running around the kitchen scooping bees out of the air. Wil stood and watched, unable to move. She crunched down on a mouthful of buzzing bees… and Wil's world went mad. Buzzing filled his ears; it made his teeth vibrate and his fingers tingle. Bees were dying – and not just in the kitchen.

Wil grabbed Faerydae's arms. 'What did you do?' he shouted. She didn't answer.

'What did you do to the bees?' he repeated through clenched teeth. He suddenly realised he was shaking the silent child. He stopped, but didn't let go. The hobgoblet began to howl.

'It was Galorian. He started it. He lit the fire!'

Wil let go and pelted straight through the swarm of angry bees in the kitchen out into the night. Mhaddphat continued to swoop and munch.

Wil could see a smouldering[59] skep in the middle of the little courtyard; he could feel the terror of the bees trapped inside. Some were escaping through a tiny opening at the base of the basket but Wil knew they weren't getting out quickly enough. There were two more skeps; the bees inside those were frightened too but thankfully they were not on fire. Wil picked up the burning hive and ran to the water trough. He looked around for a bucket or even a cup: the only thing he could find was the bell by the door. He yanked it from the wall with one hard tug and dipped it into the water. At the first bell-full, smoke and steam billowed up into Wil's face. The steam scalded his hand but he kept pouring water by the bell-full. At last the buzzing in his ears stopped. The bees were calm.

Wil put all three skeps under the drooping branches of the biggest apple tree he could find, next to two others that were already there. As he put the last skep into place, a bee settled on Wil's hand. His badly scalded skin immediately started to blister and peel but he didn't brush the bee away. Another came, and another and without really knowing why Wil reached into one of the undamaged skeps and pushed his hand into the waxy honey inside. The pain disappeared.

Behind him, what was left of the swarm in the kitchen billowed out into the courtyard like a puff of thick black smoke; they were followed by Mortimer, who was walking really quickly. Then Wil heard the two hobgoblets wailing again. Mhaddphat was already shouting.

'I'm not really sure what happened just now, Wil, but, er,' said Mortimer as he past Wil. 'I think it's time to go!'

'Oh, ...er, right,' said Wil. The sound in his head had gone but the soothing honey felt so good.

'Uh, Wil, I don't want to rush you here, but...' said Mortimer, pointing towards the tower. 'I reckon we can still get in if we go back now.'

'EIGHTY!' The voice seemed to explode from the open door of the castle kitchen. 'HE'S ONLY GIVEN ME EIGHTY! WHAT AM I GOING TO DO WITH EIGHTY QUAIL EGGS? OH MY GAAWDD!'

Mortimer shrugged, 'Or perhaps not!'

CHAPTER SIXTEEN

Unexpected Pets

Seth did nothing to hide his disappointment as Wil and Mortimer approached the city gate.

'You didn't get Tally then?' he asked needlessly.

Mortimer glanced at Wil.

'No. Let's just say the plan didn't quite work. Please tell me you had more success, Seth. How's Gisella?'

Wil looked around – Gisella was nowhere to be seen.

'Seth, she's not with that Jev idiot again, is she?'

'No!' said Seth, looking rather pleased with himself. 'No, actually I went off to find Tanith, which I did; and Gisella stayed here to watch our stuff. And while she was waiting, guess what?'

His expression suggested that he really did expect them to guess.

'She found Tally,' said Mortimer. Seth beamed.

'Yes!'

'Where?' chorused Wil and Mortimer.

'Up there. Where you've just been!'

Seth pointed towards the golden tower.

'She's in that balcony thing above those trees. I really thought you'd find her.'

Wil squinted back towards the high wall of the castle garden; the tower shone in the bright morning sunlight. His stomach tightened: the Alcalma would happen that night and he knew now that they had very little chance of getting Tally back to Saran before the moon crossing.

'How do you know she's there, Seth?' asked Mortimer.

'Because Gisella heard that egg seller talking to someone when he got back to his stall; she told him that Tally was being a complete nightmare and she'd be glad when the Alcama came because at least she'd get some peace.'

Wil went cold.

'Peace? What did she mean, Seth?'

'I'm not sure. Anyway, Gisella said that the woman was surprised people hadn't heard Tally's bad language down here because you can see the city gate from the window in her room. And if you look up there,' Seth pointed towards the castle, 'there's a window behind that balcony... and it's the only one that you could see the gate from.' Seth nodded. 'I bet that's where she is.'

'Well, at least we know she's still alive,' said

Mortimer. 'It's just a shame that we were so close and didn't know it! So where's Gisella now?'

'Well, I found Tanith – I said I found him, didn't I? They're keeping him with the other animals for the Unexpected Pets contest on the other side of the city square – I told Gisella. You should see it; it's massive and they've got this huge–'.

'Seth!' snapped Mortimer. Then he spoke much more slowly. 'Where are Gisella and Tanith?'

Seth was far too excited to notice Mortimer's irritation.

'She's gone to keep an eye on Tanith; she took Phinn, Mia and Farrow there, too. Said they'd fit in better, you know, with the other unusual animals. She told me to wait here for you two with Rhoani and Shadow. I can't wait to get back down there. Some of those creatures are awesome!'

'Well, I just hope Gisella hasn't had any more rat beer!' said Mortimer.

'Oh, don't worry about that,' grinned Seth. 'Before she went I offered her a drink of elder wine and she was sick behind those bales again!'

Without waiting a moment longer Seth set off down yet another packed street. Up ahead, Wil could hear the sound of cooing birds, and suddenly a flock of doves took off into the air. Everyone looked up except for a small boy who, Wil noticed, very carefully lowered the lid of a huge and now completely empty basket and crept away into the crowd.

Behind the basket a shop window was filled with cages of chickens, Fell hens, turkeys, pheasants, and Rockmoor quail – Wil realised that they were back on Bell Street once again and heading down towards the city square.

Right in the middle of the square, Wil could see a huge stage with a high fence of thick metal bars and a high gate in the middle of the side nearest to them. All around the city square itself he could see hundreds of stalls selling anything from rat beer to boiled eggs; in others he could see animals. The smell was awful but the noise was much worse... deep booming barks, yaps, caws, cries, mews, yowls and baying; all this plus music coming from every direction. There was also shouting – lots of shouting.

'What is that?' asked Wil. Just in front of them, a tall, very thin woman dressed entirely in white was holding something in her arms. It had a child's face but its body was covered in silky, jet-black fur. It looked at Will with huge green eyes; the woman looked too. Both she and her little companion had long, cat-like ears – that creature's ears were black tipped with white fur; the woman's ears were tipped black on her pale skin – they looked like they had been painted. The woman was wearing a delicate silver band on her slender wrist; from it swung a fine silver chain that was attached at the other end to an identical band around the animal's neck. She stroked the animal's head with fingers as white as snow and fingernails like daggers.

'We are Fayarie,' she said, blinking slowly. She had the same bright green eyes as her pet. 'We can swap our form but we can never be the same.'

Wil reached out to stroke the little animal. 'What's its name?' he asked. The animal gave a spitting hiss and lashed out with a needle claw. Wil pulled his hand back quickly. The woman laughed softly.

'Take care, those claws can rip a man apart,' she said and turned away, still talking. 'Her name is Olan. I am Olath – we are sisters.'

'Wow!' said Seth, wide-eyed. 'What does it – you – eat?'

But the woman disappeared into the crowd without giving an answer.

Two elderly men bustled through the gap she had left; they were deep in conversation.

'Well, I'm sorry to argue, Twyford, but that cry was unmistakable. That cat-like caw – classic,' said one. 'And the bright red underbelly – a mature male, I've no doubt.'

'Yes, Meldon, the Lesser Crested Ridge Creeper is …'

They passed by and their voices could be heard no more.

A little further on, they came to the animal pens. Seth was already peering into the first pen. Wil caught up and looked over Seth's shoulder. He could see two dogs half-buried under a mound of straw. They were munching on a long bone and, by the size of their heads, Wil could see they were much smaller than Phinn.

'Well, I can't see anything unexpected about them,' he said. One of the dogs grabbed the bone from the other and started to growl. Two scruffy men who were standing at the edge of the stall stopped talking.

'Torris, be'ave! Share or I'll 'ave that orff you!' snarled the man nearest to Wil.

Torris dropped the bone and got to his feet. Both heads were attached to one very muscle-packed body.

'Yep,' said Wil with a nod. 'That was definitely unexpected!'

'What's is it?' Seth asked the men.

'A Drangfell Pinscher,' answered the man without looking round.

'How old is it?

'Three.'

'Are they easy to train?'

'No.'

'What do they eat?'

The man turned slowly and looked Seth up and down. 'Inquisitive boys,' he said and turned back to his

130

friend. A little way ahead, Mortimer called out over the crowd.

'Wil, Seth! I can see Gisella. She's over there.'

Mortimer was pointing towards the corner of the square, but all Wil could see was a long-legged animal with the head and horns of an antelope that was happily munching on a net stuffed with holly leaves.

Wil and Seth struggled to keep up with Mortimer as he strode through the crowd. There were people and animals everywhere. Wil stepped backwards to move out of someone's way and bumped into the person behind him while someone else stood on his toe.

'Don't these people sleep?' asked Wil, hopping on one leg.

Seth didn't seem to notice. He was far too busy looking at the strange sights around them.

'Wow! Did you see that?' he said pointing back over his shoulder as he tried to keep up with Mortimer. 'It was like a massive deer but with a bull's head. Did you see the sign? *Beware of the poo!*'

'A bonacuss!' exclaimed Mortimer. He looked genuinely horrified. 'Why would anyone think it was a good idea to bring one of those? Everyone knows their dung is extremely dangerous!'

'I didn't!' said Seth.

'I did,' said Wil. He stepped out of the way of a

woman who was trying to keep control of two rat-like animals the size of a Peachley sheep that Wil recognised as pranxies. 'Bonacuss can shoot their dung quite long distances. If you get it on your skin it burns like crazy and it sticks, too. So if you see a bonacuss lift its tail, run and don't look back!'

'Blimey!' said Seth. 'And I thought some of Farrow's poo could be a bit nasty!'

The pranxies were now fighting. Rhoani kicked out with his back leg. One of the pranxies dropped to the ground.

'Oh, no! I'm so sorry,' exclaimed Seth.

The creature didn't move. The woman looked delighted.

'No, thank you!' she said, wiping sweat from her forehead. 'They've been squabbling for ages.'

'Yes, but is it alright?' asked Seth.

'Oh yes. Don't worry, dear,' said the woman. 'No sense, no feeling, pranxies. I love them dearly but they are hard work. Have you seen the dragon yet?'

'Er, no, not yet; we knew there was one here though,' said Seth, looking around.

'Oh, you must see it. It's smaller than I expected – but then that's what makes it unexpected, I suppose! It really is very cute!'

Mortimer appeared and his expression didn't suggest he was about to go and admire a dragon – cute or not.

'Wil, Seth! Get a move on!'

'Oops, looks like I've got you into trouble with your brother!' chuckled the woman. The two pranxies were fighting again. She gathered up the leads and dragged her beloved pets off towards Bell Street. 'Right, come on, Kibbles, give it a rest or I'll get that horse to shut you up again!'

Gisella was standing in front of two stalls only a short distance from the fenced stage. She was wearing an orange and purple tunic that was much too big for her; even from a distance Wil could see she was worried.

'Where did you get *that*, Giz?' asked Seth, looking her up and down. Phinn looked over the low door of one of the stalls.

'It was all I could find: they'd sold out of my size. Anyway, I've just heard something terrible!'

'What?' demanded Mortimer.

But Gisella shook her head and nodded towards an exceptionally tall woman standing in front of Phinn's stall. She appeared to be wearing a bright red scarf. Wil nodded politely at her and reached past to stroke Phinn's nose. The lady looked down at him. The scarf hissed.

'Oh, don't worry about Erena. She means no harm,' said the woman quietly.

Wil took a step back; he wasn't so sure.

'I think the pegalus has unnerved her. You don't see many about nowadays, do you?' she whispered, stroking the snake's head.

Wil was just about to ask what a pegalus was when Mortimer called him.

'Wil!'

The woman with the snake moved behind Shadow and disappeared into the throng[59]. Mortimer called again.

'Wil!'

Wil turned and gasped.

Gisella and Mortimer were standing next to a beautiful golden horse… with wings!

'Now *that* really is unexpected,' said Wil. Tanith whinnied gently; Wil knew the pegalus recognised him.

Gisella started talking very quickly.

'We need to get to Tally now, Mortimer. I heard someone say that the competition will be judged this afternoon. They also said that Rexmoore has a prisoner – a young girl. They are saying that she is a witch.' Gisella looked at Wil. 'Do you think they are talking about Tally, Wil?'

Suddenly a bell started to ring and voice called out over the crowd.

'Oyez, oyez!'

Wil didn't hear whatever Gisella said next. A man dressed in a red and black cloak edged with gold braid was standing in the centre of the stage, high above them. Behind the man, Wil could see a thick wooden pillar surrounded by smaller logs. The man was holding a bell in one hand and a tightly rolled scroll in the other. He rang the bell again and unrolled the scroll. The crowd in the square were suddenly silent.

'Oyez, oyez, oyez,' the man called again, his voice echoing around the vast square.

'Hear ye all.

Lord Rexmoore greets you as his guests.

At noon,

This festival will commence with the Unexpected Pets contest.

A bar of purest gold will be the prize,

So come for the spectacle and feast your eyes.

Bragg hounds, marbussal and a dragon too,

But for those behind the bonacuss, mind that poo!'

Everyone in the crowd laughed. The town crier waited for quiet and then continued.

'But don't wander too far

After the award of the bar –

Lord Rexmoore has a treat in store.

As the moons cross, evil moves through the city this night

But we shall be saved by a fire burned bright –

Here be the pyre[60]

See fingers twitch

When we light the fire for the burning of a... WITCH!'

Wil, Gisella and Mortimer stood absolutely still as the crowd around them cheered in excitement.

After a few moments, Seth looked into the silent stall.

'Did you hear that?'

CHAPTER SEVENTEEN

The Golden Tower

Wil didn't know if Tally was the witch; he also didn't know if Imelda knew that Tally had been born at the Alcama. But he did know that they had to get Tally out of Armelia, just in case. He also knew that their only real chance was to get Tally while she was still at the castle and go out of Armelia the way they had come in – through the gully under the wall – *before* anyone noticed that she'd gone!

Mortimer shook his head.

'It's just too risky, Wil.'

'But Wil's right, Mortimer,' argued Gisella. 'We'll never get her out from down here, there are just too many people. And don't forget we've got to get Tanith out too. It would be much easier if we wait until the competition is over and just walk out of the gate with him, like everyone else will with their pets. I've heard that everyone thinks the dragon will win anyway. I bet no one will try to stop us!'

'And once Tally and Tanith are both out of the town they can fly back to Saran,' said Wil, feeling more confident about his plan now he knew Gisella thought it was a good idea. He looked up at the sun; it was nearly mid-day already. 'Look, Mortimer, it's the only chance they've got of getting home before the moon crossing tonight!'

Mortimer shook his head and tapped a pile of straw with his toe. 'It's just too risky.' Then he pinched his bottom lip between his thumb and forefinger and strode to the other side of the stall, stopped and turned to face them.

'Right, this is what we're going to do.'

Seth was sulking and Mortimer was running out of patience. He took a deep breath.

'Look, Seth, you need to stay here with Gisella, Rhoani and Farrow. Wil and I will get Tally. Wil can show Tally the way out of the city through the canal, using Phinn and Mia, like we got in. As soon as I know they're safely away from the mill.' He gave Wil a worried glance then looked back at Seth. 'I'll meet you by the bonacuss stall with Rhoani. Gisella, get Tanith out of the city as soon as the bonacuss is loose.'

Gisella nodded but Seth was still cross.

'But why can't *I* go with you to get Tally? Wil could stay here with Gisella.' Wil bent down to check that

138

his knife was in his boot; Gisella looked suddenly embarrassed. Mortimer put his hands on his hips.

'Because, Seth, Wil can't ride! And *you* can't swim – or had you forgotten that small detail!'

'And anyway, Seth,' said Gisella, more kindly. 'If you and Mortimer are going to let that bonacuss out, you will need Farrow – Mia and Phinn are just too inexperienced.'

Seth kicked the ground with the heel of his boot.

'Oh, OK…, I suppose.'

'Right,' said Mortimer before Seth could change his mind. 'I'll be back as soon as I know that Wil and Tally are going in the right direction. We won't have very much time before someone notices that Tally's missing, so we're going to have to move fast, Seth. I need you at that bonacuss stall – I'll be there as soon as I can.'

Wil declined Mortimer's offer to ride with him on; he was still surprisingly sore after the long ride across Tel Harion and already he wasn't looking forward to the ride home – especially if it meant riding *and* flying at the same time!

'It's OK, Mort, I'll walk, thanks.'

Mortimer looked down at Gisella.

'If you get caught, Giz, just get out of the city and get Tanith back to Saran before the moons cross tonight.' He glanced at Seth and back to Gisella. 'You've both got your bows, haven't you?'

Seth swung his bow over his shoulder and opened his jacket – he might still be sulking but by the number of bolts Wil could see, Seth was certainly ready for a fight. Gisella nodded towards their packs; her already loaded bow was right on top of the pile. Wil had a sudden thought.

'Wait a minute, Mort.'

The rod that had fallen on his head at the Black Rock and the silk rope were still at the bottom of his bag. Mortimer frowned.

'Well, the rope might be useful, Wil, but I'm not so sure about the rod.'

Then he turned Shadow and headed off back towards the golden tower.

Gisella watched Wil click the rod into one long length.

'Where did you get *that*? And what is it?'

Wil wound the rope around his waist and tied it in a loose knot.

'Sorry, Giz, no time to explain,' grinned Wil, and he set off at a jog to catch up with Mortimer.

At the end of Bell Street Wil and Mortimer took a left turn to avoid two women who were screaming and pulling great handfuls of hair from each other's heads – Wil spotted two half empty jugs of black beer in the gutter beside them.

After two more turns the streets were deserted. Wil could hear the sound of running water.

'I think we're near the mill.'

They walk towards the sound and were soon walking on the grassy track that ran along the edge of the canal. The mill wheel was no longer turning and Wil could see that it was fixed to a huge stone building. The building had a huge stone chimney. A little oval boat was pulled up on the opposite canal bank and beyond it, going up the hill towards the half-built tower, two donkeys were dragging a cart up a rough track. The cart was piled high with gold – *lots* of bars of gold. Mortimer gave a slow whistle and whispered.

'Hey, Wil, I think this might be where they make those gold bricks.'

Suddenly he heard – or felt – a scream. Was it pain… *fear*? No, it was laughter – cruel laughter. It lasted only a moment before the sound of gently trickling water once more filled the air.

'Wil, *Wil*, are you OK?' Mortimer was still gripping hold of Wil's arm. He had nearly toppled into the canal with the shock. Leaning on the staff, Wil shook his head and listened again. He felt sick.

'D-did you hear that?'

'Crronk!'

Confused, Wil looked around. Pricilla was perched

on the top bucket of the motionless mill wheel. With another loud '*Crronk! Prruk!*' she flapped her wings and glided low over the water towards them. But just before she reached the bank, she swerved and landed on a crumbling wall.

'That bird looks like the one at Lovage Hall,' said Mortimer.

'*Crronk!*' said Pricilla.

Wil wasn't sure how much Mortimer knew about Pricilla, so instead he repeated his question.

'Did you hear that noise just now, Mort? That laugh?'

Mortimer frowned. 'What laugh?'

Pricilla took off from her perch and glided towards them, then swerved and flapped her wings towards the castle; rather late Phinn took offence and snapped at the empty air. Wil listened for the sound again but all he could hear was the water trickling over the mill race. Pricilla came back. Wil shrugged.

'Must have been a bird or something.' But Mortimer wasn't paying attention. He was watching Pricilla circling above them, calling and then flying towards the tower. She repeated the move four times.

'I think she wants us to follow her,' said Wil eventually.

'*Crronk!*' called Pricilla, circling again.

Wil nodded.

'Yep, I definitely think she wants us to follow her!'

They reached the golden tower in minutes. Close up, its smooth walls gleamed. Pricilla was nowhere to be seen.

'I just can't see what we are supposed to do, Wil,' said Mortimer, making no attempt to hide his frustration. 'Are you sure that bird wanted us to follow her?'

Wil didn't answer.

'Look, you can stay here if you want, Wil, and try to work out what that bird wants but I think I'll go back to the castle garden. I reckon I can get in through that door at the back of the kitchen – did you see it? I saw that Mhaddphat woman at the egg stall again just now so with any luck there won't be anyone to get in my way.'

Wil bit his lip. What was Pricilla trying to tell them? Unfortunately Wil's own ability to read the minds of animals was at that moment not working at all – although he'd always suspected that reading Pricilla's thoughts was rather more up to her, than him!

'OK, Mort,' he said, hoping that Pricilla might be a bit more helpful if Mortimer wasn't around. 'But I bet Mhaddphat left the hobgoblets tormenting the bees!'

'Oh, don't worry about them. I've got some of Martha's treacle toffee. It'll glue their teeth together for weeks!'

***

As Mortimer and Shadow galloped back towards the walled garden with Mia following behind, Phinn sat back on his haunches and looked at Wil.

'Well, boy – all I need to do now is work out just what Pricilla was trying to get me to do!'

From where Wil stood, the golden tower seemed reach the clouds. He could see the tiny balcony tucked about halfway between him and the sky. The staff suddenly felt much heavier than before and an idea crept into Wil's mind. Not really knowing why, he let go of the staff; it clattered to the ground, broke into three pieces and lay in the shape of a triangle.

'Crronk, crronk, prruk!'

Wil looked up. On the edge of the balcony he could see Pricilla's black shape and he knew what he had to do.

'Ohh! Well, come and give me a hand!'

'Crronk!' replied Pricilla, but when Wil looked again there was no sign of the raven. He sighed.

'Great! That bird is very useful when she wants to be,' he said to Phinn. 'But if she doesn't want to be...'

He reached for the triangle and with a snap! it was once more a rigid staff. He weighed it in his hand. Then he slid one of the bolts out from his boot and took a few steps backwards. He looked at the tower again. The balcony really was a long way up.

Wil tried three times to get a bolt through the railing at the edge of the balcony; and each time he and Phinn had to run as the as the missile bounced off the stone below and fell back to the ground. His fourth attempt, however, went straight over the ledge high above.

Now that he was sure he could reach his target Wil tied the rope to another bolt, leaving enough to fasten to the end of the staff. He slid the bolt into his bow, took a step back and looked at Phinn. The hound's unblinking amber eyes studied him through a pair of straggly eyebrows.

'Yes, I know,' said Wil. 'I think this is what they call a long shot[61]!'

He released the bolt.

To his surprise the bolt went straight through the balcony railings, taking the staff with it. He heard a clatter and smiled.

'Well, I'll be!' he breathed.

The silk rope dangled from the balcony almost to the ground. Wil tugged on the rope then wound the end around his hand and leant backwards – the rope remained fixed to the balcony above. There was still no sign or sound of Pricilla.

'Right, Phinn. Wait here. I'll go and get Tally then we'll go and find Mortimer.' He looked at the balcony high above his head and back at Phinn. 'Unless he's up there already!'

The climb up the sheer tower was not easy but luckily the rope held. As Wil climbed he couldn't help wondering why everything he did lately involved heights!

About halfway up, a huge spider crawled out of a wide crack that was working its way from the balcony down to the ground like a vein. Wil very nearly let go of the rope!

He reached the little balcony panting and sweating. The triangle had done its job as an anchor. With one final effort, Wil clambered over the rail and flopped onto the balcony – to be greeted by a round of applause.

At the back of the balcony, a narrow door opened onto a dark room. The applause slowly stopped and Wil heard the same shrieking laugh he had heard by the mill. Suddenly he felt very cold.

'Oh, do come and join us.' It was a boy's voice. 'We were wondering how you'd get in – nice idea with the stick!'

Wil slowly got to his feet but he caught the triangle with his foot. It sprang back into its rigid length and the weight of the rope still dangling down the side of the tower dragged it through the bars. Wil just had time to see the staff plunge into the ground a few feet away from Phinn who was asleep – the Fellhound did not stir[62]. Both Phinn and the staff were an *awfully* long way down.

'Oops!' said the voice behind him. Wil turned. The Jackal was standing in the doorway grinning smugly; he was a lot cleaner than the last time they had met and his rags had been replaced by smooth purple velvet. 'Wil, come and meet Mother. Oh, and by the way, I'll take that bow… and the rest of those bolts.'

CHAPTER EIGHTEEN

Hats and Horrors

The dark interior of the tower took Wil by surprise after the brightness of the gold and the sunlight outside and for a moment couldn't see anything. He was aware of something fluttering and distressed to his right; he was also aware of something else – pain, hate, darkness – he wasn't sure, but it felt... oddly familiar. His mouth went dry.

'*Crrrronk!*'

Somewhere else in the room a woman shrieked. There was clapping, again. Wil's sight cleared and he could see Pricilla, pegged to a large wooden table by a bolt – *his* bolt – right through her wing! She flapped, but the bolt held her in place. Wil spun back around. The Jackal was looking extremely pleased with himself.

'Mother and I guessed she was a friend of yours by the din[63] she was making,' he drawled, loading another of Wil's bolts into Wil's crossbow. 'Nice bit of shooting by the way. I thought your preferred knives?'

Wil couldn't believe his eyes. Had he really shot Pricilla? And The Jackal was very different from the last time they had met; he couldn't see Tally but... he could feel a strange tingling in his mind again – there was something in the corner of the room behind the clapping woman... and it smelt really bad!

The woman suddenly jumped up.

'A hat!' she exclaimed. Wil was confused. She was already wearing a hat. It was a beret covered with little oval strips of pink material. 'It'll make a very nice hat. Those feathers – black. Lovely! I need a new hat.'

'Yes, Mother,' the boy answered. 'What an excellent idea. That's why I caught her... for you. For a new hat.'

Wil felt relief and hate all at the same time. *He* hadn't speared Pricilla to the table – The Jackal had. And he'd done it for his mother's entertainment!

'You'll pay for that, Jackal... or whatever your name is!' hissed Wil.

'Oh, I thought The Jackal made me sound quite romantic. And anyway some of that was true... my name *is* Colin. The bit about being found in the flour sacks and being called Miller was just my little joke. Ha, ha!'

He stopped laughing suddenly and aimed the bow at Wil's heart. 'Actually my name's Tinniswood. I believe you killed my father.'

The woman clapped again even more enthusiastically than before.

'Oh, you're so clever, Colin darling. My clever, funny Colin. A new hat for Mommy. So clever and kind!'

So, thought Wil, watching his bow, it had all been a trap – and Wil had walked right into it. He had actually felt sorry for this boy; he'd trusted him! Wil felt like a complete fool.

Whatever was in the corner moved; excruciating pain shot though Wil's entire body. Beads of sweat erupted on his forehead.

'Where's Tally?' he demanded, trying to ignore the agony.

He could smell the same noxious stench again, stronger this time.

'Poooohhh!' cried the woman waving her hand over her nose. 'Snuffy's made a smell! Make the smell go away, Colin, make it go now!'

Colin reached for a scent bottle and sprayed it around his mother's head and shoulders. A strong but not unpleasant smell hit Wil's nostrils.

'Tally?' The boy frowned and scratched his head as if trying to remember something. 'Ooh, if you mean the headstrong, foul-mouthed *thing* that we used to get you here…' He walked out onto the balcony. 'I suspect Lord Rexmoore and his charming wife are getting the crowd ready for her big moment, as we speak.'

'What?' choked Wil.

'Yeees,' sneered Colin. He was enjoying this. He held out his right hand to admire his now clean and beautifully manicured nails. 'They've gone down to judge the competition before lighting the bonfire. I think it's a marvellous idea, don't you – burning a witch for the Alcama.'

'Tally is not a witch!' Wil hissed through gritted teeth.

Colin wrinkled his nose, he seemed to have forgotten Wil's crossbow which was now pointing at the floor.

'Weeell, I'm not sure that's strictly true, now is it, Wil? I mean, that temper is pretty evil for a start! Imelda tells me it's some sort of anniversary today too, now what was it?' He put his finger on his lips and studied the ceiling. 'Oh, that's it – the day she was born… and, well, she did arrive on a flying horse – pretty *unexpected*, wouldn't you say?'

'Flying horse! You have *seen* some of those pets down there, haven't you?' demanded Wil.

'Yes, but no one else can speak to their pets!' retorted the boy.

'I speak to Phinn all the time!'

'Yes, but you don't have actual conversations with him. You know, sentences… answering questions!'

'Answering questions!' Colin's mother repeated, with a theatrical nod.

At that moment the really bad smelling thing came out from the corner. 'Snuffy-woo!' cried the woman, with a delighted smile. Colin stepped back towards a door on the other side of the room and raised the crossbow. But this time he wasn't pointing it at Wil.

Pain and rage overwhelmed Wil. Suddenly he found it very difficult to breathe.

From out of the corner limped the familiar black shape of a Wraithe Wolf. The Jackal laughed again.

'Well, how's that for unexpected, Wil Calloway?'

Wracked with pain now, Wil looked from the wolf to the boy and back again. Colin's mother clapped her hands in joy.

'So bootiful,' she whispered. 'Snuffy, come to Mommy. Ooo, sooo cute.'

But Snuffy did not look remotely cute to Wil. As the wretched animal dragged itself into the light, Wil could see why it had not leapt to attack them. Around the wolf's neck was an iron collar so tight that Wil could hear the animal struggling for breath; an iron muzzle had been fixed around its jaws – how, Wil did not even try to imagine – and where there should have been a barbed, razor-sharp claw on each of its front legs, Wil could see wounds crusted with dried blood.

Colin's mother did not seem to notice the animal's terrible condition. She bent to her knees, threw her arms around the wolf's neck and hugged it tightly. The wolf let out a low growl and tried to flick its head around to bite, but the collar and the muzzle stopped it from doing any harm.

'Meet the winner of this year's Unexpected Pets competition, Wil,' said Colin with a cruel smile. 'Mother wins every year. Last year I got her an albino[64] sabre tooth tiger – exceptionally rare, you know.'

'But I thought the competition wasn't until later – and this is NOT a pet!' exclaimed Wil, as he shared its pain. Colin's mother held her arms tight around the wolf's neck and giggled. Colin signed.

'Well, I'm afraid she's simply got to win, Wil. You see, she always wins because she gives the gold bar back to Imelda. She's just not interested. No, hats are Mother's first and only love...,' he shrugged. 'She's very excited. Doesn't get out much... you see, she hasn't been too well for a while. The Unexpected Pets Competition is her one big treat of the year.'

'So what happened to the sabre tooth tiger?' asked Wil. Although he wasn't sure he wanted to hear the answer.

'Oh, it was marvellous. It won, as usual. Afterwards we got enough fur from it to make two hats *and* a cloak,' answered Colin. 'I wasn't too keen on the cloak though, white is so difficult to keep clean. But the hats were a huge success. We had one each.'

Wil felt sick.

'And what will you do with Snuffy-woo?'

'Another hat, of course! They're all unique, you know. She's got quite a collection; although the dwhyley turban smells atrocious when it gets warm! We've got the claws from this one already, as you can see. We're planning to use the teeth too. I mean – two sets from one mouth – I think this one will be an absolute classic!'

'So what about me?' asked Wil, unable to avoid the question any longer.

'You?' said Colin, pretending to look surprised. 'Oh, yes. Um, you're staying here. Imelda's going to ask you about Lady Élanor's legacy after the competition.'

'And how are you going to stop me from escaping when you go off to the competition?' asked Wil, making no attempt to hide his dislike of this cruel, arrogant boy. Colin slowly turned and aimed the crossbow at Wil.

'I'm going to shoot you in the leg to stop you running awa–'

The tower door exploded off its hinges, hitting Colin in the back. Wil's bow flew out of the boy's hands as Phinn bounded into the room and jumped on top of the fallen door with Colin underneath it. Wil heard the bow skitter across the floor but couldn't see where it went. Colin's mother shrieked and let go of the wolf in order to clap wildly.

'Oh, Colin. A dog – a new hat!'

Her shrieking laugh echoed around the bare room and she continued her insane applause.

Still on top of the door, Phinn wagged his huge tail and gave one deep bark; a moment later Mia, followed by

Mortimer, appeared in the doorway. Mortimer looked at Wil, then Pricilla, then the clapping woman, and finally at the pathetic Wraithe Wolf – one of its wounds was bleeding again.

'Can I borrow your bow, Mort?' whispered Wil. He was feeling faint now and it was taking all his strength to stay conscious.

Without a word Mortimer threw the loaded bow to Wil and in the next moment the wolf lay dead. The pain raking through Wil's body disappeared immediately.

Colin lay motionless under the door. Mortimer put a hand to the boy's neck. 'Still alive,' he said with a quick nod. Wil could tell it was a question but he shook his head.

'No, leave him.' Wil glanced back at the dead wolf. 'Although I am very tempted!' he added bitterly.

Then Colin's mother began to wail[65].

'Nooo. Snuffy-woo, my Snuffy-woos. No prize for Mommy. Nooooooo.'

Wil yelled over the din.

'We've got to get back to the square, Mort.'

He grabbed the Wraithe Wolf's back legs and dragged it onto the flattened door. Colin groaned.

'They'll be waiting for this lot so hopefully we've just bought ourselves some time,' he said, running to the table where Pricilla was lying quite still. Wil's hands shook as he pulled the bolt out of the wood as carefully as he could. 'We'll have to leave the bolt in her wing until I can get to my bag,' he said, tucking the raven under his arm. 'Right, let's go!'

Pricilla gave a pitiful '*Prruk*'.

Mortimer grabbed Wil's bow from the edge of the balcony.

'You might find this useful then,' he grinned. 'Can I have mine back now?'

Wil stepped over the dead Wraithe Wolf. 'Right, this time we really are going to get Tally!' he announced and stamped very heavily across the door. Behind him, Colin's mother cried out.

'But Snuffy-woo's not playing with Mommy... what's Mommy going to do now?'

'Make a new hat!' called Wil over his shoulder.

CHAPTER NINETEEN

Lord Rexmoore

Mortimer gathered up Shadow's reins.

'I'll go on, Wil. Seth'll be waiting – there's no way we can release that bonacuss until we've got Tally. Mia can stay with you and just for a change try not to lose your crossbow!' At that moment a cheer came from the square. 'See you back at Tanith's stall,' he said, and kicked Shadow into a gallop.

There were still a lot of people on Bell Street and the market stalls were now very busy despite the crush. Poor Pricilla! It was very difficult to carrying a raven with a bolt through her wing in such a crowded space.

Wil stood in a doorway for a moment to think. He was sure that his first aid bag would have something to help Pricilla but how would he keep her safe while he went to help the others rescue Tally?

'Hi again,' said a cheery voice beside him.

At first Wil didn't recognise the smiling girl sitting behind one of the stalls, but then the ruby in her earring

157

glinted in the sunlight and the tale about the dragon's tooth and the bull came back to him.

'Have you come back for the dagger?' the girl beamed. 'I knew you would! Hey, what've you got there?'

Before he could stop her, the girl reached over and drew back the edge of Wil's cloak.

'Oh, wow, a raven,' she whispered. 'They are so intelligent. I had one once – Caroline. Is this your pet? Have you just bought it?'

'Er, no,' said Wil. Pricilla was so still he was starting to worry that she was dead. 'She's mine, er, from before. She followed me here and then got injured.'

'Oh, that's terrible!' said the girl. 'Did someone hurt her? Some people! They can be so cruel. Here, let me see.'

She held out her hands.

'*Prruk!*' said Pricilla, but she didn't try to escape the girl's fingers. Wil watched. The raven trusted this girl, he could feel it.

'Does he... she have a name?' asked the girl, carefully unfolding Pricilla's injured wing. A small boy pushed in beside Wil and reached out to touch the bird. The girl glared at him. 'There's nothing for you to see here so go away!'

The boy ducked under Wil's arm and scuttled into the crowd. Pricilla winked.

'Her name's Pricilla,' said Wil. 'So, er, so you know a bit about ravens then?'

He crossed his fingers.

'Well, I didn't have Caroline for very long – the Red Back... you know,' said the girl. She wrinkled her nose. 'They eat anything... but she was a great bird. When I first found her she had a broken leg. I fixed that...'

Wil took a deep breath.

'Look, I've got to find my friends in there,' he jabbed his thumb towards the square. 'And... well, I can't take Pricilla with me – it wouldn't be fair, she'd get crushed in no time. I don't suppose you could, er...'

The girl pressed her lips together.

'So you don't want to buy the dagger then?'

'If I had the money...' said Wil truthfully – it really was a beautiful knife.

The girl stroked Pricilla's head gently. After a moment she nodded.

'OK. I'll watch her for you. But I do want to see the moons cross so make sure you're back here in plenty of time!'

'Oh, believe me, I'll be back before then,' said Wil, thinking of his promise to Lady Élanor. *Not* being back in plenty of time would be *very* bad!

The square was now jam-packed with people wearing orange and purple costumes: capes, dresses, robes, trousers with one orange leg and one purple leg and almost everyone wore some sort of orange and purple hat.

Wil had absolutely no idea how he was going to find the others among the people, stalls, wagons and campfires. Phinn and Mia were standing so close that he could feel Phinn's breath on his arm.

Hey, Phinn, he thought, stroking the hound's ear as he tried to concentrate. *Can you find Gisella? I haven't got a clue where we are.*

Phinn raised his head and sniffed the air – Wil suspected the hound had simply caught a whiff of the wild boar roasting over a fire to their left but he decided to give the hound the benefit of the doubt. Almost immediately Wil thought about Gisella washing in the river and he tried to push the image towards Phinn... it really was a very pleasant image – Gisella's long, athletic legs; her gentle laugh; she looked pretty even when she was cross...

A gruff voice beside Wil made the memory disappear.

'You gonna stand there all day?' growled the man who was cooking the meat. Phinn was sniffing the cooking meat.

'Oh, no... sorry,' said Wil. He moved on a few stalls and tried again but Phinn didn't take any notice.

Somewhere in the middle of the arena a band began to play a very lively version of something Wil's father used to play on the flute. Wil stared at the brown woollen cloak of the man in front of him and tried to concentrate.

Find Gisella, Phinn. Find Gisella.

Wil made the image of Gisella in the river so big in his mind that he felt he could reach out and touch it. But Phinn didn't budge – in fact this time he didn't even look interested. Perhaps a more recent image might be more helpful? He thought of Gisella with Tanith, here in Armelia. He pictured Tanith's mane of fine golden strands, his kind brown eyes and his inquisitive velvety nose; then Wil thought again about Gisella; her tanned face, her soft hand resting in his. Almost immediately Phinn sniffed the air and set off around the edge of the crowd. Wil moved to follow but he bumped into a young girl who had suddenly stepped in front of him. His concentration broke.

'Er, sorry… Er, someone told me there was a dragon around here,' he said, not having to try very hard to look lost.

The girl's eyebrows rose almost into her hair.

'Oh, you mean the Ridge Creeper? Oh, it's so cute. But you're going in completely the wrong direction – it's over there, next to the pork pie wagon,' she said, pointing back past the end of Bell Street to the other side of the square. 'I'll show you if you like. Are these your dogs?'

'Er, yer. Er, it's OK. I'm sure I'll find it,' said Wil. 'Phinn, come, *this* way.' But Phinn took one step forward in the other direction and Mia was now beside him. A man behind them tutted and a woman shook her head.

161

'You'd think 'e could take 'em round the back. I can't see anything with them in the way!'

Another woman pursed her lips and nodded in silent agreement. Wil turned back to the girl.

'Think I'll give the dragon a miss. Don't want to cause any trouble,' he said and with an apologetic grin ducked into the crowd thinking very hard, *Go! Phinn, Mia. Find Gisella!*

Wil was surprised at the number of unusual animals in the square and everywhere people were talking, eating, playing music or drinking; others were fighting or dancing – although in some cases it was actually very difficult to tell the difference.

The noises and the smells were overwhelming and, struggling to keep up, Wil was beginning to wonder whether Phinn and Mia really would be able to find Gisella: after all Phinn hardly knew Gisella, and Wil had no idea how long she had been working with Mia before the misunderstanding with Mortimer. Wil had just decided that they were going the wrong way when a snarling, gnashing dog fight broke out in the pen he had just passed.

'Right, that's it. Give me that bone, Torris!' The owner of the Drangfell Pinscher vaulted[66] over the rail into the pen. 'And this time you ain't 'avin' it back!' Then the man vaulted back out of the pen gripping a huge bone in his thick fist. 'Bloomin' dogs!'

Wil breathed a sigh of relief; they *were* on the right path.

Somewhere a bell chimed. The entire square went suddenly quiet.

Another voice Wil had heard before boomed out over the tightly-packed upturned faces.

'Oyez, oyez, oyez.

Hear ye all.

You've heard the bands and laughed at the jokes,

But before the witch goes up in smoke,

There's gold to be won and animals galore,

So without further ado let's close our hands[67]

And welcome fair Imelda and Lord Rexmoore.'

While the town crier's announcement was met with some half-hearted applause, owners and animals burst out of every stall. There was a loud crash and a shout as a wagon was upturned and Wil was carried forward by the flow of people heading for the arena. Thank goodness, he thought, that Pricilla wasn't still tucked in his jacket.

A canon exploded somewhere above the crowd. Everyone stopped as the deafening boom echoed between the castle walls and the golden tower, and before it stopped another voice called out over the hundreds of heads.

'Riiiight, now I've got your attention, I think we could do with a bit of order round here.'

Wil could see a tall, skinny man standing on the stage, high above the crowd. The man had a wide, fixed smile[68].

'Riiight,' he repeated, rubbing his hands together as he spoke. 'First of all, everyone who doesn't have an animal take three steps back.' He flicked his long fingers as if shooing[69] away children. A few people around Wil shuffled; some took a few tiny steps back but most only managed one. The man raised his eyebrows and tilted his head to one side. 'Now come along, I'm sure we can do better than that! One more step, thaaat's it. Good!'

He clapped twice then pressed his hands together again.

'Now, all those people with green rosettes move back, too.'

He wagged his finger at someone near the front.

'Yeees, madam. That includes you. Naughty, naughty! Everybody else knows that runners-up are not allowed to enter the main competition.'

Almost the whole crowd groaned. The man on the stage held up his palms.

'Sorry, but those *are* the rules.' His smile was so wide it almost cut his face in half.

A few people moved back another inch; several people around Wil swore and a lady to his right burst into tears.

'Oh, and by the way,' said the man on the stage, raising his voice slightly. 'For those who haven't met me before, I'm… Lord Rexmoore!'

No one cheered although it was obvious Rexmoore expected them to. Wil ducked down behind the very short person in front of him – he had suddenly realised that not wearing anything purple and orange could be a distinct disadvantage. Above him, Rexmoore surveyed the crowd; his smile was still wide and fixed.

'Well, I'm not sure if you heard me there but,' he called with a slow nod; wiry arms wide, palms upturned, '*I'm* Lord Rexmoore!'

Someone clapped.

Rexmoore turned to a sour-faced[70] woman behind him.

'Well, well, dear. We've got a deaf old bunch here today, haven't we?'

Without waiting for an answer he turned back, still smiling.

'We'll give it another go, shall we? I mean, there's always room on the fire for one more up here.' Rexmoore gestured extravagantly towards the stacked bonfire. Wil couldn't see Tally, which he hoped was a good thing. The woman – Imelda, Wil guessed – gave the people in the front a cruel smile. Rexmoore opened his arms once more.

'*I'm* Lord Rexmoooooore.'

The crowd gave in and cheered loudly – although Wil, now desperately trying to go backwards, was sure he could hear people booing, too. By the time he reached Mia and Phinn there were far fewer entrants waiting at the gate to the arena.

Find Gisella. Find Gisella, Wil repeated in his mind.

But neither Phinn nor Mia seemed to be getting his message. They had stopped, their amber eyes fixed on the arena. Wil cursed under his breath. It was very difficult to see – let alone hear – what was going on up on the stage. One thing was obvious, though; there were a lot of very unhappy people between him and Lord Rexmoore.

'You watch,' said a man, 'It'll be that Tinniswood woman again. It's the same every year. All those gold bars she's won – reckon she could build her own tower by now.'

A few people around him nodded. A boy about the same age as Wil put his hand on the shoulder of the girl next to him and stood on his tiptoes.

'You know, I don't think she's there,' he said, standing on his tiptoes for a better look. Wil breathed a sigh of relief and prayed that The Jackal and his mother were still in the tower where he had left them.

'I bet that's why Rexmoore's faffing[71] about,' said the man who had spoken before. 'The old girl's late.'

'Prob'ly got something so dangerous this year that they can't bring it up 'til the last minute!' said another

166

voice. 'Remember that sabre tooth tiger. I nearly wet myself when they brought that thing in last year!'

'Oh, hang on,' said the boy. 'Something's happening...'

Suddenly there was a *very* enthusiastic cheer. Wil tried to get a better view but stopped short of leaning on the girl's other shoulder.

'What's happening?' someone asked. 'That woman arrived, has she? Come on, tell us what she's got.'

The boy leaned harder on the girl, who didn't seem to mind.

'No!' he said. He dropped back down. His eyes were shining with excitement. 'It's the witch. They've just brought on the witch!' Then he was back up on his toes again. 'Blimey, she looks a right handful!'

Unable to contain himself any longer, Wil put his hand on the girl's shoulder and was just in time to see Tally kicking out wildly. Two men were dragging her backwards towards the bonfire; another man was doubled up on the floor. Rexmoore and the remaining entrants to the Unexpected Pets competition were standing back at the edge of the arena including... Wil's heart almost stopped... Tanith and Gisella!

Then a wave of rage hit Wil's mind; it was like nothing he had ever experienced before – even his collision with the eagard had felt like a gentle summer breeze compared to this. Anger burned through his limbs; his eyes were blind and his brain screamed. The pain through his whole body felt like it would never stop. Somewhere, through this red-hot mist, he could hear barking. He tried to concentrate on it, to make it come nearer. But it vanished, and the hissing mist overtook him completely.

CHAPTER TWENTY

The Ties that Bind

'Wil, *Wil!* Can you hear me? Wil, *please* wake up!'

It was Tally's voice… But it couldn't be Tally's voice; she was in Armelia. He – Wil – was at home in Mistleguard, he knew he was. And when he opened his eyes he would see his mother's face and smell the bread she made every morning. He loved his mother's bread. When he was little she used to tell him that she put an extra large spoonful of love in it to make it so sweet and warm and delicious. When he opened his eyes she would carve him a thick slice fresh from the oven and spread it with soft butter that would melt and drip over his fingers as he ate. His father had–

'Wil, *wake up!* Oh, Wil!' It was Tally's voice again.

But how could it be? He breathed deeply, trying to find the yeasty sweetness of his mother's fresh bread…

'Wil, *pleeease,* can you hear me?'

Wil breathed in… and out… still nothing but that annoying voice.

'Wil, *for goodness sake*, wake up! *Wil!*' The voice was very cross now – definitely not his mother's.

Wil opened his eyes very reluctantly. Utter confusion! His arms and legs were tied with chains! And Lord Rexmoore was here – dancing with a woman Wil certainly did not recognise.

Lord Rexmoore's arm was around the woman's waist and his other had held hers when he caught Wil's eye. Wil saw him say, 'Ah! At last,' before he bent and said something into the woman's ear. She dropped his hand and the music came to a halt. Behind the couple, Wil could see purple and orange stretching as far as his eyes could see. Some people at the front clapped briefly. Most didn't clap at all. The woman bowed her head and stepped back gracefully; Lord Rexmoore took three broad strides to the front of the stage.

'Ladies and gentlemen... *friends*,' he called out. And slowly turning towards Wil, he raised his arm. 'This is such a lovely surprise. Please, let me introduce... our witch's best friend... I give you... Master Wil Calloway!'

The crowd near the stage clapped politely, some shook their heads and a few shrugged their shoulders. Further back, people started chatting to each other.

Unperturbed, Rexmoore gave Wil a sly smile.

'Welcome back to the land of the living!'

Behind him someone in the crowd shouted, 'Just get on with it – burn them!'

With a delighted grin Rexmoore added, 'Well, for the moment at least!'

Then, with a nod to the musicians, Rexmoore walked back into the middle of the stage. Poker-faced[72], she took hold of his outstretched hand and they danced once more. Below them, the people danced; a few clapped in time to the tune. Everyone except Wil and the dancing woman seemed to be having a wonderful time.

Wil was confused. Why was he tied to a pole? Who was the witch and why was he her best friend? Wil could see a fence just below the stage. Beyond it he could see some very strange looking animals... and... Gisella...

with a beautiful winged horse: *Tanith* – Wil remembered.
Next to Gisella, Wil could see his Fellhound, Phinn...
and Mia. Both had thick ropes tied around their heads.
So if Mia was here, where was Mortimer...? and Seth?
Then Wil remembered...

'Tally!'

'Well, it's about time!'

There was no mistaking that acid response but
Wil's head was tied so tightly that he couldn't look
around to check.

'I've been trying to get you to wake up for ages!'

'Tally! But... how?'

Wil was now so confused he didn't know what to
ask next.

The music changed and the woman – *Imelda*, Wil
thought – dropped Rexmoore's hand, leaving his lordship
to dance alone, apparently blissfully happy in his own
company.

Imelda, Lady Élanor's aunt, Wil remembered,
walked towards Wil. She was not slender like Lady
Élanor; Imelda was skeletal. She had the same shape eyes
as Lady Élanor and Tally, but they looked scary in her
pale, thin face; and unlike the lovely cornflower blue of
her brother's daughters, Imelda's eyes were cold and
grey.

'Well, it appears that my niece has proved useful
after all,' she said with a smile that showed no kindness.

'And just when I thought she would die with nothing to show for her life. As you are here at last, that will not be the case.'

With a final twirl, Rexmoore came to a halt behind his wife and put his arm around her bony shoulders. Imelda did not look pleased. Behind them, the musicians continued to play.

'Now, my love,' said Rexmoore – sweat trickling down his temple. 'As I promised, we have the seer. *And*,' he turned to acknowledge Gisella, Tanith and the Fellhounds, 'it looks like we've got more prizes than we'd expected. Yes, I think I'm safe in saying, my own one, that your brother's legacy will very soon be ours!'

He bent and kissed his wife's neck, leaving a smear of sweat across her cheek; Imelda shuddered. Rexmoore did not seem to notice. Instead he performed an extravagant pirouette[73] and danced alone back towards the crowd before the music stopped again.

Lord Rexmoore waited for silence. Above his head the sun was sinking down the late afternoon sky, almost as if it was going to crash into the golden tower.

'Right,' said Rexmoore eventually, 'well I hope you've all calmed down after the excitement of the Unexpected Pets contest? What a result, hey! I bet you weren't expecting that one?' He raised his arms, palms up, and nodded slowly, an expectant beam splitting his face. 'And I'm sure you're all looking forward to the highlight of this year's Alcama festival?'

The cheer this time was far more enthusiastic.

'Get on with it!' called a voice somewhere to Wil's right.

Rexmoore's smile got even broader.

'Well, just before we...' he acknowledged the voice with a wagging finger, '"get on with it", as you say, The Hemlock Quartet are going to *warm* us up.' He chuckled at his own little joke. 'So there's still time to get a lantern – only one gold schilling. And, for those who think they can't afford it – think again! Can *you* afford seven years of Alcama bad luck?'

He looked skywards with an expression of mock fear and clasped his cheeks. At the same moment, hundreds of pairs of empty eyes glowed gold as sheep skulls, laid cheekbone to cheekbone, lit up the edge of the stage. From somewhere below, a band struck up. Rexmoore, barely able to contain his excitement, skipped across to his wife and swept her back into the soft light. Imelda just danced.

From somewhere behind him Wil heard Tally's voice again.

'Oh, Wil, I'm so sorry.'

Wil guessed she was probably tied to the bonfire too. But he didn't ask.

She spoke again.

'I didn't know what else to do. I've been in that tower for ages – it was freezing! That Tinniswood boy... he's been so horrid. And my aunt...' she was obviously trying not to cry, 'she says that if you won't tell her where she can find the legacy, she'll burn me, and then Tanith, *and* Gisella as well.'

'But I don't know where – *or what* – the legacy is!' Wil insisted.

'I know,' said Tally. 'But she won't believe me. I've tried and tried to tell them.'

'I heard,' muttered Wil.

'Tinniswood told me about the trap... about getting you to the tower. When they brought me up here I saw Phinn and Mia. I thought they were still waiting for you... and I... well, oh, I'm so sorry, Wil. I just had to try to warn you. But I honestly didn't think you'd react like that.'

'Like what?' said Wil – the red mist and the excruciating pain hadn't quite gone.

Tally was crying now.

'Oh, Wil, it was terrible. I thought I'd killed you – or that you'd gone mad! Everyone did.'

'What do you mean, Tally? What did I do?' asked Wil.

'You were screaming, Wil – Mia was barking and Phinn started howling. I mean, you didn't do that in the court... at the moon chase hearing. It was terrible.

You just kept screaming and… oh, dear…'

'Oh, dear, what?'

'I couldn't stop myself. I was so worried – I… I called out your name.'

Wil closed his eyes. Tally kept talking.

'If only I'd kept my mouth shut. Gisella stayed where she was. *She* didn't say a thing,' she said with a very slight meanness in her voice that Wil chose to ignore.

'Don't worry, Tally. We'd already met up with young Tinniswood anyway. Did his mother get to the competition?'

'No,' said Tally, sounding thoroughly miserable. 'Imelda was furious. They had to give the prize to that dragon down there.'

Wil scanned the fenced area.

'Where? I can't see…' Then, nearer the stage, Wil spotted an ugly lizard-like creature with a red chest and a pair of wings that looked far too small for its body.

'That!'

The only reason the dragon looked *unexpected* was because it was tiny. Anyone who had been anywhere near the Eiye Mountains – as Wil had many times – would have seen Lesser Crested Ridge Creepers far bigger than that all around Ewes Seat!

The tiny dragon extended its neck and let out a pitiful yowl. Wil could see that its long teeth were like s-shaped tusks. It was wearing a gold rosette. Its sad cry almost drowned out The Hemlock Quartet, who sang louder. But Wil could still hear the dragon – so could everyone else; many now had their hands over their ears. Wil could see the red mist again and, with a huge effort, he called out.

'Tally, stop it!'

'Stop what?'

'Trying to read my mind. I told you, I don't know anything about the legacy. You've already nearly driven me mad once – don't try it again!'

'But I'm not doing anything!'

The red mist swirled. Wil clenched his teeth in an effort to banish the pain. His arms and legs felt like they were on fire.

'Tally, I'm warning you!'

'I am *not-*' Tally began.

But Rexmoore had also had enough. He stopped dancing and stamped his foot; the singers stopped singing and the music faded away. Thankfully, the dragon went quiet too. Wil's sight cleared and his limbs cooled. He could see a man clutching a length of chain that seemed to be attached to the dragon's collar. He was also holding a large gold bar, although he didn't look very happy about it.

'If you don't shut that thing up it will lose its head!' hissed Rexmoore.

The man bowed.

'Sorry, m'lord. I think it's hungry. They... it... likes fresh meat – but no one's got change for a gold bar.'

Imelda suddenly appeared at her husband's side holding Wil's loaded bow. In less than a second, she aimed and fired down into the corral. Several people screamed; Wil held his breath – so, he could hear, did Tally.

'There,' said Imelda. 'Fresh marbussal.' She lowered the bow. 'Oh, and by the way, that'll cost you half a gold bar plus taxes. Guards, take that gentleman's gold bar and give him his change – unless he wants to buy a penny lantern!'

Wil spotted Gisella down in the corral and nearly forgot to start breathing again. Her wrists and ankles were shackled too, and Tanith's legs were bound with a thick chain. Behind Wil, Tally whispered, 'Oh, no! Tanith!'

Wil looked out at the vast crowd. There was no sign of Mortimer or Seth. It was starting to get dark – they were running out of time.

Something bright flickered to Wil's left.

Tinniswood – The Jackal – holding a burning torch high above his head, came running onto the stage; he had a very swollen, *very* black eye... and he was furious.

'Colin!' said Imelda, her voice cold but calm. She was still holding Wil's crossbow. 'It's so good of you to join us. Is your mother well? We missed her earlier; she will be disappointed not to have won the prize this year. We had such high hopes.'

Her mouth smiled but her eyes blazed[73].

The Jackal looked suddenly uncomfortable.

'I... er, I was... er... held up,' he said at last.

'Yer,' said Wil, unable to contain himself. 'A *pressing* matter!'

'Colin?' said Imelda, raising her eyebrows.

'They took me by surprise!' Colin shouted suddenly and pointed to Phinn. 'That dog down there. They knocked me out! They killed Snuffy, knocked me out and left me for dead. And Mother missed the competition, and... and...' The Jackal whirled around and pointed first at Tally and then Wil. 'And *she* isn't going to tell us where the legacy is, so I've come here to help make sure *he* does!'

Rexmoore's face lit up. Imelda looked less convinced.

'And *what* makes you think you can be any more effective than *me*? After all, Colin, you have completely failed to get any information out of my niece so far, and, correct me if I'm wrong,' she said in a voice that warned that any attempt to correct her would be a very big mistake, 'your father *completely failed* to get any information about the legacy during his rather lengthy stay in Saran some time ago!'

The Jackal's triumphant expression threw Wil completely.

'Because,' he said, answering Imelda's question, '*I* know where Master Calloway can find his father!'

'What!' gasped Wil. 'You mean you knew he was alive and you didn't say anything!'

The Jackal chuckled.

'Well… you know… didn't seem particularly useful at the time! So, let's see… we've got your father, the lovely Gisella,' he waved his fingers towards the corral while using the burning torch as a pointer with his other hand, 'that flying nag, *both* your dogs… have I forgotten anyone… oh, yes, and Tally here.'

He walked to the front of the stage and pretended to search the crowd that had completely lost interest by now. Then he returned and stood right in front of Wil.

'And, Wil, I know that Seth and Mortimer are out there too. I just hope they won't do anything foolish.'

The town crier tiptoed onto the stage with his hand in his bell to stop it from ringing.

'Ah, hem.'

He bowed and spoke in a whisper as he addressed Lord Rexmoore directly. 'My lord, with all due respect these people all wait, as was promised on this due date. The burning of the witch the party will make, but I fear more delay a foul mood they will take.'

The crier finished his hasty rhyme and bowed.

The bell... thought Wil; the hint of an idea started to form in his mind.

Rexmoore frowned.

'Yes, but the moons are nowhere near to rising,' he said, looking up at the cloud-dotted sky with a frown. 'They're just going to have to wait. Bring on the jugglers and drop the price of rat beer by a groat, that'll keep them happy!'

The town crier gave a doubtful nod and backed away in silence.

'So, what d'you think, Wil,' snarled Tinniswood. 'Your father – in exchange for the location of the legacy? Oh, and we might even let your friends *and* your pets live!'

Wil didn't know whether to cry or laugh.

'But I don't know where, or even what, the legacy is!'

Imelda laughed.

'Oh, but you do, Wil Calloway. I know you do. You see, Sir Jerad sent word. I know you are a seer. You *will* lead us to the legacy whether you want to or not.'

'And to make sure you do,' Imelda added, 'we will kill each of those you care about, one by one, and *not* terribly quickly... until you see that no matter how long it takes, really, the only way that you will be able to stop the killing... is to do as we ask.'

The Jackal danced inches from Wil's face.

'So, Calloway, what's it to be?'

'You know, Colin,' interrupted Imelda, her tone still sugary, 'as we have the lovely Tally all ready... and a crowd desperate to see Armelia's first witch burning in... ooh, quite a long time.' She turned towards her husband who was once again listening to the band. She turned back – her expression impossible to read. 'Let's see if the smell of smoke will make young Master Calloway talk.'

The Jackal bowed so low his nose almost touched his knees.

'Be my guest, my lady. I am sure Wil's father, at least, can wait a *little* longer.'

Wil had to make a supreme effort to stay calm; an idea was just starting to take shape and he needed a clear head if he was to have even the slightest chance of making it work.

CHAPTER TWENTY-ONE

The Burning of the Witch

'No! I'm sorry, my love, but I absolutely forbid it!' said Rexmoore with a little stamp of his foot. 'It's not even dark! We won't get the full effect – I mean, the people at the back won't see the flames!'

'Or hear the screaming,' sneered The Jackal.

'I can see that, my lord,' said Imelda in the same patient tone that Wil had heard Lady Élanor use when Tally was being difficult, 'But the crowd is getting restless.'

The Jackal surveyed the mass of purple and orange below them and added, 'They'll all be running around scaring each other once the moons cross anyway, my lord. If we leave the burning until later it might not be such a show.'

But Rexmoore stamped his foot again.

'Now look here,' he said. 'I don't ask for much all year, Imelda, but this is *my* festival...'

But Wil wasn't listening. It was getting dark now. He needed to get a message to Phinn; his plan depended on it. Wil closed his eyes.

Phinn, when I say... find Mortimer, he thought.

'Well, *I* don't get much the *rest* of the year,' retorted Imelda.

Get ready, Phinn. Get ready.

'Agh! I can't believe you said that. I give you everything! Why do you think the castle is a wreck – to pay for your precious golden tower!'

Get ready, Phinn. Get ready.

'What, that half built effort! You told me it would be ready by this Alcama – just like you did last Alcama *and* the Alcama before that!'

Get ready, Phinn.

'I think you'll find, if you *think* for a moment – you can do that, can't you? – that it wasn't even started then!' argued Rexmoore.

The effort to concentrate through the blazing row was making Wil feel sick. He swallowed hard and opened his eyes. In the corral below, Phinn was rubbing his head against Gisella's back – and by the look of it, he was pushing quite hard. Wil watched. Phinn was trying to get the halter off!

Gisella, trying her best to stay on her feet, looked up at Wil. She was really getting pushed about and didn't look at all happy. Wil gave a tiny shake of his head and winked.

On the stage Rexmoore had his hands on his hips.

'Me! *Selfish!* For all these months I've had to put up with that cousin of yours... and her hats! Eccentric, you said! I can think of at least one other name for it!'

'That is my family you're insulting!' hissed Imelda before calling, 'Colin, light the bonfire!'

The Jackal moved. Wil couldn't see him. Tally shrieked.

'NO! Get that thing away from me. You... NO! I will rip your entrails out with my teeth when I get free!'

The Jackal's spiteful giggle rang out over the now silent crowd; all eyes watched the bonfire – *Perfect,* thought Wil.

Below him, Gisella seemed to suddenly realise what Phinn was trying to do and hooked her finger into the rope halter. The Fellhound slowly backed away and the rope slid over his ears.

Wait! thought Wil.

Phinn stood and watched.

Although Wil could not see what was happening on stage, Tally's language suggested things were not going well. He could smell smoke; the crowd were cheering wildly, and amidst the chaos Imelda and Colin were dancing and laughing like children. Wil couldn't see Rexmoore but he could hear his Lordship shouting. He was absolutely furious. It was time.

Phinn, find Mortimer. Release the bonacuss!

The words had hardly left Wil's mind when, in one

bound, Phinn leapt over the corral fence. The crown parted as he landed and sped away, but to Wil's amazement no one gave chase. One of the guards pointed up at the stage. Several people laughed; the action was behind Wil – the witch was burning!

With Phinn on his way, Wil had to move quickly. He tried to ignore the sound of Tally, who was still screaming obscenities, but at least that meant she was still alive. He needed to get another image into his mind–

'So, Calloway, any *ideas* yet?' Imelda's voice broke Wil's concentration. She and The Jackal danced past.

'Yer, untie me and I'll show you!' snarled Wil.

'Now, now, boy, there's no need for threats,' said Rexmoore watching his dancing wife. 'You could help yourself, and your friends, by telling us where the legacy– oh no, oh, goodness...'

Suddenly The Jackal stopped dancing.

'Mother!'

Imelda tripped over The Jackal's foot.

Wil heard a childlike voice drifting through the smoke.

'A hat! Look, Colin, Mommy's got a new hat. Ooh, so warm. A pretty new hat for Mommy...'

Someone in the front of the crowd screamed and The Jackal, Imelda and Rexmoore all ran towards the side of the stage. A woman – The Jackal's mother,

Wil guessed – started shrieking, 'No, not my hat. You can't have it! Get your own. No! Don't do that! Aarrgh!'

Doing his best to ignore the unseen commotion, Wil shut his eyes tight and concentrated.

'Wil, do something,' yelled Tally. 'This wood's wet but it's drying fast. Wil, please, you've got to do something!'

But it was no good, he couldn't do it. He couldn't get them to come.

Behind him, over Tally's frantic pleas for help, Wil could hear The Jackal's mother – whatever was going on back there, she was not happy!

Then, at last, he heard another noise – a faint buzzing... the chains around Wil's hands and feet sprang apart. He clawed at the binding around his head. In seconds he was free. The buzzing got louder. He looked down. Bees were crawling across the padlock at his feet and out of the keyhole of the lock that had fallen from his wrists.

'Wil, bees! There's a swarm of *bees!*' yelled Tally.

'I know!' Wil grinned.

It took him a moment to locate Gisella through the smoke. As his eyes finally spotted her, the little dragon once more began to wail. Wil thought about the chains around Gisella's wrists. A black buzzing cloud trailed down into the corral.

A voice behind him yelled, 'Wil, anytime today!'

Bright orange flames were almost touching Tally's feet. Wil plunged his hand into his boot – to his amazement his knife was still there. He began to hack at the ropes that held Tally to the stake[74]–

'Look, he's freeing the witch,' called a voice from the crowd.

'Stop 'im,' cried another.

'Call this a burning?'

People started to boo. Something soft and squidgy hit Wil on the back of the head: a rotten tomato plopped to the floor.

'Oh, no you don't!' The Jackal took Wil clean off his feet and away from the bonfire.

Tally screamed. The crowd roared. The little dragon wailed.

'This is more like it!'

'Go, my son!'

'Let her burn, let her burn, let her bu-urn,' they sang.

Wil and The Jackal crashed to the floor. Wil's hand banged against a stray log and he let go of his knife.

'Guards!' The Jackal yelled. 'Guards! '

Wil punched out and caught the boy hard across the cheek, just missing his black eye; but for all Wil was the bigger of the two, The Jackal was on top, with his knee planted firmly on Wil's other arm.

'Guards!' screamed the boy. 'Can I have a hand up here!'

But no one came. The Jackal punched and punched. Wil felt his cheekbone crack. The crowd were going wild with excitement. Then suddenly, in a blur of grey and the sound of air being knocked out of a pair of lungs, The Jackal was knocked high into the air. He landed somewhere past the edge of the stage, followed by Phinn.

'Phinn, no!' yelled Wil. If Phinn caught The Jackal now he was sure to finish him off and Wil needed the boy alive – Wil needed to find his father.

On his knees, Wil fought to catch his breath. The fire crackled greedily; the crowd were yelling. Smoke filled his nose and with a deafening crack, the stake collapsed and gave in to the flames...

Wil sank into a crouch and wept – it had all been for nothing. Tally was dead.

How was he going to tell Lady Élanor? In a flash Wil's grief turned to rage. He had come all this way and risked so much, and now she was gone. He had tried *so hard*... and failed... well, maybe there was still time to honour half of his promise. If he could just get Tanith home, back to Lovage Hall. Of course, Lady Élanor would never forgive him, but–

'Are you going to stay there all night?' asked a

cross voice. 'I mean, it wasn't even a real fight, Phinn saved you almost as soon as it started. Ooh, that cheek looks a bit painful–'

'Tally!' Wil was on his feet before she'd finished speaking. 'How?'

Tally grinned.

'If I was in trouble, do you honestly think those hounds would just sit there panting?'

'But what... Phinn got you out of the fire?'

'He's a massive Fellhound, Wil – what do you think he did! He's a bit singed[75] though, but it'll grow back!'

'Oh, so that's what I can smell – burning hair!' said Wil.

'Er, no actually.' Tally walked to the edge of the deserted stage. Beyond her, the square was almost empty too. There were overturned carts, wrecked stalls and the smouldering remains of campfires everywhere. The little Ridge Creeper was wandering loose, abandoned and by the sound of it, very unhappy. 'Someone let a bonacuss loose.'

So Tally was alive and his plan for Phinn to find Mortimer worked. But Wil felt exactly like the day Rexmoore's men had taken his father, and the pitiful cry of the Ridge Creeper wasn't helping one bit!

'So where are they – Gisella, Mortimer and Seth?'

Wil said, trying to ignore his strange mood.

'Well, Tanith is down there with Mia and... Oh... oh, dear. That looks like Gisella.'

Tally stared down into the demolished corral with wide, unblinking eyes.

'Wil..., it was the bonacuss... she couldn't get out of the way...' Tally concentrated. She shook her head. 'No... Imelda... Imelda grabbed her... Wil, Imelda used Gisella as a shield!'

CHAPTER TWENTY-TWO

Bonacuss Poo

Without stopping to consider the height of the stage, Wil jumped. Phinn followed in an easy leap.

'Don't worry,' Tally called after him. 'I'll find my own way down.'

But her sarcastic tone went unnoticed.

Gisella was lying face down; Mia was nudging her with her huge nose but despite the Fellhound's best efforts, Gisella didn't move. Wil didn't know what to do but knowing he needed to do something, he gently lifted her hair from her face. Her normally tanned cheek was pale as stone but her neck was spattered with green liquid. Carefully Wil lifted Gisella's shoulder; her orange and purple tunic was green with thick slime. The smell was overpowering.

'No, don't!' shouted Tally. She was scrambling over broken planks and struts that had not that long before been the steps onto the stage. 'Wil, don't turn her over! If that stuff gets any more air she'll lose her skin!'

Wil let go as if he'd been stung and Gisella slumped back into the dirt.

Tally hopped over a piece of shattered wood.

'Oh, dear! Orange really isn't her colour, is it?' said Tally. Mia plodded over to greet her. 'It's bonacuss dung, Wil. Eli has told me about it. They farm them on Rockmoore Downs. There's only one cure for bonacuss poo burns.'

She stopped abruptly and watched the wandering dragon on the other side of the square; it was eating something and had, at least for the moment, stopped that mournful crying.

'Well?' prompted Wil.

'Dragon urine,' said Tally.

'What! They've got dragons on Rockmoor Downs? How... where...?'

'Brom's Lair – it's where the Giant Redback breeds. Eli told me that, too.'

Wil blinked. 'So, how do we get a sample from our little friend over there?'

Tally took a quick look around the wrecked wagons and stalls and headed for an upturned wagon a little way off. She returned with three dead hares.

'With fresh meat and a little patience!' she beamed.

Wil was surprised at how easy the dragon was to catch using the hares.

'It's small for a Ridge Creeper, isn't it?' he said throwing the last hare into the air. The dragon – not much bigger than a small, very fat, pony – caught it just before it hit the ground and crunched happily.

'Well, maybe it's young,' said Tally. She was holding five rather dirty jugs that she had just found in a deserted bar nearby.

'We can't use those, Tally, they stink!'

The jugs did smell very strongly of rat beer. Tally sighed.

'Honestly, Wil, this will work.'

'But will she be OK?' Wil checked that Gisella was still breathing. 'Why is she unconscious? Is it the fumes?'

'Nah,' answered Tally. 'Tinniswood's mother hit her with a Wraithe Wolf's head. She was yelling something about Gisella trying to steal her hat.'

The green slime was oozing into the dust where Gisella lay.

'Won't it get worse the longer that stuff's on her?'

'She'll be fine. Lying in it will keep the air off so it's the best place for her right now,' said Tally, sounding slightly mean.

'But it's all up her neck,' said Wil.

'Mmm, I'm pretty sure it's only the dung that's harmful… the slime, I mean. Eli said that the splashes just make the skin peel. I'm pretty sure it'll heal,' said Tally, holding a jug under the dragon. But nothing was happening.

'Well, can you get this thing to hurry up if you're only "pretty sure"?' said Wil. He could see silver light from the twin moons brimming over the city walls like an overfull cup. Trying to match Tally's uncaring tone, he added, 'Lady Élanor made me promise that I'd get you and Tanith back to Lovage Hall before the moons crossed. Don't think there's much chance of that now.'

Tally nearly dropped one of the jugs. 'What? Why didn't you mention this earlier, Wil?' Her sudden shock surprised Wil. 'What *exactly* did she make you promise?'

'Er, I... I can't really remember,' Wil stammered 'Try!'

Beside him, the little dragon gave a pitiful yowl. Wil suddenly started to feel sad again.

'Um, well, she just made me promise to get you home.' He watched the dragon as it waddled among the wrecked wagons. 'She said that you and Tanith would be safe if you are at home with her – at Lovage Hall... er, Tally, I think you might need that jug!'

To Wil's relief, the dragon filled all five jugs while its pitiful cry echoed around the empty square. Phinn and Mia lay with their chins on the dirt; their eyebrows flicked as they watched and waited.

'Right,' said Tally, making her way back to Gisella. 'It's quite easy – just pour the urine on every bit of green. I'd do it but if my sister wants Tanith and me back at the Hall before the moons cross, we *really* need to be there.'

'But it took us a day and a half to get here,' said Wil. He suddenly felt desperately lonely. 'How will you get back in time?'

'Wil, don't you know anything about pegaluses – they can cover huge distances *very* quickly – as the *raven* flies, you could say!'

The word *raven* hit Wil like a bolt.

'Oh no! Pricilla – Tally, Pricilla got injured. I left her with someone.'

'Who? Where is she?'

'I... I don't know.'

'What? *Who* you left her with? Or *where* she is?'

The dragon stopped yowling and stuck its snout into the wreckage of another wagon. Wil's mind cleared a little in the sudden quiet.

'Er, well both really.'

Tally looked appalled.

'You mean to say that you gave my sister's precious raven to a stranger so that you could rescue your girlfriend?'

'Now hang on, Tally! Actually I came to rescue you, remember!'

'You say!' retorted Tally. Behind her a huge timber prop under the stage toppled to one side.

'Blimey, if you two make any more noise

Rexmoore's men will be back here in a flash[76] – loose bonacuss or not!' grinned Mortimer, crawling over the broken timber. He was followed by Farrow, who had a green stain across her bottom, and then Seth.

'Hi, Tally,' said Seth, before Mortimer could speak again. 'You OK?'

'Oh yeah, I'm great thanks,' answered Tally without a smile. 'Been trapped in a freezing tower made of gold for days with a nutty woman with an obsession for hats!' Seth looked nervously at Wil. Tally continued. '*Then* I got tied to a stake while Nutty Woman's son tried to burn me alive! Then Gisella's rather inconveniently got herself covered in bonacuss dung; Wil's *lost* my sister's raven and... *and* I've just been told I'm due home before the moons cross. Me? I'm great, *thanks!*'

'Oh,' said Seth quietly. 'That's OK then.'

Mortimer stepped out forward holding Wil's hunting knife.

'Hey, Wil, I found this under the stage. Thought you might need it. What's happened to Gisella?'

'The bonacuss – Imelda used her as a shield to hide behind.' Wil took the knife and slid it back into his boot. 'But it's alright because Tally said that all we need to do is pour dragon wee over her and she'll be fine.'

Tally snorted.

'I did *not* say she'd be fine! I said she wouldn't lose all her skin – well, not permanently. She was, after all, also smacked across the face with a hat made out of a Wraithe Wolf's head.'

'What?' said Mortimer and Seth together.

'The Jackal's mother,' said Wil.

'Ah!' said Mortimer. 'Right, well... er... can I help. I guess she won't need these just yet, then?' He held up Gisella's crossbow and a handful of silver-tipped bolts.

'Er, no,' said Wil. 'Apparently we have to be quick. You hold, I'll pour.'

Mortimer pushed the bow behind the nearest upturned stall and carefully rolled Gisella over. With a brief glance at Tally, who ignored him, Wil trickled the pale yellow liquid over Gisella's neck and tunic. The slime steamed and turned pale pink.

'You'll have to be quicker than that, Wil,' snapped Tally. 'You're saving her skin – not getting her ready to meet your mother! Give it all a good splosh[77]!'

Not convinced that Tally really cared about Gisella's health at that moment, Wil tipped the jugs. There was a lot more steam and, at last, Gisella opened her eyes.

Tally put her hands on her hips. 'See. I would say she'll be as pretty as she was before but–'

Mortimer interrupted. 'Tally, look at the moons. You need to go!'

'Is Wil going to come with me?' said Tally, not moving an inch. 'After all, he did *promise* to get me back to my sister.'

Before Wil could say anything Mortimer came to his rescue.

'Seth'll go with you, Tally. He's lighter than Wil. Tanith will be able to fly faster.'

Wil suddenly felt very strange... very, very angry; he could see the red mist again – something was coming... and whatever it was, it was absolutely livid. He tried to speak but even simple words were almost impossible to say.

'Does anyone... know... what... er, happened... to the... er... bon... bonacus?'

Tally ignored him and folded her arms.

'Unless Wil come with me I'm not going!'

Mortimer stepped one step towards her and nodded to Seth.

'Get on Tanith, Seth. Tally, I'm sorry, but you and Tanith need to get to Saran. Get on Tanith now or I will lift you onto that pegalus!' Behind him, the two silver moons looked as though they were balanced on the battlements.

For a moment Tally looked like she was going to argue. She glared at Wil.

But Wil didn't notice.

Several very bad things happened all at once.

CHAPTER TWENTY-THREE

Out of the Sky

'Get them!' shouted Imelda. 'Kill the hounds! Kill them all except the seer!'

Something flew past Wil's ear and thunked into the ground behind Farrow. Phinn was on his feet in an instant – a second later his terrible howl filled the air.

'No!' breathed Wil. But the ground began to tremble and out of the shadows, firing green slime as it charged, thundered the bonacuss. Mortimer skipped backwards, firing bolts as he went.

'Get behind that wagon! Seth, get Tanith over there – NOW!'

'Phinn! Phinn's been hit!' shouted Wil.

'I know, but he's on his feet,' yelled Mortimer.

Wil scooped Gisella up into his arms and hurtled towards the wrecked stall. Bonacuss dung was spraying everywhere. He ducked down to avoid getting plastered. Seth was already on Tanith; the pegalus reared – just in time. Green slime splattered over a huge pile of sheep skulls on an abandoned stall behind them.

'Just give me a bow, Wil,' whispered Gisella. Wil nearly dropped her in surprise.

'Giz, you're–'

'A bow, Wil! And get Tally on that horse!'

Wil thrust her own bow and the bolts towards her and poked his head out from behind the flimsy[78] barricade. Imelda had Tally by the hair – and by the look of things Tally was fighting back! A little further away The Jackal was loading his catapult with whatever was near. Something hard smacked against Wil's temple.

'Ow! Giz, can you hit The Jackal from here?'

Gisella took aim, then moved her bow slightly.

'Which Jackal do you want me to hit? I can see two,' she said and fired without waiting for an answer. There was another howl, this time from The Jackal.

Wil nodded. 'Well, you got the right one, but I think you only got his arm.'

'I'll try harder next time,' said Gisella, with a slightly cross-eyed grin. 'Now go and get Tally!'

On the far side of the square, the bonacuss was turning for another charge. The little dragon was standing right in the way. Imelda was still struggling with Tally; and Mortimer was grappling with one of Rexmoore's guards who seemed to be winning. Amid the chaos, Wil could see all three Fellhounds. They were simply standing around the dragon.

'What the–' Wil was interrupted by Gisella's shrill voice.

'Wil, *get Tally,* I've hit Imelda. Get Tally on Tanith!'

Wil scrambled out from his cover but Tally was already pelting towards them pointing up at the sky. Imelda, The Jackal and the guards were all running too... they were running *away.*

The bonacuss charged.

'Wil, *DUCK!'* screamed Mortimer.

From out of the black sky plunged a dragon – a huge and very angry dragon.

But Wil didn't duck. He knew it would be OK. Phinn, Mia and Farrow knew, too – unfortunately for the bonacuss, it didn't know very much at all.

As the massive dragon soared into the sky, the light of the moons blazed red across the scales of its vast chest. In the square the little dragon, quite unharmed, was surrounded by the three Fellhounds. The bonacuss lay dead and smouldering; a sweet smell of roasting beef filled the square. It was suddenly very quiet.

'Gosh, that smell's making me hungry. Have we got time for dinner?' said Seth.

'No!' answered Wil, Mortimer and Gisella together.

'Tally, I haven't got a clue what's going on but you

and Seth are going – *now!*' said Mortimer and he picked Tally up, almost threw her onto Tanith's back behind Seth and slapped Tanith hard on the rump. 'Lovage Hall, Seth, and don't stop 'til you see Lady Élanor!'

Wil didn't think he'd ever seen anything as beautiful in his life as Tanith spreading his huge, golden wings – with one graceful beat the pegalus was in the air and in three more he was high over the city, just a black shape against one of the glowing moons.

'If they get back in time I'll eat my boots,' said Mortimer, shaking his head.

'But I thought Tally said–' began Wil.

'Yes, but, Wil, it's freezing and there are hungry eagards out there; and, in case it's slipped your mind – a dragon in the mood for a barbecue has just turned up!'

In the black sky above them, Wil knew that the huge dragon was circling, although, to his relief, it didn't seem in the least bit interested in Tanith.

'It's a Redback,' said a voice.

Out of the shadows at the edge of the square, stepped the dragon tooth girl – and under her arm was Pricilla.

'I know,' said Wil.

Mortimer looked from the girl to Pricilla and then to Wil.

'She'll be back,' said the girl.

'I know,' said Wil again.

'It was the call, wasn't it?'

'Er, yes.'

'The red chest was a bit confusing. They normally go red as they get older. I think it's stressed. But those teeth are way too big for a Ridge Creeper.'

'Er, excuse me interrupting,' interrupted Mortimer. 'But could someone tell me what you're talking about?'

'The dragon, it's a baby Giant Redback,' said Wil, nodding over at the little dragon. 'The hounds knew it was an infant. They surrounded it to protect it from the bonacuss... I... I've only just realised.'

Suddenly the white rage Wil had felt earlier disappeared; all he wanted to do was protect that little dragon. He knew that the Fellhounds would help. He looked around. If anyone attempted to harm the baby dragon at that moment Wil knew he would kill them – no matter who it was.

Wil sensed that the Redback was nearby, but that she was not going to attack – not yet. She wanted her baby back but for the moment she seemed to understand that her baby was safe; she trusted the hounds. With Tally on her way back to Saran they had to get out of Armelia but Wil knew that they couldn't just leave the little dragon. He had no doubt that if... *when* she came back, she would give the order to kill.

Something else was nagging at Wil – a dull ache –

he looked over at Phinn. The Fellhound's amber eyes stared at his master; an arrow was still sticking out of his shoulder and his front leg was wet. In the dark it was only now that Wil realised it was wet with blood.

'Is that dog alright?' asked the dragon tooth girl.

'No, it's been shot,' said Wil simply.

Gisella frowned.

'Wil?'

'It's Phinn, Giz. He's OK… for now.'

Wil knew that any attempt to move the hounds away from the dragon now would put them all in danger. So, much as couldn't bear to watch Phinn suffer, it would be a lot worse if he didn't wait.

As if she had read Wil's mind, the Redback swooped again, incinerating[79] the remains of the stage on her way past. There was a loud scream and three of Rexmoore's men tumbled over each other to escape the burning timber. Behind the wagon Wil knelt on something unpleasantly limp and furry – another dead hare.

'I don't think we're too safe here,' said Mortimer, watching the guards running away across the square. 'I reckon Imelda'll be back soon and I've only got four bolts left.'

'There's more in Tanith's stall with the rest of our things,' whispered Gisella.

'Does this mean that I'm going to miss the moon crossing party?' asked the girl.

It was Imelda who answered her question.

'Oh, no! My dear, quite the opposite. You'll be one of the stars of the show!'

Wil spun around. Bobbing lanterns swung among the dark buildings on the edge of the square – the low glow making a perfect hiding place for the ink-black shadows.

Another voice echoed out of the golden gloom.

'Right, men. The next time that overgrown bird comes down, shoot it with everything you've got. Shoot everything!' Rexmoore boomed. 'Just don't hit the seer!'

Without a word Wil scooped up the dead hare and stepped out from behind the overturned wagon.

'OK,' he called out. All around the edge of the square sheep's head lanterns seemed to be floating in the darkness – golden light waking their dead eyes. 'Let my friends go and I'll come quietly. I know where the legacy is – I'll tell you when they're safely out of the city.'

'No! Wil-' squeaked Gisella. But Wil heard a muffled whisper from Mortimer and she said nothing more. Mortimer seemed to have guessed Wil had a plan.

'I also want to see my father,' Wil continued loudly. 'That's the deal. My friends go free and I see my father.'

'Your friends?' called The Jackal. 'What about your *precious* dogs?'

'They can fend for themselves,' said Wil. Gisella

squeaked again. Wil gripped the limp hare and thought hard.

Pricilla, make a noise. Can you make the baby dragon cry... please?

Apart from a very reluctant *Prrukk!* Pricilla remained silent.

'So, do we have a bargain?' Wil called. In his head he tried again.

Please, Pricilla – oh, and sorry I left you but you wouldn't have been safe with us! If we're all going to get out of this, we really need your help. Pleeeaase.

To Wil's amazement the next voice to speak was... Fermina Fairfax's!

'I don't think you're in a position to make deals, Wil Calloway. And as one of the people with you is *my* daughter, I am sure, when she knows that I am here and safe, she will not want to go *anywhere!*'

'Mother!' Gisella gasped. Wil heard a quiet 'No' from Mortimer but Gisella stepped out from behind the wagon.

'Daaarling!' purred Fermina. 'Have you missed Mummy? We really must have a little chat about your choice of friends, my dear, now that we will be living here... in the castle.'

'What!' gasped Gisella.

'Prrukk!'

Not just yet!

207

'Yes, dear. And we've got so much to catch up on. In a way I must offer my thanks to young Calloway here – I mean, he may have taken away the only person I ever loved–'

'What!' said Gisella again. 'But my father–'

'Look, these reunions[80] are all very heart-warming, but really,' interrupted Imelda with an impatient sigh. 'Look, dear, to be brief; your mother met my cousin, Sir Jerad Tinniswood. She fell in love with him and killed your father. Unfortunately his mother didn't like your mother so there was no wedding. Sir Jerad heard about Wil's talent when he was in Saran prison. He told your mother, and then Wil killed him. So your mother told me and, well, here we are. OK, that's sorted – guards, get him, kill them!'

Now, Pricilla! Please!

To her credit, the din Pricilla made was enough for a whole flock of ravens. Within seconds the baby dragon, startled by the sudden noise, began to yowl. Arrows rained down but in the dark, luckily, every one missed its target. Silently Wil gave the order.

Phinn, Mia. Get the dragon to the tower – as close as you can! Farrow, follow!

High above, the Redback felt the change. She hovered for a moment and listened. Then she dived.

Wil could feel her panic.

He's OK. They will keep him safe.

208

Arrows came from everywhere. Rexmoore had brought more guards, and they were advancing fast.

'Mortimer, get to the horses. Take the girls and meet me at the kitchen garden. Try to get Rexmoore's men to follow – or at least some of them!' Wil shouted. In his head he kept repeating, *They will keep him safe. They will keep him safe.*

This time the Redback came in so low that Wil felt a claw on the top of his head. Arrows bounced off her scaly belly like harmless matchsticks. She soared over the charred bonacuss, flexed her long talons and snatched up two screaming guards. With one beat of her massive wings all of the lanterns went out and she skimmed over the city wall, knocking another body off the ramparts[81] as she passed. Then she let go. The screaming ended abruptly with two loud splashes. The dragon wheeled around for another pass; Rexmoore and Imelda turned and ran. The guards followed, falling over each other in their haste to avoid the dragon's fiery breath. The baby dragon's yowls got even louder.

In the chaos Mortimer, Gisella and the dragon-tooth girl crept away into the shadows with Pricilla, quiet once more; her job was done.

Wil concentrated on the black shape of the dragon circling high above Mort Craggs.

OK. Now, trust me and follow your baby.

***

Swinging the dead hare around his head, Wil walked out of the square and towards the castle. The hounds and the baby followed. Above them, the Redback seemed to realise what Wil was doing. Every time any of Rexmoore's men got near, she swooped and unleashed a bolt of fire. Soon half of the city was on fire.

After the dragon's third well-aimed salvo[82] Wil decided that she really did know what she was doing. On the ground, the baby dragon kept trying to grab the hare. Wil kept walking. The little dragon's cries got louder, while Phinn, Mia and Farrow protected him. The moons above them moved ever closer.

All around them burning buildings crackled; glass shattered in the intense heat; the dragon above roared and the dragon on the ground wailed. Yet the streets were now empty and the glowing sheep skulls in every window were the only audience for Wil's lonely walk.

Phinn stumbled. Another roof burst into flames. Overhead, the Redback roared.

Wil had never concentrated so much in his whole life:

Just a bit further, I promise. Follow me and you'll get him back.

CHAPTER TWENTY-FOUR

Wil's Plan

Wil led the way across the huge lawn that marked the boundary between the city and the castle. Mort Craggs towered high above them. Wil felt very vulnerable in the vast space, but the attacks had stopped. Rexmoore and his men were nowhere to be seen.

Up ahead, Imelda's precious tower reflected the flames of the city like a blood red beacon. Very soon they would be right under the tower – but as Wil whirled the hare over his head an echo of Phinn's pain ripped into his own shoulder. The Fellhound couldn't go on much longer.

'Wil, *Wil!* Over here!'

Wil spotted Gisella crouching in the shadow of the castle wall.

'How– What are you doing here?' As he spoke freezing air hit his lungs – the Redback was somewhere high in the icy sky above Tel Harion. 'Where's Mortimer and that girl?'

Wil kept swinging the hare and moving towards the tower.

'I don't know,' whispered Gisella, stumbling over unseen stones to keep up. 'I went to get our – ouch! – stuff… couldn't carry that much but, ooh, ow… got your bag and a load more bolts.'

'Any idea where Rexmoore and Imelda are?' asked Wil, being careful not to mention Gisella's mother.

'They've gone to th–' Gisella started to say but Wil couldn't hear any more; the baby dragon was crying again. Round and round went the hare – Wil inched closer to the castle wall. Gisella moved closer.

'… but The Jackal's around somewhere,' she was saying. 'I nearly bumped into him back there. Luckily your large friend – ouch! – set fire to the roof above us and he made a run for it.'

'So do you think Imelda's expecting The Jackal to bring me in then?' said Wil. Gisella laughed.

'Possibly. But if I find him again, believe me, he won't be able to!'

Wil grinned. Spoken like a true Fellman.

'Look, Giz,' he said. 'Phinn's not going to be able to walk for much longer but I've got a plan for the Redback… but first, er… I need to find my father. Can you get Phinn out of here? Keep the bag – it hasn't let us down yet. I'll find you when we're ready to go.'

'Well, I can't say I'll be going to look for my dear

mother anytime soon,' said Gisella, obviously trying to sound like she didn't care. 'But Wil, Fellhounds always stay with their masters, especially if either's injured!'

For a second Wil lost the rhythm of his swing. The little dragon snatched the hare from his hand. Wil cursed.

'Oh, Wil, I'm so sorry, that was my fault,' said Gisella, stepping out into the light.

Wil had no idea where the bolt came from because it smacked into Gisella with such force that she spun away before she hit the floor. But he did hear a familiar voice.

'YES!'

Moonlight lit up the balcony above Wil's head and shone down on the bow in The Jackal's hands – it was Wil's bow!

'I must get one of these; they really are quite effective, aren't they!' the boy chuckled.

Behind him, Wil could hear the baby dragon crunching the bones of the dead hare. The Jackal dropped another bolt into the bow and aimed, but not at Wil.

'Right, well, we'll start with that whinging reptile – Mother, how do you fancy a dragon skin hat? You haven't got any dragons, have you?'

'I hope your aim's good then?' called Wil.

The Jackal held the bow in place but didn't fire.

'And why is that?'

'Because dragons are very hard to kill with a bolt –
very deep hearts,' said Wil, his mind racing. 'I thought
everyone knew that.'

Behind him, he could hear the infant snuffling
around for more food; Phinn, Mia and Farrow were still
standing guard. Wil could also hear the sound of fighting
from the mill.

'Sounds like they're having fun down there,' said
Wil, desperately trying to think what to do.

The Jackal glanced in the same direction.

'Oh, it's the peasants; moaning about taxes *again* –
it's just so dull. Lord Rexmoore's gone to sort it out. I said
I'd come and find you,' he said with a bored sigh. 'I mean,
these people: they live in the city for practically nothing,
have a festival laid on *every* year... and when they're
asked to contribute... you should hear the moaning. Oh,
well, we're short on labourers for the tower anyway so it's
a case of pay up or... oh yes, I forgot, you know the rules,
don't you, Calloway!'

'So where's Imelda?' Wil demanded.

In the damp darkness, Gisella groaned then she
coughed – it was a bubbly, liquid-filled cough that made
Wil's stomach knot.

'Ooh, that doesn't sound too healthy, does it?' said
The Jackal. 'Listening to that cough anyone would think
that girl has just been shot in the chest... they'd be right
of course!' His cruel laugh rang out in the darkness.

Wil took a step back. If only he had something… some sort of weapon. He would go up there and…

Then he saw it; right in front of him in the moonlight – the staff! It was sticking into the soft ground where it had landed earlier – absolutely straight… *spear-straight*, thought Wil. And next to it, in a perfect coil, was the silk rope. Wil tried not to smile. He was sure The Jackal hadn't seen it. The Jackal took aim again.

'Anyway,' he said, 'lovely to chat, Wil, but I'm rather busy. Mmm, now which first… yes, dragon first, then your dogs, then… well…' He leaned over the balcony and listened. 'I don't think your girlfriend's going to need another bolt. So what's it to be, Wil the Seer? You can talk now, or I'll shoot first and you can talk later.'

There was no more time. Wil snatched up the staff and hurled it up at the balcony. He heard the click of a trigger and a dull grunt. Wil's bow thunked into the soft ground just in front of him – the bolt hadn't fired.

Then something very heavy slammed into Wil's back and his world went black.

Face down in the wet grass, Wil could feel hot air blowing over him – then in – then back out again. It wasn't any sort of wind – it was breath.

'Dragon! Did you say dragon, Colin?' The Jackal's mother's insane voice drifted down from the balcony above. 'Has that nasty boy got a dragon? Oh, Colin, you are sooo clever – another hat for Mommy!'

Keeping his face in the cool grass, Wil opened his mind – after all, he thought, if he was going to be eaten by a Giant Redback, he might as well know what she was thinking at the time! But the dragon wasn't thinking about him at all. All Wil could feel was relief and a very, *very* strong sense of warm love – the Redback and her baby were reunited and *she* really didn't care about anything else.

Wil lifted his head.

The Redback was nestled right up against the old castle wall. She really was enormous; she even made the golden tower look pretty small. She gave a contented groan – almost a purr – while her baby flapped its tiny wings and butted against her.

Somewhere the riot was still raging and a lot more of the city was now ablaze. But where was Gisella? On his hands and knees, and desperately hoping that she hadn't been crushed by the scaly giant, Wil crawled forward, patting the soaking grass. He heard a gasp and a weak gurgling cough – she may not have been flattened but, by the sound of it, Gisella was in a very bad way.

Wil found Phinn first; lying with his long back against Gisella's body, keeping her warm. He was panting hard. Wil felt the arrow sticking out of the hound's shoulder; it wasn't too deep but by the hound's sticky matted coat Wil guessed that Phinn had lost a lot of blood.

Wil didn't need to turn Gisella over to see where she had been hit – the bolt had gone right through her chest; its silver tip was sticking out of her back.

'Don't die,' he whispered. 'Don't die, either of you.'

A tear trickled down his nose and dripped onto Gisella's neck just below her ear. With a bloody finger, he followed it down the line of her soft cheek to her chin where it dripped and disappeared into the grass. Through the blur of tears Wil could see Gisella's hand, clutching the pink silk bag.

While Wil didn't expect Gisella to react when he reached for the bag, he wasn't expecting her fingers to feel so cold. He delved into the pink silk – his own hands shaking almost uncontrollably – hoping that they would pull out a miracle. Almost immediately his fingers closed around something soft.

As always, a little label hung from the soft bundle of what felt like soft duck down. With tears still running down his face, Wil peered at the label; the words swam in front of him. He dropped his hands and took a deep breath.

Well, you're going to have to stop this blubbing, mate, or you're never going to be able to help them.

So he wiped his eyes with his sleeve and took

another deep breath. But on reading the label, his heart started to pound. The label read:

Brindey Goose Down
Snap the arrow and the bolt as close to the skin as you
can without disturbing the wounds.
Pack this down around both wounds and get
experienced help as soon as possible.
Best before: unknown, probably eternity

Not knowing what else to do, Wil re-read the label and set about Gisella's wounds. He snapped the bolt head as close to the wound as he could and packed the down around the shortened shaft sticking out from her back. The instant the down touched the wound he could feel it becoming wet. Convinced he'd done something wrong, Wil grabbed at the dressing – the down had set rock hard; there was no more blood.

Dressing the entry wound was more challenging. He rolled Gisella onto her side. Despite his shaking hands, he worked quickly and by the time he'd finished the goose down was almost completely used up; although, to his relief, the bleeding from both wounds had finally stopped.

Next, Wil turned to Phinn. As he had guessed, the arrow wasn't deep and slid out of the wound when Wil tried to snap it. Phinn gave an indignant yelp and licked

Wil's hands as if to politely request that he didn't do it again, and with soft words of reassurance Wil packed the hole with the remaining down.

With the wounds dressed, Wil turned again to the silk bag. This time it gave up a bottle that Wil had seen before and he remembered Mortimer's bright green tongue – it was the medicine used to treat blood loss. Wil curled back Phinn's top lip and tipped a few drops between the hound's teeth before giving the rest to Gisella – he had no idea how much blood she might have lost, but feeling the stickiness of the grass underneath her, he didn't think he could do any more harm.

The sound of galloping hooves made Wil reach for his knife – the distinct advantage of sitting under a gigantic dragon, with two enormous dogs, seemed to have passed Wil by.

As the rider approached the Giant Redback spat a jet of orange flame. It missed Mortimer by only a few feet.

'Erm, I know this might sound like a daft thing to say, Wil, but you do know there's a dragon behind you, don't you?'

'Yeah,' shrugged Wil. 'I had a sort of a plan but Gisella and Phinn got hurt and it doesn't seem like such a good idea now. Where's the girl with Pricilla?'

'Who?'

'Oh, um, I meant Lady Élanor's raven... her

name's Pricilla. I thought you knew?'

Shadow took a step forward. The Redback growled.

'I don't think your new friend likes me,' said Mortimer. Shadow stepped back two steps. 'Oh, yeah, the girl – she took the bird and went back to see if she could save anything from her stall. The city's a mess, Wil! What hasn't been burned,' he raised his eyebrows towards the Giant Redback, 'has been picked clean by looters[83] on their way to the mill. It's chaos. They're taking every bit of gold they can lay their hands on. Rexmoore's men are completely useless.' He shook his head and laughed. 'You should see Imelda – she's livid. I don't think they've had much practice with rebellion around here.'

'Any sign of The Jackal?' asked Wil, wondering if his makeshift spear had actually hit its target.

'No,' said Mortimer with a frown. 'Come to think of it, I saw that woman – the one wearing the Wraithe Wolf head for a hat – she was taking a gold brick into the mill – very odd. She didn't seem to notice the riot at all!'

Wil looked up at the balcony; The Jackal was still up there somewhere, he was sure. 'Mort, can you look after Gisella and Phinn. I need to find that boy – he knows where my father is and I'm not leaving Armelia without him.'

'And what about your *little* friend here?' said Mortimer, pointing behind his hand. The Redback was now dozing, her scales bright in the light of the burning city – somehow her baby had managed to clamber onto her back and was nestled behind her folded wing.

'She'll be fine as long as you don't try to move him,' said Wil, pointing to the infant dragon. 'Any ideas about how we're going to get out of here?'

Mortimer let go of Shadow's reins and slid to the ground.

'Absolutely none.'

CHAPTER TWENTY-FIVE

The Many Faces of Death

Wil wasn't surprised that the castle kitchen was deserted; although he was surprised by the absolutely delicious smell in the silent room. Outside, a huge dragon had just set fire to the whole city while its people ran riot; and yet, in Lord Rexmoore's warm quiet kitchen the cooking continued.

In the middle of the vast kitchen table was the biggest pie Wil had ever seen – although, it wasn't a pie. There was no pastry and it seemed to rise up out of the dish as if it had been inflated. Whatever it was though, it smelled wonderful.

Suddenly starving, Wil grabbed the nearest spoon. He had never tasted anything so delicious – or so hot – in his life. It must have just been taken out of the oven. He was just about to take another mouthful when he heard the sound of heavy footsteps crunching across the courtyard. He dropped the spoon right into the dish and ran – behind him the steaming pudding rapidly deflated.

Wil put his foot on the first of the golden steps that

spiralled their way up the centre of Imelda's precious tower; behind him someone started shouting.

'OH MY GAWD! MY SOUFFLE. FIRST MY EGGS AND NOW MY SOUFFLE. GALORIAN, IF THAT WAS YOU... GALORIAN, GET YER. FAERYDAE, WHERE'S YER BROTHER! OH MY GAWD...!'

The stairs led up to the little room with the balcony that Wil had been in before; he looked at the golden walls and the steps that continued up beyond the doorway and guessed that the unfinished tower was meant to be a lot higher. Anger flared in Wil's stomach. He thought about the shabby city – the canal that was used as a well for drinking water *and* as a toilet; he thought about his mother, and many others across Thesk desperately trying to save enough to pay every time Rexmoore's thugs came knocking. Men had died – were still dying – just so that Rexmoore could please his wife.

The door that Phinn had demolished earlier was still on the floor. Snuffy's tail stuck out from under one end. From outside, the moons, even closer now, cast a bright, silver beam that cut the darkness in half like a knife making the room's dark corners as black as coal. Silence. Wil pulled his knife from his boot.

'I know you're in here,' he said. 'If you take me to my father, I will spare your life.'

A flight movement in the farthest corner gave away The Jackal's hiding place.

'And did... you give my... father a similar... choice, Wil... Calloway? Or... did you just... kill him in... cold blood?'

The voice was weak; uttered as if the speaker might be making a choice between a breath and a word. Wil was pleased – it sounded like The Jackal was suffering just like Gisella.

'Your father gave *me* a choice,' spat Wil. 'And I took it.'

A shiver ran down his spine as he remembered the freezing river, Sir Jerad Tinniswood on the rocks taunting him – Esk Falls dragging Tinniswood away. Wil shook his head to push the memory away – his only concern now was to make sure that the boy survived long enough to get Wil to his father so that he could take everyone home. The boy in the corner coughed horribly.

'And if... I take you... to your... father... will you... save me?' he whispered. The Jackal's voice suddenly sounded sad.

'I... what do you mean, save you?' asked Wil, confused. 'You seem to have it pretty good here – Imelda's favourite nephew, Mommy's little *prince!*'

The Jackal tried a scornful laugh but quickly gave in to another gruesome cough. Eventually he spoke again. 'My aunt... loves gold; ...my mother,' he spat the

word, 'loves hats... in case you... hadn't noticed? And...
the woman... who loved... my father... hates me for...
being alive instead of... him.'

'And Lord Rexmoore?' Wil knew it was a lame
question, but he was fighting a creeping guilt that had
already made him lower his knife.

The Jackal attempted an answer, coughed and spat
into the darkness before answering in a bitter whisper.

'You know... I really do think... he loves...
Imelda... Sad, isn't it?'

There was a gasp, a loud clatter and the sound of
something sliding.

'Jackal? Colin?'

Nothing – not even the sound of the boy fighting
for breath.

Wil took three steps forward; his foot kicked
something hard, knocking it into the wall – there was a
familiar click and something shot past Wil's knee and
bounced off the door post behind him. It was a bolt – The
Jackal had had a second bow!

Wil had killed the only person who could have taken him
to his father. What was he to do? The light from the rising
moons crept across the dark floorboards. It touched The
Jackal's bloody finger lying in the dust and then one by
one lit up the letters of the still sticky words 'THE
MASON'. From the moment Wil had gone into that

room The Jackal could have killed him, but instead he had left a message.

'Thanks,' Wil whispered, and walked from the room without looking back.

In the dark corridor next to the kitchen, Wil spotted a door under the stairs. He guessed that The Jackal's mother must have used it earlier to get to the mill because the only other way would have taken her straight past Wil outside in the grounds.

Wil tried the door – it opened.

The passageway stank of mould and Wil's arms and face immediately felt damp in the clammy air. An occasional glow-worm provided only a very dim light, and twice Wil slipped on what he hoped was either moss or mould. What was strange, though, was that Wil was walking up hill, not down towards the mill as he had expected. There was also no sound of the riot that was still going on outside; what Wil could hear was the slow, rhythmic ping of a hammer hitting metal. And it was getting louder with every step he took.

Wil gripped his knife. Despite the cold, damp air, Wil was clammy and hot. His heart beat in time with the hammer. The climb grew steeper and the air got colder.

Finally, in the distance Wil could see a pin prick of light that spread like a fan as he got nearer, turning the surrounding dimness into pitch blackness. Not knowing where he was going, Wil reached out. The wall was covered with damp mould. He slipped again and landed heavily on one knee.

His groan of pain seemed to travel all the way to the light at the end of the tunnel and out into... Wil wasn't sure he wanted to find out.

Then... the tunnel groaned back – a long, hollow moan, as if the sufferer had endured the pain for far too long.

Was this an Alcama ghost? Wil's heart was pounding now. He tried not to imagine who had made that terrible noise – just in case he was right.

The end of the tunnel came too quickly now.

Suddenly, Wil was at the entrance to a huge barn. It was freezing. One solitary sheep's-head lantern burned in the doorway – its light only a little brighter against a dozen candles flickering inside. The regular ping of the hammer echoed out from one unlit corner; in another lay the source of the pain-wracked groan.

Wil ran towards the groan, hesitated, and lifted a filthy sack. The eyes that looked up at him were the saddest, palest blue. This was not his father. Wil dropped the cloth and took a step back. He had seen those eyes before – in the painting above the fireplace in Lovage Hall – this was Lady Élanor's father.

'Hello, Wil. Élanor was right; you are as reckless as you are brave.'

The man's voice sounded very strange, as though it was in Wil's head, not in his ears.

'You're... are you...?' Wil started.

'Lord Lakeston, father of Lady Élanor and Talasina? Yes, of a sort[84],' said Lord Lakeston. He bowed his head with the merest hint of a smile. 'I am a revenant, Wil. Do you know what that is?'

In the dark, the hammer continued to ping.

The hairs on Wil's neck prickled. He had no idea what a *revenant* was and was starting to wonder if his lack of food and sleep were affecting his imagination. How could this man be Lord Lakeston? Tally had told him her father was dead.

The hammering stopped.

The man in front of Wil gave a solemn nod.

'Yes, Wil, you are right. I am dead.'

The hammering started again. This time the rhythm was less regular, higher too, as if a smaller tool were being used.

Lord Lakeston continued.

'I understand that you already know something of my family history, Wil – about how my beloved wife's sister took the rule of Thesk while I grieved.'

Wil nodded.

'And how Lady Élanor and Talasina came to live in Lovage Hall?'

Wil nodded again.

'And you also know that there is a secret that protects my daughters, although Talasina knows nothing of its content?'

'The legacy,' said Wil.

A thought struck him. Suddenly he was angry.

'Oh, I see.' Wil gripped his knife ready to fight. 'You're one of Rexmoore's men. So, Imelda's still trying to get that blinking legacy – well, for the last time, *I don't know where – or what – it is!'*

The hammer continued to ping; the man continued to look at Wil without blinking – those eyes really did remind him of Lady Élanor and Tally. But no, this was definitely some sort of trick. The man stood up. Wil's knife shone in the lamplight. Lord Lakeston stepped forward – straight into Wil's blade.

Wil felt the knife slide between the old man's ribs.

'No!'

Without altering his gaze, Lord Lakeston stood for a moment and then calmly took a step back. The knife was clean.

'Years ago a soul seller came to Armelia,' said Lord Lakeston, moving away towards the pinging hammer. 'My beautiful wife, Rosalind, was already dead. Even then, Imelda's control over Rexmoore was terrifying. It was only a matter of time before she took my girls. Thankfully she did not know about their strange gifts – but I knew Imelda would never be a loving mother.' His eyes narrowed and he showed his teeth as he spoke. But his voice remained quiet and steady. 'So, I struck a bargain – the legacy to which you refer, and its protection.' Lord Lakeston shook his head. 'And before you ask, no, I will not tell you – I cannot. I was allowed to share the secret with two others. The price was my soul.'

Wil stood, wide-eyed in the dismal gloom.

'But what happens if…' Wil hesitated, 'If one of the secret keepers… dies?'

'Only then can their burden be passed on,' said Lord Lakeston.

'But what would happen if they *accidentally* told someone else – if it slipped out?' asked Wil, still struggling with what he had just seen, let alone what he was being told.

Lord Lakeston moved to the doorway and stared out into the dark.

'That cannot happen, Wil Calloway. That was part of my bargain. You see, the soul seller sealed their lips – they could not tell even if they wanted to – if their lives depended on it. Not until their dying breath.'

Wil stayed silent. His knife had just gone into this man's heart – and yet there was no blood. He was still standing and speaking. Lord Lakeston's words filled Wil's mind. Only the beat of the hammer filled the air.

'So Imelda would have to *kill* Lady Élanor to get her to give up the legacy?' Wil asked after a few moments.

Lord Lakeston closed his eyes and a single tear dripped down his cheek.

'Yes, Wil.'

'Or to give up the other secret keeper?'

Lord Lakeston nodded.

The hammering stopped. *Silence* filled the silence.

'That boy – Tinniswood's son – he told you about your father?' said Lord Lakeston after a moment. The sudden change of subject threw Wil.

'Er, yer,' he answered. 'Well, he said he knew where he was – he was going to take me to him. But then I...'

The words caught in Wil's throat. Lord Lakeston finished the sentence for him.

'You killed him.'

A shadow passed over his Lordship's face.

'I will take you, you need to know.'

An icy blast whipped through the open door. The lantern went out. The man in the corner continued to chip away and, as they passed, Wil could see that he was carving something across a large, flat stone.

'The mason!' whispered Wil. He moved to look at the stone but his Lordship grabbed his arm – for a dead man, his grip was extremely powerful.

'No, Wil. Come with me. Leave him, he can't tell you anything.'

'But... *he's* the mason. The Jackal left a message...

he can tell me about my father.'

Lord Lakeston stopped, but this time did not face Wil when he spoke.

'He cannot tell you, Wil. He cannot speak. *I* wrote the message.'

Then he strode away, leaving Wil to run to catch up.

By the time they eventually came to a halt, Wil knew what he would find. There were headstones[85] as far as the eye could see. Uniform lines, all with a name and the words 'Taxes paid' carved in beautiful, precise lettering. Some of the stones were covered with thick, green moss; some were engulfed in ivy and some were so new they were not even coated in the evening dew; one, at the end of the second row back, had tiny green shoots around its base – crocus, thought Wil, his mother's favourite. The word 'Calloway' blurred in Wil's tears; as with all the others, below the single name, the words 'Taxes paid' had been skilfully carved.

'He's been here all along,' said Wil in barely a whisper. 'The Jackal... he knew. He knew and he kept promising – using my father to make me tell them something I just don't know.' He choked out the last few words. He was glad The Jackal was dead – he was glad it had been him – Wil – who had killed him. He hoped The Jackal's mother would find him and that her heart would break...

'He was angry too, Wil,' said his Lordship gently, as if reading Wil's hate-filled thoughts. 'He was lonely and angry and he used the only thing he could to hurt you. And he picked you because he couldn't hurt anyone else – no one cared. You are better than that, Wil. You are better than any of them. Go now and help your friends. Go and keep my daughters safe. You cannot do anything to help your father now, I am sorry. But you can help them.'

Wil felt a cold hand on his shoulder.

'You really are dead, aren't you,' he whispered.

'Yes, Wil – if you can call this a death. Being a revenant is an eternity of half-death.'

'But at least *you* get to see your daughters!' said Wil bitterly. He turned and walked away back towards the barn. 'It was you – at Black Rock – wasn't it? You gave me the staff.'

There was no answer.

Wil turned around – he was alone among the headstones. High above him the two moons were sliding into one.

CHAPTER TWENTY-SIX

The Redback's Wrath

'Blimey, Wil, I thought I was going to have to come and rescue you again!' said Mortimer as Wil charged towards him across the grass – completely forgetting to stay in the shadow of the castle wall.

'Sorry, Mort, thought I'd stop for a bite to eat,' Wil lied. He was struggling with the surreal experience of meeting Lord Lakeston while, at the same time, trying to believe that his father really was dead – the last thing he wanted to do right now was talk about any of it.

He handed Mortimer a wooden bowl full to the brim with what looked like green scrambled eggs.

'What's this?' asked Mortimer, sniffing the dish. His tired face brightened. 'Ha! I was right. Quail egg soufflé... and... asparagus. Yum!'

'Oh, I brought you this, too' said Wil. He handed Mortimer a silver spoon. 'How're Gisella and Phinn?'

Mortimer scooped up a huge spoonful of the soufflé.

'Well, Phinn's getting better all the time. He tried to get up a few minutes ago but I managed to stop him.'

He popped the loaded spoon into his mouth and added thickly, 'Oh, this is delicious! Want some?'

'No thanks,' said Wil. True, he was tired and hungry but he felt too worried to eat. 'And Gisella?'

Mortimer stopped mid-spoonful and frowned.

'Not too good. You did give her that blood stuff, didn't you?'

'Yeah,' said Wil. He knelt down and put the flat of his hand on Gisella's cold and clammy cheek.

'So, you, er, didn't find your father then?' asked Mortimer.

'No,' said Wil abruptly. 'But The Jackal won't be bothering us again – Gisella'll be very pleased about that!'

Then he changed the subject.

'We really need to get her home,' he said, although putting Gisella on a horse right now was probably the worst thing they could do – but he couldn't see that they had any other choice.

Wil looked around; the Giant Redback and her baby were dozing peacefully, as were Mia and Farrow. Even the riot seemed to have calmed – other than flames reaching like tentacles out of the roof, the mill was quiet now; and, elsewhere, the city smouldered in a macabre[86] peace. It was then that Wil spotted the little boat that he'd last seen down by the mill pond.

'Why's that up here?'

Mortimer popped the last mouthful of soufflé into his mouth and then waved the spoon at Wil.

'Because I think I know how we can get everyone out of here,' said Mortimer, and patted the silk rope that was neatly coiled beside him. 'I've checked – this should be long enough – just!'

Mortimer finished explaining his escape plan. Wil went very quiet. True, they had to get out of Armelia and true, there was no way Gisella could ride a horse; also true was the fact that Phinn was unlikely to be able to gallop too far for too long.

What wasn't so clear to Wil was how to make a dragon take off; how to ride a dragon; or how to make sure that a boat carrying Phinn and Gisella tied under said dragon didn't fall – *if* they ever did get into the air.

In the west, the two huge moons were drifting together on their way to becoming one, before passing and continuing their solitary journeys among the stars for another seven years.

Mortimer's voice jolted Wil from his worries.

'Well, come on then. Grab the other end of this rope!'

'Er, maybe we should get Gisella and Phinn into the boat first?' said Wil, desperately trying to think of a different plan.

'Good idea,' said Mortimer with a firm nod.

'Then, as soon as this rope's attached to the dragon's leg you can get up there and we'll get her to take off.' He bent to lift Gisella.

'No!' Wil said so abruptly that Mortimer jumped up, drew his sword and glanced over his shoulder. Wil stepped forward.

'It's alright, Mort, I, er, I'll do that.'

Wil carefully gathered Gisella into his arms before Mortimer could object.

'Suit yourself,' said Mortimer. 'But you're going to need a hand with Phinn.'

'Er, yeah… of course, thanks.'

They laid Phinn next to Gisella in the boat and wrapped Gisella's cloak around her as best they could. Mortimer had also brought up some sacking which they packed around the pair; Wil was still trying to think of an alternative to Mortimer's mad plan.

'And you're sure you can get both horses, Mia *and* Farrow back to Saran on your own?' he asked. Mortimer looked offended.

'Gosh, yes! I'm a Fellman, Wil!'

'But you won't go over Tel Harion now, will you?' asked Wil. It was, after all, the middle of the night – the favourite hunting time for Wraithe Wolves. It was also the Alcama – although Wil was sure that they'd had enough bad luck already.

'No,' said Mortimer. 'I'll go over to Grizzledale

and then come back down along Mistle Forest – other than the odd wild boar or bear, it'll be far safer than travelling alone over the Fells.'

He paused and then said, 'Was that carcass still up there?' He nodded towards the balcony.

'Yeah, no head.' Then Wil remembered. 'Oh! They'll come for the body, won't they! I forgot – dawn – Wraithe Wolves come for their dead. Mort – we really have got to get out of here!'

The little boat creaked and groaned as Mortimer pulled down on each of the rope fastenings but the knots held.

The Redback's plate-size scales shimmered like some sort of iridescent[87] armour and Wil wondered just how Mortimer was going to get her to take off. Then a shout from the mill made him turn – heading up from the canal, hundreds of torches were advancing on the tower. Wil made a decision.

'Mort, get on Shadow – you need to get going.'

'OK, Wil, I just need to…' Clutching the other end of the rope, he disappeared under the sleeping Redback and shouted from the darkness, 'Get on, Wil. And get her off the ground!'

Wil clambered up onto the dragon's back. From below, he heard Mortimer shout, 'Good luck, Wil.'

And then Shadow, Mia and Farrow were nowhere to be seen.

Right, thought Wil as he wedged himself in between the baby dragon and its mother's wing. Angry shouts echoed off the castle wall. An arrow shot past Wil's ear and wedged in the scales between the Redback's shoulder blades. She stirred. Then, without warning, she shook. Wil grabbed at the baby dragon to stop him sliding off. The arrow fell. A tiny trickle of green blood dripped down the dragon's neck. Then another arrow bounced off the Redback's snout[88] and one more hit the wall.

The Redback sat up.

Wil wedged his fingers between the dragon's scales.

'Here goes!'

With every ounce of strength he had left, Wil concentrated. Arrows whistled over his head. A spear bounced off the bow of the boat.

Save your baby, thought Wil. *They will take him. Fly. Save your baby.*

He pictured the man who had briefly been the proud owner of the gold bar – the winner of the Unexpected Pets competition.

He's coming, thought Wil. *Save your baby. Fly. They will kill you and take him.*

The Redback arched her neck. She bent her head right around and sniffed her precious baby. Then, to Wil's alarm, he felt her hot breath as she sniffed him.

Save your baby, repeated Wil silently. *They are coming. Fly. Save him.*

They were coming. Wil could see spears, knives – someone was brandishing an axe while a woman waved a pitchfork.

'There it is,' called a ragged voice. 'I told you it's *hers* – look it's guarding her precious tower!'

'Take our gold; then use your pet to burns our homes!' yelled another. 'I want my gold back!'

'Hey, you up there – that's my dragon,' yelled a third man. 'My Ridge Creeper! I paid good money for that – it owes me a gold bar!'

Making a supreme effort to ignore the approaching mob, Wil tried again.

They are coming. Fly. Take him now!

At last he felt the dragon move – just as a volley[89] of arrows stopped the rioters in their tracks. Lord Rexmoore's reedy voice called out from the balcony of the golden tower.

'STOP! You will come no further!' And then, a little quieter, he added, 'And Master Calloway, you can stay where you are... with your new pet! Guards, watch him!'

Wil's concentration shattered.

Illuminated by the merging moons, Imelda and Lord Rexmoore surveyed the crowd. Imelda spoke next.

'Every one of you will return the gold you have stolen from the mill – *every* brick and *every* coin.'

'What! Give back what was ours in the first place?' called a mocking voice from the crowd. Shouts of approval drowned out whatever Imelda said next.

Below him, Wil felt the Redback shift her weight. He let his mind fill with pictures of huge wolves, vivid red eyes; two sets of needle-sharp teeth, designed to rip and tear.

The Wraithe Wolves are coming! Save him!

Wil sensed the dragon's unease.

Imelda snarled.

'That gold is mine! You live in *my* city – you pay *my* taxes!'

A spear flew out of the crowd. The Redback grabbed it in her jaws. It snapped like matchwood as she hauled herself to her feet.

'Look out,' shouted a frightened voice. Too late. The Redback spat a jet of fire right over the heads of the crowd. People screamed and scattered. On the balcony, Imelda shrieked with laughter.

'And this is what happens to people who steal! Ha, ha!'

They are coming. Fly. Save him! thought Wil.

Somewhere along the wall Rexmoore was yelling orders – guards lined the crumbling ramparts – all with their bows drawn; each one aimed at the Redback.

Fly! Fly, NOW! Wil's mind screamed. He felt as though he would burst with frustration. If the Redback didn't take off in the next second they would all be dead, not just her baby!

Finally, the Redback flexed her huge wings. Wil braced himself. Next to him, the baby dragon slept on. But the Redback didn't take off. Wil felt a thud. The dragon's wing had hit the wall – she was too close.

Move, walk... jump! Move away from the wall... if you want to take off – move away!

But the Redback stayed where she was. Wil knew she was listening to him but she didn't take off. He could feel her rage building.

Helpless, Wil clung on. Again, she beat her giant, leathery wings; again Wil felt them smack into the wall beside them. Then, to his absolute horror, the Redback stepped backwards, only just missing the boat that was right under her.

'NO!' yelled Wil, unable to contain himself any longer.

Imelda's laugher stopped abruptly.

'The seer – *GET HIM*!'

The Redback's wing smacked against the tower again. A golden brick tumbled past Wil's ear – he remembered the large crack that he had used as a foothold that afternoon.

'Of course,' he whispered.

Whether the dragon had noticed the crack in the tower or whether she was actually trapped, Wil would never know; but once he pictured the building's weakness and suggested to the dragon that it might be a good idea to hit it a bit harder, she let loose with terrifying power.

With three more very quick and very devastating strikes, the crack opened so wide that Wil could have walked through it. Gold bricks and coins poured out onto the ground below – and with each strike Imelda's furious screams grew louder still.

The castle wall collapsed first. Guards scrambled in all directions as they fled the tumbling stones. Roaring now, the dragon clambered up onto the ruined battlements and spread her wings for one last blow. With its only support gone, the golden tower gave way. Coins slid like sand in an hourglass. The Redback leapt skywards.

As they left the chaos beneath them, Wil peered past the dragon's scaly rib-cage. He could hear Imelda's screams even over the roar of the dragon; the lawn in front of the castle now looked like a sea of gold and a dark wave of people swept over the rich pickings of the demolished tower.

The dragon soared into the night sky.

'Armelia – *taxes refunded!*' Wil yelled and whooped loudly.

The moons were almost one now. Freezing air blasted past Wil's ears as the dragon glided over the ice-covered wastes of Tel Harion. He had no idea if the little boat was below them but quickly decided that trying to peer at the underbelly of a dragon in full flight was really not a good idea.

Instead Wil tried to reach Phinn with his mind – after all, he'd managed it at the festival. Almost immediately Wil sensed that Phinn was close by – deeply unhappy about being in a boat that was a long way from the ground, being hauled along by a dragon, but nevertheless, he was close.

And Gisella? thought Wil.

His heart quickened slightly but Wil could sense that the Fellhound knew she was still alive.

Desperately worried, Wil drew his cloak tight around him. The baby dragon was tucked down behind his mother's wing on the other side of her bony spine. Wil did the same and was surprised how warm he became. He pictured Lord Lakeston's sad eyes and his own father's pathetic headstone; he thought of Mortimer galloping towards Grizzledale – to safety… and Tally…

The barn smelled of clean straw and sweet hay. Lady Élanor was standing in the stable doorway. There was no sign of Tally but Wil knew that Lady Élanor's pegalus had returned to Lovage Hall safe and sound.

The merging moons, now almost one perfect sphere[90], cast a silver-white beam that flowed into the stable through an open window. Tanith's gentle breath fogged the crisp night air and Wil could feel the pegalus's teeth as if they were his own, grinding down on the glorious meadow-fresh hay, unspoiled by its winter storage.

Lady Élanor did not move – she was watching.

The bright beam lit up one of Tanith's golden hooves. The pegalus stopped grazing.

'It is time,' whispered Lady Élanor. She stroked Tanith's velvet muzzle and wound her arms around his neck. 'Good luck.' Then she walked to the open window and looked out.

The Moon Crossing formed one perfect circle of pure gold. The stars dimmed. Tanith, suddenly sweating, pawed at the straw; a golden moonbeam hit his mane. He reared, opened his wings and... exploded into flames.

Lady Élanor opened her arms. Tears were streaming down her face but she did not look around. The flames burned orange, then blue, then bright green, then pure gold. Wil tried to scream. He wanted to run, to raise the alarm. But he couldn't. He couldn't move. He opened his mouth to shout but the only sound that came was a feeble, rasping whimper. No one heard. No one came. Tanith's stable blazed. Blinded by the smoke and gasping for air, Wil made for the window, gasped a lungful of ice-cold air and opened his eyes...

The little dragon was looking right at him. The night air was so cold it *burned*. Wil shook his head. He had been dreaming again – or, more likely, having a nightmare!

Ahead of them Wil could see the pink light of dawn – the Wraithe Wolves would be on their way to Armelia now. He remembered the sight of them streaming down from Tel Harion the night they lost Leon. He shook his head to get the terrifying image out of his mind.

Beside him the little dragon started to wriggle – he was hungry and very soon, Wil knew, he would start to make that dreadful sound again!

CHAPTER TWENTY-SEVEN

Not So Happy Landings

At almost the same moment that Wil realised it was feeding time *yet again* for the baby dragon, he realised that Mortimer's plan had a serious problem – how on earth was he going to get the boat safely back onto the ground without it being smashed into pieces as the dragon landed? He'd only ever seen the Ridge Creepers land up by Ewes Seat and they all landed on craggy ledges – usually a very long way from the ground. Wil recalled the swans landing on East Lake; their wings smacking on the water as they slid to a halt – how that might work for Gisella and Phinn, Wil decided not to think about!

They were soaring now high over The Black Rock, inky[91] in the dull, pink dawn – about half a day's ride by horse from Saran – although Wil had no idea how far by dragon.

Wil was pretty sure that the nearest stretch of water was the river leading onto Esk Falls. But the Falls were way too far from Saran to drag a boat *and* way too dangerous if he misjudged the drop!

No, somehow he had to get the dragon to fly slow and low over somewhere flat so that he could cut the rope when they were close enough to the ground and hope that the boat came to a halt before it smashed to pieces.

As Wil deliberated the various potentially fatal options open to him, the baby Redback resumed its whingeing. The Giant Redback began to swoop and weave in search of food for her hungry baby. Wil's mind swam – suddenly he felt very sick.

The words on the Brindey goose-down label had said 'get experienced help as soon as possible', and the only experienced help that Wil knew was at Lovage Hall – unless you counted Old Dulcie over in Little Howarth. But while her turnip linctus was well-known across the Hills for curing anything from a sore throat to sheep scab, Wil wasn't sure it could help with a through-and-through bolt wound.

At the thought of Gisella's life ebbing away, Wil felt like someone was dragging their nails inch by painful inch across his heart.

Beside him the hungry dragon's pitiful cry was rapidly sending its mother into a frenzy. She swept across the open ground, hunting the frozen wasteland of the upper Fells. Wil knew it was only a matter of time before she spied the deer they had seen on their frantic gallop across to The Black Rock, and that would only mean one thing – she would go in for the kill. He had no choice. He had to get into that boat and get ready to cut the rope.

Wil took a deep breath and slid down the Redback's vast ribcage. He made one brave effort to persuade the Redback to slow down before the bone-chilling air almost ripped his boots off his feet; from then on he concentrated only on not falling to his death.

Fortunately the dragon's scales were easy to stand; he gripped tight, pretty sure that he would soon be over the boat enough to let go. But what would happen if he missed the boat – or landed right on top of Phinn or Gisella and hurt them even more?…

An ear-splitting roar burst from the Redback's throat. The scales down her ribs vibrated violently. He knew without looking – she had spotted food and was going in for the kill. Wil let go.

Wil slammed into the side of the boat and felt his arm shatter. But at that moment he didn't care – he had fallen into the boat. Phinn and Gisella were tucked down in the hull[92]. Above them, the dragon's wings were hawked back. In the distance, Wil could see a lone stag standing the moorland – its antlers like fingers grabbing at the sky. The Redback dived.

Wil clutched his knife and forced himself to wait until he could see the tops of the trees level with the boat. Then he cut the rope.

The boat grazed a lone hawthorn tree, smacked onto the ground and bounced high across a grassy ridge. Terrified rabbits scattered in all directions. Wil put his hands over his head, shouting for all he was worth.

'STOP! STOP! STOP!'

The little boat smacked into something very solid; the bow[93] exploded into a thousand pieces and Wil's mind went black.

'Look, Wil, I didn't have a choice!' said Gisella testily. A nasty coughing fit prevented her from saying any more. Wil used his good arm to haul her cloak back over her shoulders; she was getting even wetter than she was already. Rain was lashing across the Fells in great sheets. It was impossible to tell where they were.

'Yes, but pulling a wrecked boat halfway across Thesker Fell!' said Wil, over Gisella's coughing fit. 'What are you trying to do – finish the job The Jackal started?'

Gisella finally stopped coughing. The rain on the back of her hand washed away a trickle of blood.

'Phinn was doing most of the pulling,' she said, wiping her eyes with her soaked cloak. 'Honestly, Wil. I'm a Fellman – we're trained for this kind of thing!'

'Oh, right-oh! I suppose you crash a lot of flying boats on a moon chase, do you – *after* someone's tried very hard to kill you!'

'I'm alright, Wil,' Gisella insisted. But her ash-white face was a stark contrast to her lips that had gone a very odd shade of blue. Wil wondered just how long she and Phinn had been pulling the boat but decided that now wasn't the time to pick a fight.

'Look, Giz, you must be exhausted. You take a turn to rest. I'll help Phinn.' He peered into the sheeting rain. 'We really can't be too far now – how long has it been light?'

'I don't know,' admitted Gisella. 'Phinn was already dragging us when I came to. It was already light.'

Wil looked at the bedraggled Fellhound. He was limping badly and, by the blood down his leg, the wound on his shoulder had been bleeding for quite a while.

252

'Don't suppose you managed to grab any food?' Wil asked.

Gisella shook her head.

'It was all I could do... to get your bag and... the bolts.'

Wil couldn't reply. The only sound he could hear was Gisella fighting for breath – the last time he'd heard that sound was just before The Jackal died.

Ignoring the agony of his own broken arm, Wil swept Gisella up into his arms and tried his best not to drop her back into the remains of the boat.

'What the...' gasped Gisella.

She moved to get out. Wil held up his palm.

'No, Giz. Stay there. Phinn and I will get you home.'

Gisella opened her mouth but another coughing fit stopped whatever she was going to say. She sat back, defeated; Wil could see she was also frightened.

'I'll get you home, Giz,' he said. 'Trust me.'

She bit her lip and struggled to speak again.

'Have you got any of that... potion we gave... Mortimer... You know... the stuff for... blood loss?'

Wil looked down at Gisella's blood-stained cloak. Gisella gave him a weak smile.

'For Phinn,' she said.

'Oh, yes! I... of course. For a moment then–'

'Wil! Give Phinn that... potion! If he's going to get us home... he's going to... need it.'

Then she sank back against the wooden plank that ran as a seat across the centre of the boat – behind it the rest of the boat was no longer there.

'Oh, right. Yes. I've... er... I've got it here somewhere,' Wil lied.

The little silk bag was wedged up under the transom. Wil moved away before he sought out the bottle that he knew was empty; when he looked back Gisella's eyes were closed.

'Don't die,' he whispered and turned away.

From behind him, almost lost in the wind, he just caught her weak reply.

'I'll try not to.'

CHAPTER TWENTY-EIGHT

Sights for Sore Eyes

Between them Phinn and Wil made reasonable progress. Downhill was relatively easy once they got up a bit of speed over the waterlogged ground; although they had to dive out of the way as the battered hull overtook them down a particularly steep slope.

The gusting wind smashed the rain into them again and again. Wil's arm was too damaged to pull anything so he had tied the rope around his waist but the thin rope quickly rubbed painful blisters across his chest and cut into the flesh under his arms.

Blood trickled down Phinn's shoulder again and although Wil did his best with what was left of the Brindey goose down dressing, with no food and very little sleep for almost two days, he wasn't sure how much longer any of them could go on.

The pain in his arm was bearable as long as he didn't move it, think about it, or touch it. The cold was also getting to his cracked cheekbone that now throbbed with every step.

'Well, Phinn,' he called into the wind, 'we left in the rain and we're going back in the rain – and it was miserable both times, too!'

At Wil's ironic laugh, Phinn moved closer to shield his master from the worst of the weather and, heads down into the wind, they trudged on together.

Wil had no idea when he fell, or indeed how he had fallen, but the next thing he knew someone was lifting him up. He screamed out in agony.

'Argh! My arm! Argh!'

His head was pounding.

A soothing voice flowed through Wil's veins like warm honey.

'Let me see.'

Soft hands gently lifted his injured arm. He winced again but this time managed not to cry out.

'Get me two branches, Bryn. The straightest you can find,' said Lady Élanor.

Wil kept his eyes shut tight against the rain and braced himself. Lady Élanor pressed on the shattered bone – the pain in Wil's arm and cheek eased.

'Hmm, a bad break,' she murmured.

'There you are, my lady. A nice bit of beech'll make a fine splint 'til we get back,' said Bryn. 'Good job Seth found Phinn – he was miles off the path! Lucky they didn't fall into Hester Beck in this weather. And poor Gisella!'

Wil opened his eyes.

'Where is she, where's Gisella?'

He sat up and shoved Lady Élanor hard with his good arm. She toppled backwards.

'Leave *me!* It's Gisella – *she* needs your help, not me!'

Lady Élanor got to her feet and brushed her muddy hands down her cloak.

'Seth has already taken her, Wil.' Lady Élanor spoke again in a tone far kinder than Wil deserved. 'Tally is with them. Now please, let me set this splint. You can see Gisella as soon as we get back to Lovage Hall.'

Phinn was surprisingly lively as they travelled back to Saran. Wil watched him trotting happily behind the horses then suddenly sprinting off ahead at a full gallop, bounding into the driving wind as if challenging it to try to stop him.

'He was worried about you, Wil,' said Bryn. Phinn came pelting towards them, darting to the right at the last minute, his tail held high.

'What have you given him?' asked Wil with a grin.

'Lady E's got a special mixture she keeps for the hounds after a hard moon chase,' said Bryn. He tapped his nose and winked. 'I just gave him a drop of that.'

Phinn bounded out of a hedge ahead of them. A furry corpse dangled from his mouth. Bryn roared with delight. 'Ere, look, he's caught a rabbit, too! Well done, Phinn!'

The Fellhound trotted over and dropped his prize into Bryn's outstretched hand, then he was off again.

'Hmm, a nice one, too!' said Bryn, weighing the rabbit in his hand. 'Martha'll cook up a lovely stew with this!'

'Or a game pie… with these!' said a familiar voice from the other side of the hedge. A moment later, Mortimer rode into view waving another rabbit in his hand. At the same time Mia charged straight past them and nipped Phinn on the back of the leg.

Lady Élanor laughed.

'I wondered how long you would be able to stay quiet, Mortimer Merridown!'

White with foaming sweat, both Shadow and Rhoani were blowing hard.

'Gosh, you've made good time,' said Wil, although looking up at the sun he realised that he must have lost a lot more of the day than he had thought.

'Not bad,' said Mortimer, smoothing his hand along the top of Shadow's mane. 'Been galloping all day. Having Rhoani *and* Shadow meant I could swap so we could keep going.' He handed Bryn a guinea fowl and the rabbit. 'So where's Gisella? Until I got closer, my lady, I thought you might be her.'

Mortimer bowed his head as Shadow danced. Wil could sense the horse's impatience at suddenly being brought to a walk so close to home.

'She will be back at Lovage Hall by now – in the infirmary,' said Lady Élanor.

'What?'

Mortimer looked at Wil.

'How?'

'Er, well, the boat probably wasn't the best idea you've had, Mort?' said Wil.

'Nonsense,' said Mortimer. 'It got you out of Armelia, didn't it? Phinn's fine and, well, what've you done? Broken your arm?'

Wil shifted awkwardly. A sharp pain shot right up his arm into his shoulder.

'Well, yes, the boat was fine. And the Redback was great,' he said trying not to show the agony on his face. 'It was just that the landing wasn't.'

'Wasn't what?'

'A landing,' said Wil. 'It was more of a crash.'

'Oh,' said Mortimer.

'And I got knocked out. Phinn and Gisella started to drag– '

'Yeah, Wil, I think I'm getting the picture,' said Mortimer, for once looking almost as awkward as Wil felt. He changed the subject. 'So how did Lady Élanor find you?'

'Phinn!' said Bryn, beaming with pride. 'Seth found him. Coming for help, he was. He was nearly home, too! Seth was on the Fells looking for you. Poor Phinn, half dead but he wouldn't give up. No. He saw Seth, turned right back round and led him right here!'

'So how did you and Lady Élanor find us?' asked Wil.

'Well, Seth was out on Tanith when he saw Phinn. Took him no time at all to get back for help.'

The gamekeeper chuckled.

'He's got a real way with a pegalus, that one. Poor Rhoani!'

The vision of Tanith in flames flashed across Wil's mind.

'Oh! So Tanith's alright then?'

'Yes, Wil, Tanith is fine,' answered Lady Élanor. 'Tired of course, after such a long flight from Armelia, but otherwise perfectly fine.'

Mortimer scraped a finger of foaming sweat from Rhoani's flank.

'Gisella'll be alright though, won't she, my lady?' He flicked the sweat into the grass. 'I know that the bolt went right through but we've come back from moon chases with far worse.'

'Yes, she will be fine,' said Lady Élanor. But there was something in her voice that worried Wil. Mortimer seemed to have missed it.

'That's good,' he said. 'Because I was thinking that she'd make a great chaser. What do you think, Wil? She's as brave as any and she's certainly got a way with the hounds.'

'Well you've changed your tune!' said Wil.

Mortimer shifted in his saddle.

'Yer, well, I was wrong. I'm not afraid to admit it. Olivia must have been upset and decided to try to make trouble. I'll speak to Leon... he'll be fine when he hears it from me.'

Wil frowned.

'You sure about that?'

From the moment they rode into the yard at the stables above Lovage Hall, Wil had refused all offers of treatment for his shattered arm and his battered cheek. His head was throbbing, too, but he needed to see Gisella. Unfortunately, his visit to the infirmary had been both brief and disappointing.

'Well, I'm sorry, Wil,' snapped Tally. 'But I couldn't keep her awake just in case you decided to turn up!' She was dressing Wil's arm as she spoke, although he was still resisting any attempts she made to look at his cheek or his head. 'She is very ill – you do understand that, don't you? We're giving her camomile and morphine in *very* large doses. So if you're *not* going to let me have a look at that bruise there's really no point in hanging around!'

Lady Élanor walked into the ward just as Tally took a breath.

'Don't worry, Wil. Gisella is fit and strong. If anyone can get through this, she will,' said Lady Élanor kindly. She studied the purple bruise on Wil's head and then glanced at her sister before she continued. 'But Tally is right, Wil. If she is sleeping, she won't feel the pain. She needs her strength to fight, not to talk. In the meantime, perhaps you should let Tally take another look at that bump.'

She moved closer. Wil backed away.

'No, it's OK. I'm fine, honestly.'

He studied Gisella's smoke-white face.

'It's just that, well, she hasn't got anyone now... you know – to... to, well, er... look after her,' he struggled.

'No,' said Lady Élanor. 'With her mother still... away–'

'Away!' said Wil. A spark of anger flared inside him. 'She's in Armelia – Imelda's new best friend. That's where she is!'

'You saw her,' said Lady Élanor, sounding surprisingly calm.

'Yes! So did Gisella! And I don't think she's going to want to see her loving mother again – *ever*!'

It wasn't until after Wil left the infirmary with his arm encased in cumbersome[94] splints that he started to wonder about Lady Élanor's reaction. If she already knew of Fermina Fairfax's whereabouts, Wil was sure she had known about Fermina's romantic links with Sir Jerad Tinniswood.

'Lord Lakeston must have told her,' he muttered to himself as he stomped back up to the stables to check on Phinn. His head throbbed.

'Who told who what?'

Wil turned. Seth was just behind him.

'Oh, nothing,' said Wil casually. If he told Seth that he'd met the ghost – or whatever he was – of Lord Lakeston, Seth would most likely march him straight back to the infirmary again fearing that the bump on Wil's head was more severe than everyone had first thought. 'Where are you off?'

Seth's normally pale cheeks went bright red.

'Oh, nowhere,' he said. 'Just thought I'd, er, check on Farrow; might pop over to see Tanith, too. Was, er, was Tally down in the infirmary?'

'Yes,' said Wil, getting cross again. 'Exhibiting the bedside manner of a Bragg Hound as usual!'

Seth's shoulders dropped a fraction.

'Oh,' he said. 'Did she, er, did she, you know, say anything about me?'

'No,' said Wil, kicking a pile of rotten leaves. 'She was horrible. I just can't understand why she dislikes Gisella so much!'

'Feather blindness?' said Morten Mortens as Seth and Wil walked into the yard. Mia was standing with Mortimer, who was recounting the story about the eagard attack to the Grand Wizen. Morten Mortens shook his head.

'Very nasty. Only seen it once myself. Poor chap lost his sight – but then he didn't have Lady Élanor watching over him.'

The Grand Wizen smiled as he mentioned Lady Élanor's name. Morten Mortens had said something before about a promise he had made to her father; maybe it had something to do with Lord Lakeston becoming a revenant? Wil started to wonder just how you became a revenant – did it hurt?

'Didn't they, Wil?' said Mortimer.

'Sorry?'

Mortimer frowned.

'Has that bump on your head made you deaf?'

'No… yer… sorry, I was just thinking about something… sorry, what did you say?' Wil did feel a bit dizzy. He sat down heavily on the edge of the water trough.

Morten Mortens peered over his glasses.

'Are you sure you are alright, Wil? Shall I ask Lady Élanor to have another look at you?'

'No, really,' said Wil, trying to concentrate. 'What did you ask me, Mort?'

'I was just telling Morten about the eagard attack; about Leon getting injured. They were coming back here, weren't they?'

'Er, yes,' said Wil. Nausea was coming and going in waves now. He took a deep breath. 'I don't think Leon was in a fit state to go anywhere else.'

The stable yard was spinning now and the waves of sickness were so bad he didn't want to risk opening his mouth. The Grand Wizen didn't seem to notice.

'Well, Oswald's sister lives somewhere up by Grizzledale – tiny place, Little Piketon, I think... only about three houses. Right on the edge of Mistle Forest – they've got a hobgoblin, you know – excellent wild boar sausages.' Morten Mortens grinned at the memory. 'I'll bet they stopped off there? It's nearer to The Black Rock than Saran, after all.'

Mortimer brightened.

'Oh, I know that place – yer, those sausages are delicious! I tried to get them to give me the recipe but no such luck. Lots of juniper, I think. Those hobgoblins know how to butcher a boar, mind – use every bit – even the stomach contents are– Wil, are you OK? You've gone very green.'

Wil bent over the back of the water trough and vomited.

'I think we'd better get you back to Lady Élanor,' said Mortimer, and lifting Wil's good arm over his own shoulder, he added, 'And I think I'll ask Martha to keep sausages off the menu for a while!'

***

Despite Wil's continued resistance, Lady Élanor finally persuaded him to stay the night in the infirmary.

'Goodness me, Wil,' she said, her pale blue eyes looking almost the crossest he'd ever seen them. 'It's not as if I'm suggesting you spend the night in Saran Jail! Now drink this!'

She handed him with a glass of bright orange liquid and watched while he drank every drop. The medicine was as bitter as lemon rind but after one gulp Wil's nausea disappeared.

Lady Élanor gave a satisfied nod.

'Right, you can change into this for tonight and Martha will return your clothes – clean – in the morning,' she said, exchanging the empty glass for a long, linen night shirt.

'I can't wear–' started Wil, but a sudden hardness in those blue eyes silenced him at once. Without another word he changed and clambered into bed.

The sheets were crisp and the cool pillow soothed his burning head. Wil could feel his body giving in. Fighting sleep now, he looked over at the opposite bed. For the briefest second, just before exhaustion completely consumed him, he could see Gisella. She was smiling.

CHAPTER TWENTY-NINE

Gisella

It was almost lunchtime the next day before Wil woke and when he opened his eyes Tally was just leaving Gisella's bedside.

'How is she?' he croaked.

Tally headed towards the door.

'As well as can be expected after having a bolt shot through her lung, being dropped from a dragon, and then being dragged halfway across Tel Hireth in the *wrong* direction in the worse storm we've had for ten winters!'

As Tally left her sister entered the room.

'Why is she cross with me *now*?' said Wil. After all, he had just played a fairly big part in rescuing her from being burnt at the stake!

Lady Élanor was bearing down on him with another glass of the foul orange medicine.

'Just ignore her, Wil. Here, drink this. If you aren't sick again this afternoon you can get dressed and join us for supper. Martha is expecting you. I have not as yet had the chance to thank you all for getting Tally and Tanith home safely… and in time.' She took the glass without looking at him. 'Mortimer and Seth have already accepted my invitation.'

Then, with a glance at Gisella, she added, 'We have made up your usual room over at the Hall.'

'Thank you, my lady,' he said, following her eyes. 'She is going to get better, isn't she?'

This time Lady Élanor looked Wil full in the face.

'Gisella has only a slim chance of survival, Wil. You did all the right things but she was out on the Fells for far too long.' She turned back towards Gisella. 'She is also battling with the news of her mother… her father's murderer.'

'How did you–' Wil started.

Lady Élanor interrupted him.

'Don't forget, Wil, I can *see* these things.' Her blue eyes held his gaze. 'Maybe she has a chance. True, she was injured during the Alcama – a time of bad luck – but she had you to take care of her and,' she looked back at Gisella, 'I am guessing you will be here for her when she wakes up?'

The room was suddenly too quiet. Wil could feel his cheeks starting to burn.

'Well, er, yer. I thought I'd stay around for a while. After all, as you said, I did try to help her.' He paused and then added, 'Do you think she'll be cross with me for the boat crashing? I just couldn't stop it. And then I banged my head and passed out and left her to try to drag the boat.' He laid his head back on the pillow. Right above him, in the corner of the bright white ceiling, he could see a spider rolling a fly into a tight bundle of silk while the fly's muffled buzz drifted through the otherwise silent room.

'She's not going to forgive me, is she?'

'And why not?' croaked a weak voice from the bed opposite.

Lady Élanor was at Gisella's bedside before Wil could turn his head. It was difficult for him to see Gisella's face while Lady Élanor looked into her eyes; poked, prodded and tried her very best to discourage Gisella from trying to sit up.

'Please, Gisella, just lie still. It is very good to see you awake so soon, but please... lie down.'

Despite the heavy cast around his arm, Wil managed to hoist[95] himself up onto his good elbow. Gisella abandoned her feeble effort to sit up and, satisfied that she wasn't about to try to spring out of bed, Lady Élanor left the room, calling Tally's name crossly and muttering something about camomile not being in short supply.

Gisella looked over at Wil.

'Hi,' she whispered.

Her weak smile made his heart dance.

'Hi,' said Wil, suddenly feeling terribly awkward.

'The others,' whispered Gisella. She gasped a few shallow breaths. 'They got back too?'

'Yes... er, well, not Leon and Oswald. Seth and Tally got back OK. Mortimer caught us up on the Fells. We were with Bryn and Lady Élanor by then. It was Seth who found you and me and...' Wil ran out of words. He wanted to tell Gisella how sorry he was about the boat and about collapsing; and about how she'd had to drag the smashed boat through the storm when she could hardly breathe. But he didn't know how to start.

Gisella waved her fingers weakly.

'It's OK, Wil... You might have... half killed me... once we got out of... Armelia, but... at least... you got me out.' With a huge effort she raised her head from her pillow and looked over at him. 'I'd be there... dead... if it wasn't for you... Thank you.'

Wil grabbed the tumbler next to his bed and almost choked on the water –luckily he was saved from trying to speak by Tally, whose sudden appearance really did make him choke.

'Oh, Gisella, I'm so sorry! I should have given you a double dose of camomile. You're supposed to sleep – to give your lung a chance to heal. I really am so sorry. Here, drink this.'

Gisella drank the cloudy pink liquid. A trickle of the medicine escaped from the corner of her mouth as she settled back on the pillow. Tally took the glass from her and headed back out of the ward.

'I hope you're not overdoing it, Wil?' she called through the open door. 'Martha's making game pie and rhubarb crumble for tea.'

And then she was gone.

Gisella's laboured breathing was deafening now in the quiet room. Wil could see that her eyes were once more closed.

With his head feeling like it was full of custard Wil lowered his legs over the edge of the bed and sat up. Once he was confident that he wasn't going to fall he stood up, very conscious of the overlong nightshirt that was dangling way below his knees.

Sunbeams shone across the neat beds – all deserted other than his and the bed in which Gisella lay fighting for breath.

In half a dozen unsteady steps he was across the room. But he didn't know whether to go nearer. He could see the pale pink smear across Gisella's cheek – a stark contrast to her white face, normally brown and freckled by the sun. Either Tally hadn't noticed the dribbled medicine or, Wil suspected, she just hadn't bothered to wipe her patient's face even though Gisella couldn't do it herself.

A clean towel hung over the end of his bed. He grabbed at it and dipped the corner into his water jug. Then he returned, this time moving closer to Gisella's pillow. As gently as he could, he wiped away the spilt medicine; then he brushed the soft towel over Gisella's eye lids – first one, and then the other. Then he dabbed the cloth lightly across her brow.

'Just don't die,' he whispered.

Without opening her eyes, Gisella lifted her hand. Her icy fingers brushed against Wil's face as gently as a snowflake. When she spoke, her voice was as quiet as falling snow.

'I told you before... I'm... trying not to.'

By the time the sun had set and the twin moons were rising into the stars, Wil's dizziness had gone. Tally had returned to the infirmary to check on him twice during the afternoon and both times had given Gisella only a quick glance. Gisella had not stirred at all and when Tally returned a third time, Wil couldn't hide his irritation any longer.

'So, is she alright Tally? Is her breathing OK?'

'Oh... er... yeah,' said Tally. 'She's Eli's patient really. I don't know that much about lungs.'

'But you've been giving her that medicine,' said Wil, careful not to sound as cross as he felt. 'Did you, um,' he took a deep breath, 'Did you give her the wrong stuff earlier?'

Tally flicked the corner of the extra blanket that Wil had put over Gisella when he had felt her cold hands.

'Well, that was Eli's fault! How was I supposed to know it was double camomile for the *whole* week!'

'I thought you could read minds?'

Tally's eyes flashed but she didn't react. She smoothed the blanket and pulled it a little further up under Gisella's chin, then gently brushed a curl of hair from Gisella's face.

'I'd never realised how curly Gisella's hair was,' she said. And with a faint *tut* turned on her heels, adding, 'Probably why it always looks such a mess.'

Supper at Lovage Hall was quiet. Lady Élanor had arrived late, having been called down to the village to tend the blacksmith who had accidentally driven a nail into his hand while shoeing one of Godwyn Savidge's horses.

'But I thought he did that yesterday,' said Martha, spooning a second helping of rhubarb crumble onto Wil's plate even though he had barely touched the first. 'Cream, Wil?' she asked, plopping a huge dollop of clotted cream on the top before Wil could decline[96].

'He did,' said Lady Élanor. She helped herself to a tiny slice of pie that Wil was convinced must by then have been stone cold. 'But today it was a very odd colour.'

Wil pushed the crumble away.

'I've given him a bottle of iodine. If it's no better tomorrow he'll have to come up here. I can't keep going off down to the village while Gisella is still...' this time her eyes did dart to Wil, 'so poorly.'

'She sounded more settled this evening, didn't she, Wil?' said Tally, her voice filled with a concern Wil knew was false. But to avoid a fight, he nodded. Lady Élanor brightened.

'Oh, good! Well, now she's having the right dose of camomile.' Tally's fork crashed onto her plate. 'I'm sure the sleep will do her good.'

'So how's Tanith, Tally?' chirped Seth. He had eaten every crumb of the pie although the vegetables on his plate remained untouched. 'Do you want to come up to check on him later?'

'No,' said Tally.

Seth's face fell. Mortimer picked at the crumble with his spoon.

'I'll go, Seth,' he said, peering out of the window at the now star-filled sky. 'Shadow was still a bit hot today. Is Bryn still up at the stables, Martha?

'Oh, yes. What with two exhausted horses, three extra Fellhounds and Tanith to look after, he'll be up there for a while yet. Can you take him that last slice of pie and some of those potatoes when you go, Mortimer?' She frowned at the sight of Seth's uneaten vegetables. 'Seth, I didn't slave over a hot stove all afternoon for you to leave those on your plate–'

A sharp knock on the door saved Seth.

'We expecting anyone else?' said Martha, inspecting the nearly empty serving dishes and suddenly eyeing Seth's uneaten vegetables in a more positive light. Lady Élanor's dismayed expression suggested not.

'Oh, I do hope it's not Godwyn again. He was in such a foul mood earlier.'

There was a second impatient rap on the door.

'Goodness me, hold your horses!' called Martha.

But she had hardly put her fingers on the latch when the door burst open and Oswald Beck and Morten Mortens tumbled into the room.

CHAPTER THIRTY

Bad News

Oswald was absolutely filthy; his face muddy and he was still in the same clothes he had been wearing on Tel Hireth. Morten Mortens was as white as a sheet.

'Morten! What is it! What's happened! Is it Leon?' Lady Élanor knocked her chair over backwards as she stood to help them.

Oswald struggled to his feet. He was shaking and Wil could see he had been crying.

'No, my lady, Leon's fine, he's outside. I left his bandages on though. What with everything else...' His voice broke and he looked to Morten Mortens for help.

The Grand Wizen went from white to scarlet.

'It's Olivia Drews, Eli. The Wraithe Wolves have taken her – she...'

'*What?*' chorused[97] everyone else in the room; Morten Mortens let out a great gasping sob.

'She... I can't believe it... she went to them.'

Lady Élanor led the Grand Wizen to a chair.

'Martha, cherry brandy, I think, for everyone. And can someone go and get Leon?'

Mortimer carefully guided Leon into the room and helped him into a chair. The bandages over his eyes were no longer crisp and white. Leon was as filthy as his father and his cloak was ripped.

Martha served everyone a big glass of cherry brandy while Oswald, Leon and Morten Mortens told the story of Olivia's fate[98].

'After we left you I decided to go south instead of going over to Mistle Forest first. It was early and the journey would be quicker,' Oswald began, calmed slightly by the brandy. He sounded as if he was telling them of an event in which he had not been involved. 'But the weather up on the Fell closed in and very soon we were lost. So we took shelter for the night,' said Oswald. 'The next morning we'd only just set off when Olivia just walked up to us. She was soaked through! She must have been in that storm – and there she was – all on her own.'

'But I thought she was going to visit her aunt,' said Tally. 'She told me the other day that she was going to stay there for a while to try to get over losing Giles.'

'And we all know whose fault that was, don't we!' Leon spat, glaring at Wil.

'Now, now, boy,' said Morten Mortens in barely

more than a warning whisper from the other side of the table. 'We've been over this many, many times.'

Leon shrugged. Oswald continued their tale.

'She just walked right up to us. It was so strange. She had no horse, no bag, no bow – nothing. She was soaked through but she didn't seem to notice. She was…' Oswald stopped to think for a moment. 'That's it, she was lost… just lost.'

Leon nodded.

'We told her we were going home and told her to come with us but she kept saying that she couldn't find him.'

'Find who?' asked Lady Élanor.

She indicated to Martha to pour some more brandy into Oswald's glass, but gave a tiny shake of her head when Martha moved towards the goblet in Leon's hand. Oswald stared at his brandy.

'Well, we couldn't work it out for ages,' he said. 'At first I thought she was talking about her father. I knew he was planning to ride over to Lower Minton with her. But she swore she'd come out alone. She just kept saying that she just wanted to find *him*. She was behaving so strangely.'

'So who was she looking for?' asked Seth, his eyes wide as he listened. 'And why was she near The Black Rock? If she was on her way to Lower Minton she'd gone really badly wrong!'

Mortimer turned to Oswald. 'So why didn't you just bring her back with you?'

Oswald clutched his glass with both hands and stared at the floor.

'It really wasn't as simple as that, boy. We managed to persuade Olivia to join us... but... then things got really bad.'

'Oh, yes,' said Leon, turning his head in the direction each voice. 'You see, without my sight I can hear things I wouldn't usually notice: sounds... smells... I knew we had gone wrong when I couldn't smell the forest anymore.'

Oswald took a large sip of his brandy. Leon continued.

'It had stopped raining. There was a really weird smell – really familiar. But father told me it was still daylight so for a while I just thought it was my mind playing tricks... and it was the day of the Alcama–'

'What smell?' interrupted Mortimer. It was obvious from his expression that he knew what Leon's answer was going to be – so did Wil.

'Wraithe Wolves,' said Leon.

Mortimer nodded. 'Cae Wheeler, this morning, said he'd seen footprints out on Thesker Fell – over by the river. I told him he must have made a mistake – Wraithe Wolves don't come this far south.'

'Well, I'm afraid he wasn't wrong,' said the Grand

Wizen gravely. 'Tell them, Oswald.'

Oswald gulped the rest of his brandy and swallowed.

'Leon and Cae were right.' He looked straight into Mortimer's face. 'They wouldn't let us get back. Every time we tried to turn towards Saran two or three would be there – on the nearest hilltop – forcing us to change course. They were herding us. As long as we kept going east they left us alone.'

'Father decided that it would be better to get to the river. Olivia was really excited – hysterical almost. I thought she was just scared, I… I was,' said Leon, his bandaged eyes sightless to the solemn faces in the room.

'It was starting to get dark and the Alcama was rising,' said Oswald. 'We decided to light the biggest fire we could and stay right by the river. The plan was to go downstream the next morning and try to get back to Saran from Goatmed Scarp. We even managed to get Olivia to calm down a bit too. It was fine… until the moons crossed.'

Oswald's voice, flat and drained of emotion, filled the quiet room.

'The fire was going well but it was eating logs. I'd only just come back from collecting more wood – I didn't dare move too far from the river. You could feel them watching,' he said with a shiver. Martha ignored Lady Élanor's disapproving frown and topped up his empty glass. He nodded gratefully and continued. 'Olivia wouldn't sit down. She just kept pacing and looking out at the hills. It was getting dark. There wasn't much you could see, even in the moonlight.' He took a sip of the brandy. 'When I got back I dropped one of the logs on my foot. I was hobbling around. So when we needed more wood a bit later, Olivia insisted she get it. She seemed a bit happier – and my foot was sore – so I agreed...' He raised his hand and pressed his eyes. Teardrops leaked down his cheeks. 'She laughed as she went. She was so happy just then. I should have realised.'

He wept. Nobody moved. Martha lowered herself onto one of the little milking stools by the fire, the brandy bottle momentarily forgotten in her hand. After a few moments, Oswald took a deep, quivering breath, his eyes on the same patch of floor somewhere in front of him.

'Leon heard it first. The howl. Then another, and another until I thought I was going to go mad. They were all around us. But then the storm hit us. I could hear Olivia calling but in that wind I couldn't make it out at first. Then I realised. She was calling Giles's name. She kept saying, "Giles, it's me. I've come. Take me with you. Giles, it's me."

'I ran out into the dark, away from the fire, but I couldn't see anything. I called,' Oswald was whispering now. 'But she just kept calling for Giles and the wolves kept howling. And then... they stopped and...'

'I heard Giles,' said Leon.

'But you couldn't have!' interrupted Seth so loudly that Martha jumped. 'He's dead... well, you know.'

'Are you sure it was Giles, Leon?' said Mortimer. 'Did you hear him, sir?'

'You calling my son a liar, boy?' snarled Oswald.

Wil glanced at Lady Élanor but her expression was impossible to read. Her fingers were pressed together so tightly that her knuckles gleamed white.

'I heard Giles,' Leon repeated. 'He called Olivia. He called her and she went to him.'

'Did he attack her, Leon?' asked Lady Élanor, her fingers still wound around each other in her lap.

Leon shook his head.

'He called Olivia out onto the Fell. There were wolves close – I could smell them. *They* got her. And you know what...' He turned his head as if looking around the room. 'She never made a sound. They dragged her away and she *never* made a sound.'

'So what happened after they took her?' asked Seth, wide-eyed. 'Did they come back?'

Oswald put his glass down and, gripping the table with one hand, pulled himself to his feet.

'You know, that was the strangest thing. Once they had Olivia, they just left.'

Leon nodded.

Seth raised his index finger.

'But that was two nights ago,' he said innocently. 'How come you've only just got back now?'

Oswald hobbled over to lean on the huge oak lintel above the fireplace. He was only wearing one boot; his other foot was bare and at least twice its normal size.

'As you can see, that log did me a bit more damage than I first thought. The horses must have taken off when the howling started. There was no sign of them after Olivia…' Oswald seemed to grind to a halt, as if it was all simply too much. He'd got his son home, he'd told his sad story and that was it – he didn't seem to have anything left. Leon came to the rescue.

'As soon as it got light we knew where we were. If they'd driven us any further we'd have gone over Nell's Drop! It's taken us ages to get back.'

'Well, what with you blind and your father hardly able to hobble, I'm not surprised,' said Morten Mortens. His eyes were wet and glistening. 'Eli, do you think you can find two beds in the infirmary for tonight?'

'No, Morten,' said Oswald. He leant heavily on the back of a chair and winced. 'One will be fine. Leon needs your help, my lady, but I… I need to see my wife.'

To Wil's surprise, Lady Élanor did not object.

'That is perfectly understandable, Oswald. But perhaps you might let Tally bind that foot to make it a little more comfortable?' She turned to Tally without waiting for Oswald to respond. 'Tally, go and get some bandages and the poplar buds – I left a new batch soaking in the pharmacy. Pack them around Oswald's toes as best you can, they'll help with that swelling.' She turned back to Oswald and the Grand Wizen. Oswald was already hobbling to the door.

'I'll send Tally down to the house, Oswald,' she called after him, and then said under her breath to nobody in particular, 'But I'm willing to bet that the pain will drive him back up here before tomorrow.'

CHAPTER THIRTY-ONE

A Friend Returns

Sure enough, before breakfast when Wil looked around the infirmary door the next morning he saw three occupied beds. Leon and Oswald were sound asleep; Gisella was lying on her back as Wil had left her the night before.

'He came up around midnight. His wife brought him,' whispered Tally, who had crept up behind him. 'Eli's pretty sure he's broken his foot in at least three places. She's amazed he managed to walk from Goatmed Scarp in anything less than a week! Did you know he sleeps with his eyes open?'

'Yes, I noticed when we were at The Black Rock – scared me half to death!' said Wil. 'And, er, what about Leon?'

Tally's eyes narrowed.

'*Gisella* is getting on just fine, Wil – as that's *obviously* who you really came to see at this time in the morning! As for Leon, he'll mend.'

'Will he be scarred?' asked Wil, remembering the

terrible marks across Leon's eyes just after the eagard attack.

'No. Eli's confident he'll be as good as new in a couple of weeks.'

Tally tucked the blankets into the end of Leon's bed, checked the knot on his new bandage and fussed with Gisella's pillows for far too long. Wil stayed around for as long as he dared.

In the end it was Martha calling them in for breakfast that broke the stalemate[99].

As usual the courtyard was bursting with vibrant colours and smells that made Wil feel quite light-headed as he made his way back across to Lovage Hall.

'Look, Wil,' said Tally, skipping up to join him. Wil got ready for another fight. But instead of telling him off or being mean about Gisella, Tally looked slightly embarrassed. Wil stopped at the kitchen door.

'I, er,' Tally started, pressing her fingers together so hard that the tips went pink. 'Well, I should have thanked you. You know, for getting me out of Armelia. I know I would be burnt to a crisp by now if you and… and the others hadn't come to get me.'

Wil shrugged.

'It's OK, Tally. I'm sure you would have done the same.'

Tally opened her eyes wide.

'Oh, yes… for you, definitely! You know that.'

'And for Gisella?' said Wil.

Tally dropped her hands to her hips.

'Oh, typical! You always have to spoil it, don't you?'

With a sweep of silver hair, she turned and marched back into the infirmary.

'Tally, oh, come on. I thought you were coming for breakfast?' Wil called after her.

A tearful voice replied, 'Tell Martha I don't want any!'

As the days went on Gisella's breathing got easier and easier. By the fifth morning, to Wil's relief, Lady Élanor instructed Tally to halve the camomile and start reducing the morphine.

When he called in to the infirmary that evening, Gisella was awake and Tally was nowhere to be seen. Oswald had gone home the previous day, just after Tally had removed Leon's bandage.

Wil nodded to Leon, lying in the bed opposite.

'Hi, Leon, can you see anything yet?'

Leon's eyes were almost their normal colour again.

'Yeah, much better,' he said with a vague wave. 'Tally said it's thanks to you that I'm not going to be blind?'

'Oh, I don't know about that,' said Wil, feeling very awkward. He knew what it must have taken for Leon to thank him – after all, it was fairly obvious that Leon still blamed Wil for what happened to Giles on the moon chase. 'Gisella helped too.'

'It was mostly you though!' said Gisella. 'It seems we've all got something to be grateful to you for, doesn't it!'

Her sunny smile made Wil's heart dance a little jig[100].

'You've woken up at last then,' he said grinning back.

'Well, a girl can only have so much beauty sleep,' said Gisella, hauling herself up on her pillow. Wil jumped forward to help.

'Here, lean forward.'

She was still bound in a thick bandage. Wil tucked the pillow carefully behind Gisella's back. His blood froze. In the middle of the binding, right over Gisella's lung, was a circle of blood the size of Wil's fist.

'Giz, are you… are you feeling OK?' he stammered. Gisella was still bleeding – or maybe the effort of sitting up had made her start bleeding again – and it was his fault.

He backed away and stood on Lady Élanor's foot.

'Ouch! I was just coming to check on my patient, Wil. Or do you think that there aren't quite enough occupied beds in here?'

Wil removed his foot from Lady Élanor's slipper, leaving mud across the delicate silver embroidery.

'So, Gisella, how are you feeling tonight?' asked Lady Élanor gently pulling Gisella forwards and examined the same bandages. 'Hmm, still some blood. But nothing to be concerned about – it was a big hole, after all.'

The sound of light footsteps in the hall outside suggested that Tally might be on her way. Wil's heart sank. He'd managed to avoid her for the past few days. But she poked her head around the door and gave him a surprisingly friendly smile.

'Hi, Wil. Hi, Gisella, good to see you're awake.'

Wil waited for a mean comment about him, or about Gisella's snoring – which Wil had put down to her lying on her back for five days. But instead Tally simply said, 'Anyone seen Seth?'

Wil, Gisella and Lady Élanor all shook their heads.

'Oh, he must be up there already,' she said and ducked back behind the door only to reappear a moment later. 'Oh, Eli, is it OK if we take Tanith out for a ride?'

'We?'

'Oh, just Seth and me,' said Tally, and before her sister could answer, she said 'Thanks,' and closed the door.

Lady Élanor looked from Wil to Gisella.

'They were out on Tanith only this morning... and yesterday, too,' grinned Wil.

Oswald Beck, still hobbling and pale with pain, came up to the Hall to collect Leon the following morning. Leon had been very quiet during his stay in the infirmary and his silence continued as he blinked his way into the overcast morning.

Oswald stopped at Gisella's bed and held out his hand to Wil.

'I know that you and Leon have your differences,' he said, gripping Wil's hand in both of his own. 'But he owes you his sight. I won't forget that and I'll make sure that he doesn't either.'

Lost for words, Wil watched until father and son were at the kitchen door on the other side of the courtyard. Then he turned to return to Gisella's bedside. There, in the hallway of Lady Élanor's pristine[101] infirmary stood Phinn, his tail wagging lazily by way of a greeting.

'Phinn, how did you get down here?' said Wil as the hound pushed his head into Wil's chest. 'I know I've been neglecting you but I think Gisella needed me a bit more than you did.'

Phinn moved closer and leant his entire weight against Wil. Wil scratched the hound's ear and Phinn groaned appreciatively.

'No, you can't see Gisella. Lady Élanor would dose me up with something highly poisonous if I let you in there. Come on, let's go back up and see Bryn.'

Phinn padded back through the main door. Wil followed.

'*Crronk!*'

Phinn stood and let out a single booming bark.

'Oh,' said Wil, with a laugh. 'You came to get me!'

Gliding down from a branch high up in the nearest beech tree, Pricilla landed a good horse's length to Wil's left.

'Oh, come on, Pricilla! You can't possibly be cross with me too? It's been bad enough having to battle with Tally. I had to leave you with that girl – what other choice was there? Honestly, you'd *never* have survived what we went through, believe me!'

Utterly disappointed, Wil retreated back towards the infirmary. Pricilla hopped after him, dragging something behind her. Wil bent down and, without being invited, the raven hopped onto his arm. There, attached to her leg was tiny roll of parchment. Wil untied the knot and unfurled[102] the paper.

> *'Please find attached – your raven. No bones broken and in time she'll be flying straight again. Got nearly all my stuff back, but the Redback dagger was lost – that's looters for you. Am safe back home. From – oh, never mind, we're unlikely to meet again.*
> *Regards,*
> *The Girl with the Dragon Tooth Earring.'*

***

Wil felt guilty and grateful at the same time; Pricilla was back and – almost – alright. He hoped that Lady Élanor wouldn't notice her slight drift to the right and decided it might be best if Bryn checked her over. So with Phinn happily leading the way, Wil set off towards the stables.

Wil walked into the stable block expecting to find Bryn but it was Lady Élanor he found instead. She took one look at Pricilla perched on Wil's arm and smiled.

'Thank you for looking after her, Wil.'

Phinn wandered back over to his own stable and plonked himself down, nose out of the door so that he could keep an eye on what was going on. There was no sign of Bryn.

'So, Tanith's alright, my lady?' he asked, suddenly feeling very awkward.

'Yes. Tally and Seth seem to be giving him plenty of exercise now he's had a good rest.'

'Oh, that's good. It was just I... well, I had a dream and–'

Lady Élanor moved to stroke the raven's healing wing.

'Tanith is fine, Wil,' she repeated, extending Pricilla's wing. To Wil's relief there was no sign of the bolt wound. 'You must work on that gift of yours. In time you will learn what is a genuine dream and a real vision.'

'Er, can I ask you something else, my lady?'

'Of course.'

'Did you, um, did you believe Leon... you know, about hearing Giles?'

Lady Élanor continued to examine Pricilla.

'Leon had suffered a terrible injury, Wil. And with the storm and... well, the Alcama can play some odd tricks on an injured mind.'

The infirmary was strangely quiet when Wil went back in. Gisella was lying with her back to the door. Wil smiled – she had not been able to lie on her side since The Jackal had shot her.

It was only when he got closer that he realised that Gisella was crying.

'Giz, what's the matter? Do you feel ill again? Shall I go and get Lady Élanor?'

Gisella did not move.

'No, it's OK, Wil. I'll be fine. I need to start doing things on my own now anyway.'

'What do you mean by that?'

Gisella sniffed.

'Well, now I'm getting better you'll be going back home. Your mother must be wondering what's happened to you by now.'

Wil watched her shaking shoulders. He didn't know what to do. True, he did have to go home soon; to tell his mother that her husband really was never coming back –

but he wasn't ready to do that just yet.

'But who's going to wonder about me?' she whispered.

'What do you mean, Giz?'

'Well, my mother's hardly going to visit, is she?' She sniffed. 'And as she killed my father, well, that sort of leaves me on my own, wouldn't you say?'

As Gisella seemed determined not to face Wil he moved around the bed and crossed his arms.

'Gisella Fairfax, if you think for one moment that I'm going to abandon you to fend for yourself, you really don't know me very well at all!'

CHAPTER THIRTY-TWO

Dome to Mother

They were all there: Lady Élanor stood with Mortimer, and behind them, the Grand Wizen, Oswald Beck and Agatha Peasgood with Seth, Tally, Mia and Farrow. Tally's own hound, Pickles, was there too.

Wil sat behind Gisella on Rhoani. For once, he'd managed to get on without too much trouble – which had amazed everyone as his arm was still in splints. Mortimer held Rhoani steady while they got ready to set off. He pointed a finger at Wil.

'Now, understand this, Wil Calloway. I'm only *lending* you my new chaser. I fully expect you to return Miss Fairfax for hunting practice once she's fighting fit. And, of course, if you feel like joining in...' Mortimer winked.

Wil risked letting go of Gisella for a brief moment and held up his hand.

'I've told you before, Mort. I've seen enough Wraithe Wolves to last me a lifetime! But if that's what Gisella wants to do,' she looked around at him with a warning glare, 'Well, that's up to her.'

'And don't forget, when you come home, Gisella, there'll be a new Fellhound to train. You think of a name while you're away!' said Bryn.

'I will,' said Gisella.

Lady Élanor stepped forward. A burgundy silk bag swung from her wrist.

'Well, you had better go, Wil, or you will be staying another night and your poor mother will be frantic.' She offered up the bag to Wil.

'Oh, I don't think I'm going to need that, my lady,' said Wil. 'Gisella's got all her medicines in her own bag.'

Lady Élanor's face was suddenly serious.

'No, Wil, this is not first aid,' she said as she pressed the bag into Wil's hand. He could feel it was full of coins.

'Lady Élanor, I can't– '

'No, Wil, you must. It is the least I can do. My father would have wanted you to have it – he would have insisted. It is because of you the legacy is safe,'

'But I didn't–'

'Take it, Wil. Give it to your mother. I have no news of Lord Rexmoore as yet but his thugs will be back to collect his taxes before too long.'

'Well, I'm not sure about that, my lady,' said Wil, recalling the screams as the golden castle collapsed into the dirt.

'Only time will tell, Wil Calloway,' said Lady

Élanor with a steady gaze.

As if knowing that they needed to go, Phinn stood at the end of the stable block and barked loudly. Wil grinned and wrapped his arms around Gisella's waist.

'I think we're being nagged.'

'Are you sure about this, Wil?' said Gisella. 'I mean your mother–'

'Look, Giz,' said Wil. 'The last time I came home from Saran, I arrived with the biggest dog my mother had ever seen and she still loves me – you, by comparison, will hardly even raise an eyebrow.'

'*Thanks!*' said Gisella. The little group on the ground laughed.

'Well, obviously I didn't mean it like that!' said Wil. He recalled the last time he had left Saran – when he had managed to upset Gisella so badly that she had galloped away – at least this time they were both on the same horse!

Gisella kicked Rhoani into a walk.

'Now you look after him, Gisella,' called Seth. 'He's on loan, too, remember!'

Tally put her hands on her hips.

'Oh, right! So you might get bored of Tanith, is that what you're saying, Seth Tanner?'

Wil gave Seth a sympathetic grin and then looked up into the grey skies – it was going to rain again.

'Right, Gisella Fairfax, let's go and see my mother!'

As they neared the edge of the woods a figure stepped out into their path.

'Lady Élanor,' said Wil, suddenly concerned. 'Did we forget something? I checked Gisella's medicines twice.'

'No, Wil. Gisella has all the medicine she will need.' She paused and then said, 'Wil, do you remember asking me if I believed Leon's tale?'

'Yes,' said Wil. 'I told Gisella, too, and she agreed with you.'

'Yes,' said Gisella. 'I thought I'd heard Giles's voice when I was lying in the boat. But I felt so ill, and in that storm – well, *everything* sounded pretty frightening!'

Lady Élanor folded her hands into her cloak and dropped her gaze.

'What you and Leon heard I cannot say, but get back to Mistlegard before dark – stay in the forest. Do not go out on the Fell.'

The hairs on the back of Wil's neck suddenly felt very uncomfortable.

'Why, my lady? What's happened?'

Lady Élanor's pale blue eyes moved from Gisella to Wil.

'Armelia was not invaded at dawn on the day you left.'

'What?' breathed Wil.

'The wolves – they did not go into the city to collect their dead.'

And for those of you who haven't read it yet…

Moon Chase

Cathy Farr

Accused of a crime that he didn't commit, teenager Wil Calloway is sentenced to join the Moon Chase to try to prove his innocence. On the face of it, this sounds easy enough, especially with the help of the huge Fellhounds of Thesk, but as Wil learns more from the mysterious Lady Élanor and her telepathic sister, Tally, he soon realises that proving his innocence is the least of his challenges – staying alive is another!

GLOSSARY
(*WHAT THE LITTLE NUMBERS ARE FOR*)

You can use this glossary to find words or phrases you don't understand. Just look for the number and you can discover what the word or phrase means and see other words you could use instead.

	What does it mean?	**Other words you could use**
[1] strode	: walking with purpose	march
[2] splooshed	: slashing liquid	splash
[3] 'im	: another way to say 'him'	him
[4] seer	: a person who can see into the future, or has special powers	prophet
[5] reunion	: a meeting of people who haven't seen each other for a while	gathering
[6] *splat*	: a wet slapping sound	slap

	What does it mean?	Other words you could use
[7] breakneck speed	: moving very fast	rapidly
[8] yulefest	: **Made up word:** a time for celebrating in winter	-
[9] rump	: bottom	rear end
[10] hobbled	: in pain while trying to walk	limped
[11] darted	: rushed to hide	hid
[12] thunked	: the sound of something hitting something solid	thud
[13] hurled	: threw with all his might	chucked
[14] barren	: nothing growing; no trees or bushes	bare
[15] delved	: looked into, using hands to search as well	searched
[16] scrumptious	: really lovely to eat	delicious

	What does it mean?	Other words you could use
[17] haunches	: the top part of the back legs of an animal	rear
[18] orb	: circle	moon
[19] a troop of mushrooms	: this is the collective name for a lot of mushrooms	-
[20] winced	: feel pain	recoil
[21] devouring	: eating because you're really hungry	gobble up
[22] mock salute	: a polite wave to acknowledge something	signalled his agreement
[23] phial	: a very small glass tube	small glass tube
[24] gibbous moon	: more than half of the moon	waxing, or growing
[25] twist (of thread)	: a piece of thread	a length

	What does it mean?	Other words you could use
[26] back-up plan	: a second plan in case the first one : fails	Plan B
[27] taken aback	: to be surprised	caught off guard
[28] needle's tiny eye	: the hole at one end of a needle	-
[29] panic-stricken	: very frightened	terrified
[30] waspishly	: mean and bad-tempered	nastily
[31] unclenched	: relaxed	relaxed
[32] sheepish	: feeling a bit foolish	guilty
[33] copse	: small tree-covered area	wood
[34] in a heartbeat	: very quickly	in less than a second
[35] slingshot	: a type of weapon for firing stones	-

	What does it mean?	Other words you could use
[36] twinge	: feeling pain suddenly	pang
[37] quaking	: shivering with fear	shaking
[38] y'know	: a short way to say 'you know'	-
[39] folk	: another word for people	people
[40] 'cos	: short for 'because'	-
[41] flogged	: to hit someone or something	beat
[42] a voice that would have chilled ice	: a very harsh way of speaking that suggests the speaker is angry	angrily
[43] lurked	: lie quietly, barely noticed	lay dormant
[44] shy	: what a horse does when it's frightened	jump
[45] world went red	: anger consumed him	lost his temper

	What does it mean?	**Other words you could use**
[46] bounced	: went on his tiptoes then back on his flat feet	jumped up and down
[47] nicked	: to take something without permission	steal
[48] culvert	: a covered stream	drain
[49] surging	: strongly moving water	flowing
[50] hurl	: throw really hard	chuck
[51] scoured	: looked really hard for something	searched
[52] downed	: drank without stopping until finished	knocked back
[53] drowned	: couldn't be heard because of a louder noise	silenced
[54] hubbub	: lots of people muttering and talking	chatter

	What does it mean?	Other words you could use
[55] rickety	: something old and not very stable	broken-down
[56] eying	: looking at	gazing
[57] contentment	: feeling happy with life	happiness
[58] barey	: A made up word for 'barley' that a child might say	-
[59] throng	: a lot of people	a crowd
[60] pyre	: a pile of wood for a fire	bonfire
[61] a long shot	: something that might work, but it might not	a forlorn hope
[62] stir	: move slightly	move
[63] din	: a lot of noise	a cacophony
[64] albino	: a person or animal that is entirely white (no pigment in their skin)	-

	What does it mean?	Other words you could use
[65] wail	: cry really loudly	sob
[66] vaulted	: jump over something	hurdle
[67] so without further ado let's close our hands	: he is asking everyone stop what they are doing and clap	-
[68] fixed smile	: pretending to smile	-
[69] shooing away	: waving your hands to make someone go away	dismissing
[70] sour-faced	: not looking very happy at all	miserable
[71] faffing	: messing around	fiddling about
[72] poker-faced	: looking cross and miserable	bad tempered
[73] pirouette	: to spin around on one leg with you arms in the air	span around
[74] stake	: a pole in the middle of a bonfire	pillar

	What does it mean?	Other words you could use
[75] singed	: slightly burned but nothing serious	scorched
[76] in a flash	: very quickly	almost immediately
[77] splosh	: a splashing sound	sploosh
[78] flimsy	: very weak	rickety
[79] incinerating	: burning so that there is nothing left at all	destroy
[80] reunions	: meetings where people get together after a long time apart	gatherings
[81] ramparts	: the top of the wall of a castle	castle wall
[82] salvo	: bombing, firing or shooting	volley
[83] looters	: a crowd of people stealing from wrecked shops and homes	thieves

	What does it mean?	Other words you could use
[84] of a sort	: another way of saying 'sort of'	-
[85] headstones	: carved blocks of stone that mark the site of a grave	tombstones
[86] macabre	: spooky	spooky
[87] iridescent	: reflecting light and shining	opalescent
[88] snout	: an animal's nose	nose
[89] volley	: lots of missiles being fired at once	bombardment
[90] sphere	: circle	orb
[91] inky	: very dark	almost black
[92] hull	: the bottom of a boat	-
[93] bow	: the front of a boat	-
[94] cumbersome	: big, clumsy and uncomfortable	uncomfortable
[95] hoist	: lift	lift

	What does it mean?	Other words you could use
[96] decline	: say no	turn it down
[97] chorused	: people saying the same thing at the same time	said
[98] fate	: what happened to someone	-
[99] stalemate	: no one has won	draw
[100] made Wil's heart dance little jig	: Wil was extremely happy and relieved	-
[101] pristine	: really, really clean	immaculate
[102] unfurled	: to unfold something that has been rolled up	unroll

Lightning Source UK Ltd.
Milton Keynes UK
UKHW03f0925140318
319416UK00003B/87/P

9 780992 850975